"My reputation is in tatters," she said. She cried for a little while longer, then turned to leave.

"There are worse things in the world," he said.

"Excuse me?" She studied his motionless profile.

She moved to get a better look at him. His strong triangular nose in particular caught her eye. It tapered to an unexpected point, giving him an erudite appearance that was reinforced by his wide, thoughtful mouth.

She wished to see his eyes, but still he would not look down at her, and it was then she noticed his forehead. Three thin black letters were tattooed across its wide expanse. *FVG* they read. *Runaway*.

She should have guessed it. He was a slave—a bodyguard for one of her guests. Vita felt suddenly very foolish.

"You are right, sir. There are worse things in the world," she said. "Much worse things. My apologies."

Finally, he looked at her, and an unwelcome rush of warmth spread beneath her skin.

Author Note

From its mythological inception in 753 BCE, the kingdom, republic, then empire of Rome seemed bound to expand forever—that is, until 117 CE, when Emperor Hadrian rose to power. He ceased Rome's expansion and sought to fortify its borders instead. One of his first projects was to build a wall across northern Britannia.

Elsewhere in the empire, Hadrian reinforced Rome's borders with fences and forts, so it is not entirely clear why Britannia warranted a wall. There is evidence of rebellion in Britannia early in Hadrian's reign, and some scholars believe the 118-kilometer-long structure was built for defense. Others believe it was built to control trade, or simply to give the legions something to do. Hadrian's biographer famously said that it was built "to separate the Romans from the barbarians."

I think Hadrian's Wall was built for another reason—a theory which I have attempted to weave into the story. It is the journey of two people who are both Roman and barbarian and both in search of a home. They must navigate barriers from within and without in order to find what they seek. Perhaps they will also find love...

I hope you enjoy the story!

GRETA GILBERT

—

The Roman Lady's Illicit Affair

HARLEQUIN
HISTORICAL

HARLEQUIN®
HISTORICAL™

Recycling programs
for this product may
not exist in your area.

ISBN-13: 978-1-335-50580-4

The Roman Lady's Illicit Affair

Copyright © 2020 by Greta Gilbert

This edition published by arrangement with Harlequin Books S.A.

For questions and comments about the quality of this book,
please contact us at CustomerService@Harlequin.com.

Harlequin Enterprises ULC
22 Adelaide St. West, 40th Floor
Toronto, Ontario M5H 4E3, Canada
www.Harlequin.com

Printed in U.S.A.

Greta Gilbert's passion for ancient history began with a teenage crush on Indiana Jones. As an adult, she landed a dream job at National Geographic Learning, where her colleagues—former archaeologists—helped her learn to keep her facts straight. Now she lives in southern Baja, Mexico, where she continues to study the ancients. She is especially intrigued by ancient mysteries and always keeps a little Indiana Jones inside her heart.

Books by Greta Gilbert

Harlequin Historical

Enslaved by the Desert Trader
The Spaniard's Innocent Maiden
In Thrall to the Enemy Commander
Forbidden to the Gladiator
Seduced by Her Rebel Warrior
Saved by Her Enemy Warrior
The Roman Lady's Illicit Affair

Harlequin Historical Undone! ebook

Mastered by Her Slave

Visit the Author Profile page
at Harlequin.com.

For Michael James Gordon,
with all of my love.

Chapter One

Rome—122 CE

When Vita spotted the woman's loincloth on her husband's desk that night, tears of laughter filled her eyes. It was just that the cloth looked so silly draped over Magnus's stylus pen, which stood inside its wooden holder as usual.

Another woman's intimate garment on top of her husband's erect pen—what could be more humorous?

Ha!

She set down her oil lamp and plucked the mysterious loincloth from its perch. It felt expensively soft—probably Egyptian—and its fine embroidered waistband had been enhanced by gilded beads.

Gilded beads!

It was obviously the undergarment of a woman of elevated status—likely an equestrian—or at least someone who aspired to that lofty class. And Vita's husband had obviously aspired to the woman—probably on top of that very desk.

Ha, ha!

Vita considered the female guests who had attended

their banquet that evening. There had been only three: all beautiful, all of rank and all very much married.

Not that a woman's marital status had ever deterred Magnus. A consummate adulterer, he seemed to appreciate the company of maidens and married women alike.

And they appreciated him, for part of his job as a commanding *vigile* of Rome was to keep its women safe.

To most women, Vita's husband was not Magnus, but Aeneas or Adonis—a musclebound tower of a man whose physical power was matched only by his heroic deeds, which were eclipsed only by his classic good looks. In sum, Magnus could have nearly any woman he liked—and often did.

Still, a tryst in the *tablinium* was reckless, even for him.

Ah, Magnus.

So who had it been this time? Gaeta, the olive merchant's wife, with her fluttering laughter and piles of curls? Or Numeria, the tax collector's wife, who often stuttered and blinked in his presence? Perhaps it was Lollia Flamma, the architect's wife, whose nubile beauty was wasted on her much older husband, or so Magnus had commented once.

Whomever Magnus had chosen as his paramour that evening, there would have been few opportunities to disappear undetected. And the lovers had escaped to the *tablinium* of all places! Instead of retreating to a quiet corner, they had occupied the centrally located office where Magnus attended to household business.

Household business indeed! But when could the two have possibly…conducted it?

Vita thought back to her husband's movements that evening, but she could hardly remember anything beyond her guests' frowns and groans.

Bad food, terrible service, lack of wine—how could she have possibly detected her husband's transgression when she had been so busy watching her own reputation crumble into ruin?

Surely he had left clues? He always did. She only needed to think back to the banquet and try to remember them. She closed her eyes and willed herself to return to the disastrous gathering. All at once she was there, hovering outside her *triclinium* while her guests bit into her disastrous first dish...

'These dumplings have the savour of defeat,' Gaeta was whispering.

'Conjured in the Underworld for certain,' tittered Numeria.

'Come now, ladies,' said Lollia, 'the dough would make a lovely sandal leather.'

There was a smattering of quiet giggles as Vita swept into the room. 'My dear guests, the oysters are on their way,' she announced, pretending she had not heard the women.

'Well, that is good news!' said one of the husbands.

'I think I shall save room for them,' said another, setting his dumpling aside.

Vita smiled as she prepared to tell her guests the truth: that the dumplings were an accident that had resulted from the inebriated condition of the woman she had hired to cook. But in that instant the oysters arrived, distracting everyone's attention.

Thank the gods—the oysters! Surely the Ostian delicacies would erase the memory of the failed dumplings from her guest's minds. Borne on trays by two Germanic freedwomen whom Vita had hired at the urging of the cook, the fresh oysters were an unassailably elegant addition to the banquet. Still, Vita's guests were frowning.

Jupiter's thumb—the oysters' shells were still closed! Worse, the Germanis had forgone the special knives Vita had provided them for the task and were attempting to open the creatures with their own fingernails.

'Is that how they do it in Germania?' Gaeta clucked.

'We are fortunate they are not using their teeth!' Numeria added.

'Filthy barbarians,' Lollia mumbled.

Vita smiled joylessly. Her own mother had been a barbarian. Brought from Britannia in chains during the reign of Emperor Domitian, she had been bought and sold many times before finally landing in the household of the man who would become Vita's father.

'You can complain all you want,' said one of the husbands, 'without barbarians Rome's fields would be fallow and its chamber pots full. It is why our new Emperor must continue to conquer their territories.'

Another husband shook his head in disagreement. 'The Empire is overstretched as it is. Emperor Hadrian is right in fortifying its defences—especially along the Germanic frontier.'

A spirited discussion ensued and Vita tried not to listen. The Roman expansion had been forged in misery and enslavement, cruelty and death, yet most Romans spoke about it as if it were a table game.

She busied herself filling her guests' cups of wine, though she could not seem to pour quickly enough to keep them full. She emptied the last drop into her husband Magnus's own cup. 'The problem is not along the Germanic frontier, but the Britannic one,' he was saying. He drank the liquid down in a single gulp. 'Hence the wall Emperor Hadrian will build there soon.'

'It is true, then?' Gaeta asked. 'Hadrian is building a wall across Britannia?'

'I have heard that it will stretch over seventy miles, from one sea to another,' Numeria said.

'Humph,' grunted Lollia's husband, Lepidus.

All eyes turned to the bald, grey-bearded man, who had recently acquired a high post as a military architect in Hadrian's army.

'I honestly do not see the purpose of a wall so far north,' Gaeta commented at last.

'To separate the Romans from the barbarians, of course,' Numeria replied.

'That is not the reason for the wall,' grumbled Lepidus. He picked up a grape and began to peel it.

'It is obviously an excuse to busy the legions,' Magnus commented. 'Without a war to fight, the soldiers will have nothing to do.'

'That is not the reason for the wall, either,' Lepidus muttered, continuing to peel his grape.

'Its purpose is obviously to control trade,' said one of the husbands. 'Taxes over battle axes.'

'That is not the reason, either.' Lepidus held up the peeled grape and studied it, as if holding a miniature world in his hands.

'Surely it is for defence,' said another husband. 'Those barbarians in the north are a different breed. Or have we already forgotten the Battle of Teutoburg Forest?'

Across the room, one of the Germanic women gasped. The oyster she was opening shot into the air. It soared over the couches to the far wall, where it landed at the foot of a bust of the first Emperor.

Someone laughed. Another groaned.

'A bad omen,' Lepidus said.

There had been a sudden roll of thunder outside—a

late summer thunderstorm—and the Germanic women shrieked. They shoved their trays at Vita and rushed from the lounging chamber in a panic.

'Where are you going?' Vita had cried and they had replied that the banquet was cursed.

It seemed they were right, for the rain began to pour through the atrium ceiling so effusively that it soon began to overflow the pool designed to catch it. An embarrassing flood filled the atrium, reaching all the way to the entrance of the *triclinium* where Vita's guests reclined.

'Too bad I forgot my fishing net,' one of the husbands jested and Magnus said something about Vita neglecting to empty the cistern regularly. 'We would not have a flood if my wife would keep this house properly.'

The statement was utterly untrue. Vita emptied the cistern of its collected rainwater on the *kalends* of every month and Magnus knew it. The flood was a result of the build-up of sediment—too much sediment for Vita to be able to dispose of on her own. She had been urging Magnus to hire someone to remove it for years.

Vita had been unable to say anything in her own defence, however, because by that time her arms were nearly collapsing beneath the weight of the two heavy oyster trays she held.

'More oysters, anyone?' she asked, with perhaps a little too much cheer. Her guests only stared into their cups.

'I will return in just a moment,' she told her guests, then waded across the atrium towards the kitchen, trying to keep her spirits up. It was then she remembered the Falernian. A cup of fine wine could solve most crises and Falernian wine was the finest there was.

When she rounded the corner of the kitchen to fetch

the special amphora, however, she discovered it lying empty on the floor beside the slumbering cook.

'What have you done?' Vita shouted, but the woman only snored.

Her heart pounding, Vita ran out of the kitchen towards the entry hall. She needed a breath of fresh air and a moment to collect herself. Swinging open her front door, she rushed outside, crashing headlong against a barrier that might have been Hadrian's Wall itself.

She gasped and stumbled backwards, nearly tripping on her own feet. 'Curses!' she gasped. Regaining her balance, she peered up at a broad-chested pillar of a man standing motionless outside her door. The rain poured down over his short brown hair, plastering it to his skull and continuing down his stony profile.

'Excuse me,' she commented, but he made not a single movement to acknowledge her. She wondered for a moment if he was even alive. He seemed more statue than man: a rain-chiselled warrior, frozen in time.

'Is there something wrong with you, sir?' she asked. 'Can you hear me?'

He slid her a glance, as if noticing a tossed apple core.

'Are you not going to apologise?' she asked.

'For what?'

'For bumping into me!'

'I did not bump into you,' he stated, returning his attention to the pouring rain.

By the gods, he was right. It was she who had bumped into him. What was wrong with her?

'Apologies,' she said. 'I am not myself today. I have just come to get a breath of air.' The man stared out at the pouring rain, unmoved. 'My banquet is a disaster, you see,' she continued. 'The food is bad, the service has escaped and there is a flood in my atrium.'

She did not know why she had felt the need to confess herself to him. He was a stranger, likely a bodyguard for one of her guests, and surely did not care to hear of her woes.

Still, tears began to fall down her cheeks, mixing with the rain. 'My husband loathes me. Our friends find me ridiculous. No matter how much I try, I can never please them.'

She gazed out at the rain, wishing it could somehow wash away the memory of the banquet from her guests' minds, as if it had never taken place. She wished she could wash away the memory of the last ten years, in truth.

'My reputation is in tatters,' she said, 'and so is my marriage.'

She searched his face for some sign of a response, but it remained as still as a mask. She followed a drop of rain down the bumps of his arms and on to the paving stones at his feet.

She wiped her cheeks and turned to leave.

'There are worse things in the world,' he said.

'Excuse me?'

He shook his head, dismissing the words.

'Apologies, but what did you just say?' Vita insisted.

She moved into his line of sight and gazed up at the features of his face. To her surprise, they were broad and pronounced, like those of a politician or man of the stage. His strong triangular nose in particular caught her eye. It tapered to an unexpected point, giving him an erudite appearance that was reinforced by his wide, thoughtful mouth.

That mouth—it seemed full of opinions, though his lips seemed far too sensual to support anything it said. She wished to see his eyes, but still he would not meet her gaze. It was then she noticed his forehead. Three thin black letters were tattooed across its wide expanse. *FGV*, they read. *Runaway.*

She should have guessed it. He was a slave for one of her guests, most likely Lepidus, who was the highest-ranking man there. It was probably Lepidus who had ordered the man's tattoo, for the old equestrian architect had many slaves and was known for his brutal punishments. Vita felt suddenly very foolish.

'You are right, sir. There are worse things in the world,' she said. 'Much worse things. My apologies.'

Finally, he looked at her and an unwelcome rush of warmth spread beneath her skin. His brownish-green eyes were large, yet perfectly proportionate to his other outsized features. Still, they dominated his face, along with all of Vita's attention. They seemed to see inside her somehow.

'My guests are probably missing me,' she muttered. 'Again, my apologies.'

She should have been more careful in stepping around him, but in her haste she misjudged the distance between them and somehow her hand grazed his.

She jumped to the side, startled. It was as if she had just passed her hand through a blaze. She could still feel it burning as she rushed back through the door without even bothering to close it behind her.

She was halfway down the entryway hall when she heard the man call back to her.

'Do not despair,' he said. 'All will be well.'

She pretended not to hear, but the words echoed in her mind, fortifying her, and she could not get the vision of his earthy green eyes to leave her memory.

'Where have you been?' Magnus demanded as she stepped back into the *triclinium*. 'We need more wine.'

'There is no more wine.' She did not recognise her own voice: there was no apology in it. 'We have plenty of *posca*, however,' she added, reaching for a pitcher of the bitter, vinegary drink. Magnus scowled.

'No wine?' someone whispered and she noticed several sets of rolling eyes. There was a smattering of *tsks* from nameless lips.

'I fear we must take our leave,' Gaeta blurted, adding, 'on account of the rain.'

'We must also depart,' Numeria piped up, 'before the Appian is plugged with mud.'

'And the frogs!' shrieked Lollia. 'They will turn the streets into a theatre of corpses!'

Thus the banquet ended even before the first hour of night—a mark of shame if ever there was one.

Now, many hours later, the shame of Vita's failed banquet seemed small in comparison to the humiliation represented by the loincloth in her hands. It seemed that Vita's husband had taken his latest lover inside their very home.

Still, she felt no closer to determining when the tryst had occurred, or who the woman was, though she did remember watching Magnus's eyes assess Lollia from behind as she departed with her husband and their towering bodyguard across the rain-washed plaza.

It had been right before the moment when Magnus had turned to Vita and slapped her hard. 'Useless woman,' he had said, then he, too, had strode off into the grey glow of dusk.

'Useless woman,' Vita muttered now, touching one of the loincloth's golden beads. It was not the first time Magnus had called her that, nor would it be the last.

In truth, she had never questioned the epithet. Magnus was the *paterfamilias* of their household, after all, and he knew best. If he said she was useless, then she was—it was something she had always accepted.

Now she wondered if the label was truly warranted. It was true that her hostess skills were not the best in Rome. Nor was she a good cook, or a clever conversationalist, or even close to young or pretty any more, but was she really useless?

She could sew, after all, and quite well. She earned enough *sesterces* from the sale of her fine capes that she was able to keep their household stocked with oil and wine. She covered the costs of their other expenses as well, including the services of the fuller and baker, and even the annual demands of the tax collector. The proceeds from her sewing supported their lives in many different ways, so why did Magnus call her useless?

She lifted the loincloth to her nose and breathed in the scent of the cloth. Lavender, perhaps mixed with a bit of myrrh: it was the smell of a useful woman.

'I want a divorce,' she spouted. She looked up, vaguely expecting a thunderbolt to strike—or a hand against her cheek.

Instead, she caught the alabaster gaze of her venerable great-grandfather. Her father had gifted her the bust on her wedding day and, though she rarely visited it, now she gave it a soldier's salute.

'Permission to speak, Commander.'

'Permission granted,' said her illustrious ancestor. 'State your subject.'

'My husband, Commander,' said Vita.

'What is the matter?'

'He has been faithless to me throughout our marriage. He does not see the contributions I make to our household. He finds me loathsome and is often compelled to deliver me blows. He calls me useless.'

'I see,' returned the hollow-eyed centurion, who had once served in the army of Julius Caesar.

'I wish to divorce him,' she said, 'with your permission.'

'I have no argument,' replied the visage. 'Where will you go?'

Vita had no idea.

In Rome, the vast majority of marriages were *sine manu* unions. The wife went to live with her husband, but remained beneath the control of her father throughout the marriage, making divorce easy and common. To leave her husband, a woman simply packed up her dowry and returned to her father's home to await her next pairing.

But Vita's father had insisted on a *cum manu* contract with Magnus, transferring his authority over Vita, along with her dowry and all her possessions, to Magnus himself.

'If you divorce Magnus, you will become homeless,' remarked the centurion.

'I am aware, Commander.'

Too aware. It was part of the reason she had stayed with Magnus all these years. When her father had given her away to Magnus for good, he had supplied Vita with an unusually generous dowry: the very home in which they lived. It was the reason Magnus had agreed to marry her at all, though she had not known it at the time. She had mistakenly believed he had married her out of fondness.

'I will find somewhere to live,' she repeated, as if simply saying her desire aloud could somehow make it come true. 'I will do that first, then I will divorce him.'

'A sensible plan, but are you certain?' asked the bust. 'The Rubicon River, once crossed...'

Vita nodded, aware that she would likely spend the rest of her life living in squalor, struggling to survive on her own. It was a reality that had kept her tethered to a man who did not want her for too long, but not any more. There were some things in life more important than comfort—dignity, for example.

She held the loincloth above the lamp as if illuminating a sacred text. Two small initials came into view. They were as white as the fabric itself: *L.F.*

Lollia Flamma—Magnus's latest lover.

Mystery solved. Vita scolded herself for not seeing it sooner. The young, raven-haired socialite was the highest ranking of Vita's female guests that night and also the most beautiful.

She remembered how Magnus had watched Lollia depart that evening. He had departed himself immediately afterwards, had probably followed Lollia all the way to her home. The two had then sneaked back to Aventine Hill together and made love in Magnus's *tablinium* while Vita slept.

Ha, ha, ha!

Vita waded towards the centre of the atrium and glanced up to observe the sky.

Holy Minerva, it was beautiful. Most nights, the smoke of a million cooking fires clogged the air of Rome, but tonight the smoke seemed to have been swept away by the rain, revealing a swathe of glittering stars.

They seemed endless and full of possibility—like freedom itself.

She was going to divorce Magnus. Perhaps not today, but soon.

She had held out for years, telling herself that she

did not need his affection. It was enough to live in a fine home in a respectable neighbourhood with high-ranking acquaintances and a husband whose profession was admired.

Still, what did any of it mean if she did not have her own dignity? She turned the loincloth over and over in her hands. Four walls, a bed mat, a secure place to keep her sewing—it was all she needed.

Finally, she had decided. She would find herself a place to land, then she would fly from Magnus's life and never look back.

'Do not despair,' she whispered to herself. 'All will be well.'

She closed her eyes and in the place of stars she saw a man's green eyes. They were staring into her soul, re-assuring her.

A sound split the silence. A tiny peep echoed from somewhere near, followed by a high-pitched giggle. Vita froze.

There it was again—another peep—though this time it was deeper and throatier and much closer to a moan. Perhaps the drunken cook had begun snoring again.

'Oh, Magnus,' a soft voice cooed.

Perhaps it was not the drunken cook.

'Shush, woman,' whispered Magnus. His voice ema-nated from the *triclinium* where the banquet had taken place. 'You will wake my wife.'

Vita held her breath. He was there in the *triclinium* lounging area with Lollia, not five paces away, *in fla-grante delicto*!

Vita glanced about, wondering where she could con-ceal herself. If she waded out of the atrium into one of its surrounding rooms, the lovers would be sure to no-tice the sound of her squeaking sandals on the tiles. If she stayed put, they would soon pass by the atrium and see her there.

She had to hide, but where? She stepped on to the edge of the cistern and gazed down into its dark flood-waters. 'Come, we must get you home,' she heard Magnus say.

There seemed only one place to go. Vita took a deep breath, then slid downwards into her home's flooded rain well.

She held her breath as water surrounded her and mud enveloped her to the thighs. She could hear the sound of footfalls and whispering voices above her. They seemed to be moving away from her. They were leaving, thank the gods. She had done the right thing.

Still, she hated herself in that moment. She was help-less, a coward. Even in this small unused corner of her home was the record of her failure—so much sediment that Vita could barely move.

She reminded herself that it was not all her fault. Magnus had ignored the cistern as well, never once of-fering to help her clean it. Thus the sediment had accu-mulated: the collected detritus of a marriage gone bad.

Her breath was running out. The movement above her had ceased and so had the whispers. The two lovers had finally departed, or so she hoped, for she could no longer hold her breath. She pushed herself to the sur-face, gripping the side of the cistern and drawing in air as she opened her eyes.

There they were—her husband and his lover—stand-ing at the edge of the flooded area, staring down at her.

Magnus opened his mouth to speak, then burst into laughter. 'Vita? Have you gone mad?'

Vita lifted herself up out of the cistern and stared

down at her mud-drenched skirt. She wondered briefly if the answer to his question was yes.

'You are a thing of the swamp!' He laughed and nudged Lollia, who laughed softly, then cast her guilty eyes to the floor.

'Is that all you have to say, Husband?' asked Vita. Her heart was pounding.

'What more is there to say?' He turned to Lollia. 'Apologies, my darling. As you can see, my wife has lost her wits. Come, let us flee this madhouse.'

Her husband took his lover's hand and moved to leave.

'I divorce you, Magnus,' Vita muttered.

Her husband turned. 'Excuse me?'

'I divorce you, Gaius Magnus Furius—for your cruel heart and selfish ways. I divorce you for betraying me all these years. I divorce you, as Jupiter is my witness. We are divorced!'

She glanced down at Magnus's fist, fully expecting it to land on her cheek.

Instead her husband only grinned. 'Gods, Vita, what took you so long?'

Chapter Two

That night, Ven tossed and turned atop his bed mat, unable to find his rest. The heat of August was always difficult to endure, but this night it was as if the air itself were boiling. It was producing a kind of fever inside his mind, making him think of unimportant things. The *vigile*'s wife, for example.

Each time he closed his eyes she was standing before him, staring up at him with those inscrutable eyes. What colour were they—brown or green? And why was it so important to know? She was just another spoiled Roman woman, after all. She had crashed into him that afternoon in a flurry of self-absorption and then barraged him with complaints, just as Roman women always did.

'There are worse things in the world,' he had told her, aware that he risked a lashing for such insolence. In truth, he had hoped she would just go away.

She had not gone away, however. Instead she had studied him closely and when she had noticed his slave's tattoo she had instantly repented. *'You are right, sir,'* she had replied. *'There are worse things in the world. Much worse things. My apologies.'*

The statement had been unexpected. In his twenty

years as a slave, no Roman had ever apologised to him, though the real surprise had been in the tone of her voice: there was not a drop of condescension in it. It was as if she were not addressing Ven the slave, but Ven the man. By the gods, she had even called him 'sir'.

Sir.

It had caused his concentration to momentarily weaken and he had noticed the rain. It had been pouring over them both, soaking them through. He noticed it travelling over the bumps of her red lips and braiding down her lush, full cheeks. It ribboned its way down the locks of her sandy hair and on to her tunic, which had begun to cling tightly to her flesh.

Something inside him had roared to life. For a moment he was not a slave, but a man—a strong, lusty man standing beside a beautiful woman in a late summer storm.

Even now, the strange memory was keeping him awake.

He stood up and began to pace. His master's *tablinium* was large—it took six long strides to cross—and was open to both the atrium on one side and the sheltered garden on the other. Still, Ven was grateful for the small measure of privacy it offered.

In exchange for his services as a bodyguard, litter bearer, secretary, law clerk, architectural assistant and escort for his master's wife, he was allowed to sleep on the floor of his master's office at night.

Ven reminded himself of his good fortune. He could have been working in a field beneath the blazing sun after all, or slaving in some wretched mine counting the days until his death. Instead, he was educated and healthy and he laboured in the service of a rising man.

Many men—slaves, freedmen and citizens alike—had it much worse.

Still, all he could think about was the feel of rain on his skin that evening, and a woman's brown-green eyes looking into his. Suddenly the *tablinium* did not seem large enough. He stepped out of it and into the atrium and stared up at the sky.

Holy Taranis, the stars were beautiful—like freedom itself.

He looked away, reminding himself not to fall beneath their spell. Twice he had tried to escape his servitude and twice he had failed. His first attempt had earned him a tattoo: *FGV. Fugitivus*. It stretched across his forehead like a surrender flag.

His second attempt had earned him scars—a veritable spider's web across his back. One lash for each mile he had made it out of the city. Ten arguments in favour of the notion that there are some things worse than death.

There was just no escaping Rome. The fool who tried faced an army of half a million free souls, all of whom had an interest in keeping the equally large slave population in check.

If Ven were caught again, he would not be given a third chance. He would be crucified along the Via Appia leading into the city. He would be left upon a cross amid hundreds of other errant slaves to die slow, public deaths.

So much pain. Rome's men doled it out like grain, in bucketfuls, and thus kept their barbarians bent in submission.

Such was Rome itself, Ven thought. It plunged its fist into the world's belly and would not be satisfied until all humanity buckled.

Speed and dexterity were not enough to escape such a foe. One also needed a cache of provisions, a potent

disguise and a lifetime's worth of Fortuna's good favour. One also needed a fire burning inside one's heart.

Ven stared up at the stars once again, testing himself.
He willed away his sense of awe and the yearning that
followed in its wake. Yearning led to desire and desire
was the most dangerous kind of fire there was. The stars
were not beautiful, or hopeful, or wondrous, or so he told
himself. They were just tiny points of light in the dark
night sky. They represented nothing.

And he would be a fool to think he could ever out-
match the power of Rome.

There was a soft squeak somewhere near. The front
door creaked open and Ven slipped into the shadows, his
mind racing. Had a robber managed to get past the night
guard? Ven could hardly believe it. The large Scythian
guard was one of Lepidus's few paid servants. The ill-
tempered mercenary would not miss the opportunity to
apprehend an invader and prove his worth.

Perhaps the sound had come from the guard himself, stepping away from his post? Ven hoped it was
the latter. He was in no mood to apprehend an invader
on this night.

He held his breath as he followed the sound of footfalls towards the atrium, considering how he might take
down an intruder. He held his breath and braced himself as a familiar profile stepped into view. Incredibly,
it was Lollia Flamma, his own *domina*.

He exhaled, sinking deeper into the dark, and watched
in puzzlement as the young woman moved down the hall
and disappeared behind her bedchamber door. There
was only one explanation for such secrecy: Lollia had
taken a lover.

What other reason might a beautiful young woman
have for sneaking about at night behind the back of

her much older husband? Ven imagined that the young woman and her lover had created some diversion for the Scythian, then huddled briefly outside the entryway of Lepidus's home saying their goodbyes. Stealing time.

An image of the *vigile*'s wife slipped back into his mind. It was as if the time they had spent together had been stolen, too, though the theft had been accidental. Still, the thought caused a strange warmth to envelop Ven's chest.

He did not know why she continued to bother him so. They had spent only a few accidental moments together, most of which had been filled with her meaningless chatter. He could picture her standing in front of him now, the rain pouring over her head, her expression aghast. *Excuse me!* she was saying. She was excessively short to the same degree that he was excessively tall and she'd had to tilt her head back as far as it would go just to see him.

The memory struck him as comical. She was like a stout little dagger staring up at a towering spear, vying for attention.

And her eyes—so luminous against her rain-washed skin.

More warmth. This time it was spreading through his limbs, surely the return of that cursed fever. He did not appreciate its heat. It reminded him too much of desire, a dangerous emotion for a slave. Her eyes were not any more luminous than any other eyes, or so he told himself, and there was nothing funny or special or endearing about her either. She was just another spoiled Roman woman after all. She meant nothing.

Besides, he would probably never see her again.

And thank the gods for that.

* * *

Vita was awake before the dawn, beset by happiness. It had sneaked up on her in the night, a beggar demanding coin. She found her pockets were full.

She tried to remember the last time she had felt so light-hearted. It occurred to her that it had been the very day she had met her husband—her *ex*-husband—Magnus.

She remembered the meeting vividly, though it had been over ten years ago now. She had been sitting inside her mother's weaving room, unable to concentrate on the threads.

'Are you Vita?' he had asked her, stepping into the doorway. She had not replied, had not even looked up, for she had been in no mood to speak. Though it had been many months since her mother's death, Vita had remained frozen inside her grief.

'I am here for an audience with the Senator,' Magnus had explained. 'Where might I find him?'

'In the *tablinium*, of course,' Vita had muttered.

'And your mother?'

'My mother?' Vita had gazed at the row of threads, feeling the heat of tears on her cheeks.

'Forgive me,' Magnus had said. 'I refer to the woman of the house—your father's wife. It is just that… I have a gift.' He had produced a bouquet from behind his back.

'Lavender flowers?'

'You stare at them so keenly. Do you favour them?'

'No, it is just…lavender was my mother's favourite flower.' Finally, she had looked up at him. Standing before her had been the handsomest man she had ever seen.

'And your father's wife—where might I find her?' he had asked.

'Lounging in the *triclinium*.'

'Ah, gratitude,' he had said, then, incredibly, he had held the flowers out to Vita. 'Please, take them.'

'Are they not for my father's wife?'

'My gift to your father and his wife is something else.' He had flashed her a dazzling grin. 'The flowers are for you.'

Vita had been confused. 'Excuse me, but who are you?'

'I am Magnus,' he had pronounced, 'your new husband.'

They had wed just five days later inside her father's *tablinium*. Discretion had been essential, for Vita's father was a senator of Rome and Vita was not a legitimate child. Vita had only thanked the gods that her father had chosen Magnus for her mate. He was strong, handsome, witty, refined. Vita found it hard to believe that such a dashing young man would take such an interest in a plain woman such as she.

She had never been so hopeful than on the day their hands were joined and, when they arrived outside the house with which her father had endowed her, she was overwhelmed with emotion. 'I can hardly believe you chose me,' she had told him. 'I cannot wait to make a home together.'

'A home? This is a palace,' Magnus had remarked. 'I can hardly believe it is mine.'

'Ours,' Vita had corrected.

She should have known then that he did not care for her. He had married her for the house, nothing more. It gave him exactly what his humble beginnings had not supplied him: a place to entertain, a symbol of his status, a family history he could feign. It was everything he needed to forge his own road to success.

Vita had merely been a bump in that road.

What a fool she had been! But no longer. Now, after ten years of misery, she had finally divorced Magnus. He was never going to love her—she had known that for years—but now she realised he was never going to respect her either.

Life was short and she wanted more.

The sun touched her cheeks and seemed to set them aflame. She was divorced! Joy pounded inside her heart.

She squinted against the bright sunlight. This was how the sun greeted her every morning, for her bed-chamber was located on the eastern side of the house. Magnus had wanted it that way, for it caused Vita to wake before him each day. Thus she could prepare his breakfast and empty his chamber pot and ready his clothes for the day—all before he woke.

Vita had little desire to do much readying of anything today, however. She was a divorced woman after all. Divorced!

Though perhaps she should have waited to announce her decision. 'You have five days,' he had told her the night before and she had been shocked.

'I thought it was sixty,' she had replied.

'Five,' he had had said through clenched teeth.

If only she could have held her tongue, she could have saved herself a good deal of worry. She had heard it was difficult to find a room in Rome and now she had only five days in which to do it.

Still, she could not let her worry ruin her good cheer. She crossed to her small window and peered out at the neighbourhood—a garden of brick and stucco bathed in dawn's yellow light.

The view was lovely, though much was still in shadow, including her doorway itself. As she gazed down into that ill-lit space, her heart filled with a strange delight.

Only a few hours before, she had been standing there beside a man who had found her...worth reassuring.

Perhaps she was making too much of their short interchange. Perhaps the warmth she had felt when his hand grazed hers had been an invention of her own mind—a remedy she had concocted to soothe her weary heart.

In truth, it had been the darkest moment of her life. She had been standing on the cornice of a cliff whose bottom she could not see. He had reached out his hand to her and somehow held her steady.

'Do not despair,' he had said. *'All will be well.'*

It was as if he had loaned her his very spirit in that moment—sent it travelling from his hand to hers. It had rushed up her arm and spread throughout her body, warming the back of her mind, the headwaters of her tears. It had wrapped around her heart like a cloak.

She tucked the memory away. The moment was gone, as was the man, surely never to return. He had eased her heart, that was all. And that was enough. She would find a place to live. In five days, she would be safe inside a room in some towering *insula*, with no one to answer to but herself. She would not despair. All would be well.

She lifted her gaze to the plaza beyond the alley. A troop of men carrying a tall ladder marched past a mother with a babe on her hip. The mother turned away, stepping into a large gathering of pigeons. They rioted into flight and the babe shrieked with delight.

The city would be beautiful today, as it always was after a rain. The air would be clear, the fountains bursting, the streets washed clean of their grime. It would be the perfect day for a walk.

A walk: what a lovely idea. How she would enjoy a walk! She could reacquaint herself with Rome's neighbourhoods and investigate her options for dwellings.

Why not go for a walk? She was a divorced woman now, which meant that she no longer answered to Magnus. She could do whatever she liked.

She could pretend she was a tourist! A Roman citizen born in the provinces, visiting the city for the first time. She could smile and gasp at the sights: the Flavian Amphitheatre, the Circus Maximus, the Roman Forum.

She could spend all afternoon at the baths, by Jove! She had always wanted to experience the Baths of Trajan—the newest complex in the city—but had never found the time. Magnus had always come first, followed by her sewing.

Today, however, she was in no mood for either. Nor was she in the mood to clear the flood in the atrium, though she knew she would not have Magnus's aid.

The kitchen also needed attention. It had gone from messy to disastrous after her efforts with the dumplings. It would all need to be cleaned and set in order soon, lest it be overrun by vermin.

She turned away from the window and sighed. There would be no wandering today, it seemed, and the hunt for a dwelling would have to wait. There was housework to be done.

She paused at the entrance to the kitchen and gave the household god his usual helping of grain. 'Protect all inside this house, goodly Lar,' she entreated.

'Ow!' replied a voice.

Vita strode into the kitchen in pursuit of the sound, then stumbled against a large sack that had apparently been stuffed with bones. 'Ow!' the sack repeated. Catching herself against the wall, she peered down at the howling obstacle. 'Go away!' it groaned.

'I will not go away,' replied Vita, 'for this is my own kitchen!'

The sack rolled over and sat up, blinking in the morning light. 'Gods, what is the hour?' asked the dishevelled cook.

'It is the second hour of the morning,' said Vita. 'Why are you still here?'

The woman scratched at her tangled black locks, then cast a look of longing at the pockets of Vita's tunic. 'What? You expect to be paid?' Vita asked. 'You drank twenty *denariis'* worth of my Falernian wine!'

The woman's expression contorted with confusion, then disbelief, then seemed to settle on denial. She opened her mouth and released a pocket of air, then lay back and curled into a ball, as if to resume her slumber.

'Oh, no!' Vita stalked across the kitchen, dipped a cup into the water bucket, then returned and dumped the water over the woman's curly head.

The woman sat up, sputtering 'Why did you do that?'

'What is your name?'

The woman appeared not to know. 'It is...ah... Avidia, madam,' she said, as if realising it herself. 'Avidia Secunda.'

'Well, get up, Avidia Secunda! This is not the corner tavern!'

Avidia struggled to her feet and Vita was reminded of the woman's formidable height. Her wet black curls hung almost to her shoulders and seemed in great need of a comb. Beneath her tattered tunic, scabs of bed lice peppered her skin.

'Where am I if not the tavern?' Avidia slurred. She looked thoroughly perplexed. By the gods, she was still drunk!

'You are in the home of the Commanding Vigile of the Regio III District of Rome,' said Vita. 'You were hired to cook for a banquet, but you passed out drunk before you could do it.'

'Did I?'

'I laboured sewing capes for many months to purchase the wine you drank.'

'You did?'

The woman placed her finger on her nose and closed her eyes. 'Forgive me,' she mumbled.

'Forgive you? You abandoned me with the dumplings! They were the reason I hired you at all. You said that you made dumplings—'

'—that the gods themselves could pine for,' muttered Avidia. 'Dear Minerva.'

Vita dipped the cup back into the drinking water bucket and handed it to her, and she drank the water down in a single gulp. 'Forgive me, madam,' she said.

Now Vita felt more foolish still. She was speaking with a lice-bitten woman in a ragged tunic who had drunk herself into oblivion. Surely the woman had graver problems than a failed banquet.

'Come, I will see you out,' Vita said and the women made their way to the exit.

'The wine,' Avidia said in the doorway, 'and the dumplings. Everything. I am truly sorry.'

Vita dug in the pocket of her robe and placed five brass *sesterces* in the woman's palm. 'You are forgiven.'

The woman stared in disbelief at the handful of coins. 'May Jupiter bless you, madam.'

'Do not use them to buy wine!'

Avidia blinked her glassy eyes and shook her head in confusion.

'Have a nice day,' Vita said.

'And you, too, madam.' She began to move slowly across the plaza, apparently lost in though. Avidia had not gone five paces when she turned suddenly back to Vita. 'May I ask you a question, madam?'

'Of course.'

'When you hired me, you said you were a terrible cook, yes?'

'That is true,' said Vita.

'Why not purchase a slave to cook for you?'

It was not the first time Vita had been asked the question. A woman of Vita's rank was expected to own a slave or two—especially given the size of home she kept.

Vita selected her words. 'I shall answer your question with a question of my own,' she said. 'In the manner of the sophists.'

'Very well,' said Avidia gamely.

'Why do you not indenture yourself to someone?'

'Enslave myself for a time? Is that what you are asking?'

'Yes. Or am I wrong to assume you have debts?'

Avidia sighed. 'You are not wrong.'

'Then why do you not simply indenture yourself? You would have a roof over your head and food to eat. You could pay your debt over time. You would not have to seek out paid work.'

'But I would be the same as a slave. My life would not be my own.'

Vita grinned. 'Freedom is precious, is it not?'

'It is.'

Vita paused. 'My mother was a slave.'

Avidia studied Vita's face, as if seeing it for the first time. 'Ah.'

Avidia's silence belied her thoughts. She was obviously Roman, her *gens* as legitimate and ancient any other. Vita's confession had instantly reversed their roles, making Avidia the higher-ranking woman and conferring upon Vita a particular kind of shame.

Still, Vita did not regret her confession. She noticed the broken blood vessels meandering down Avidia's cheeks. She could read years of sadness in the creases around the woman's mouth and the bags around her eyes seemed accustomed to containing tears.

There would be no judgement from Avidia—only compassion. 'I divorced my husband last night,' Vita added. 'I have nowhere to go.'

Avidia grasped Vita's hand reassuringly. 'Well, I suppose congratulations are in order,' she said. Her face lit up with a genuine grin and she ran her hand through her mane of black curls. 'I would offer you a place to stay, but I am afraid I sleep on the floor of the tavern most nights.'

Vita gave Avidia a grateful bow. If she could find a large enough place to live, perhaps she could help Avidia off the tavern floor herself. 'Magnus has given me five days in which to find a place. I just need to find something safe and inexpensive.'

'Safe and inexpensive? Unlikely bedfellows in Rome. The cheapest *insulae* are in the Subura, but bad men roam that neighbourhood at night.'

Vita swallowed hard. 'Perhaps I can start by asking here in the Aventine. Surely the local matrons will know of something—possibly nearby.'

'In that case you should not go knocking on doors until the afternoon,' stated Avidia. 'Just now all the matrons will be at the baths.'

Vita turned and gazed down the entryway at the flooded atrium. All the matrons of the Aventine in one place? Perhaps the clean up could wait.

'Come, dear Avidia,' she said. 'Let us go for a dip.'

Chapter Three

When the *vigile*'s wife wandered into the warm *tepidarium* that morning, Ven thought he was seeing a ghost. A halo of steam surrounded her as she padded noiselessly across the tiles and he felt certain that she was not walking, but floating.

An unfamiliar lust gathered within him as his ghostly vision crossed to the warm pool—itself obscured by a cloud of vapour. The soft-footed ghost slipped off her drying cloth and hung it on a hook.

Blessed Isis, there she was, all of her, standing a pool's length away from him, blurry in the mist, naked but for a loincloth. He feared to blink, lest she disappear into the steam.

Not a ghost, but a goddess.

It was the only way to explain what he saw. She was a divinity in the flesh, for no intangible spirit could have played host to such a generous apportionment of attractive curves. Her breasts alone were a revelation—so round and full, like abundance itself. They ruled over a pillowy stomach that spread into lush, wide hips and succulent thighs that seemed the perfect staging ground for worship.

She stepped into the pool and started towards him.

He redoubled his efforts on his *domina*'s back, which he was supposed to be rubbing. Still, he could hardly concentrate on the task and continued to look up as she approached, his heart beating faster.

His own imagination had outdone itself. Red lips and dark brows were coming into view, along with long ropes of hair the colour of the sandy earth. It fell around her generous breasts, caressing her perfect pink nipples.

She was an incarnation of divinity for certain, a dangerous ghost that he had summoned from the netherworld to remind him of what he could not have.

'What is wrong, Ven?' barked Lollia. 'Why have you stopped rubbing?'

'Apologies,' Ven muttered.

'My legs.'

Ven moved to the other side of the massage bench, turning his back on the vision. His *domina*'s legs! What was the matter with him? He was a slave, after all. The only goddess he served was the one sprawled before him.

The other was just vision—a meaningless fantasy he had conjured in his mind for a reason he could not guess. He cleared his mind and concentrated on his task, willing his ghostly siren to disappear for ever.

Vita hung her drying cloth on a hook and stepped into the warm pool. Her whole body relaxed as she let its balmy waters carry her worries away. There were precious few bathers today: a handful of swimmers and just a smattering of loungers on the benches at the far end of the expanse. It was the perfect morning for a swim.

Vita smiled as she dunked her head under the water and stretched out her limbs. She had always loved to swim. Her mother had taught her to swim before she could walk, or so she had told Vita, and as a young woman Vita had often come to the baths.

Still, it had been at least ten years since she had allowed herself the pleasure of a dip and she could hardly contain her joy.

She began to tread the water, moving her arms and legs rhythmically, in the manner of a frog. How silly she must have looked, yet she did not care. Beneath the silken water she felt graceful for a change and the limbs she had always condemned for their short thickness felt buoyant and light. Beautiful, even.

She burst to the surface, then turned to discover a well-coiffed woman floating nearby, frowning.

'Apologies, madam, if I splashed you,' Vita said.

'You did not, thank holy Neptune,' said the woman, who had invoked the name of Neptune as if he were a personal friend.

'You would not happen to know of any rooms for rent nearby?' The woman's frown deepened.

'You are a provincial?' she asked Vita. 'A tourist?' She gave Vita an assessing look. 'From Baetica? Pannonia, perhaps? One of the three Gauls?'

'The Aventine,' said Vita.

The woman's frown bloomed into scowl and she floated away into the mist.

Vita told herself it was of nothing. There would be other women with whom to discuss possibilities for shelter. If she could not find any here in the *tepidarium*, she would certainly find them in the more popular *caldarium*, where Avidia was already sitting sweating away her woes. Surely between the two of them they would stir up some information, for what was the purpose of the baths if not for the smooth exchange of it?

Vita sank beneath the water once more. She could

hear the low roar of the boiler, which lay in the large open area beneath the baths. It did not just warm the pools, but the walls and floors, compelling the bathers to rest.

There was no rest for those who made the heat, however. The slaves who serviced the boiler were invisible, yet indispensable, just like the boiler itself. She imagined those slaves feeding precious wood into the great stone beast, their bodies awash in sweat. It was they who most needed a bath; they who most deserved a rest.

Vita pictured her own mother, who had been brought to Rome as a slave from distant Britannia. She refused to go to the baths, even after Vita's father had freed her. 'The other women would notice my tattoo,' she had always protested, pointing at the tiny stains of servitude on the side of her neck.

'But you, my darling,' she would tell Vita, 'you shall be freer than I ever was and I want you to spend your life at the baths!'

Vita came up for air and smiled sadly. So much for spending her life at the baths. Not long after her mother died, her father had married her to Magnus, who had gently informed Vita that she was too fat to go bathing.

Not wishing to make a fool of herself, Vita had made a habit of bathing inside her own bedchamber using water and a bit of soap.

She liked to think her mother would have approved— especially of the soap. She had always thought it strange how Romans cleansed themselves with olive oil. 'And have you seen those terrifying instruments they use to scrape it off their skin?' her mother had often remarked. 'They are like the tools of demons!'

Today, Vita would purchase a vial of olive oil from an attendant, rub it over her skin, then diligently scrape it off with one of those demon tools. It had been a long time since she had wielded a *strigil* and she only hoped that nobody would notice her awkwardness in handling it. Mostly, however, she hoped that nobody would notice her body.

It was the reason why, as Vita started her way up the stairs leading out of the pool, she scanned the lounging area for the most private possible bench. Unfortunately, the bench closest to the wall was taken. On it, a woman lay on her stomach and appeared to be receiving a massage from a tall man wearing a slave's short tunic.

Vita had not noticed the two before, probably because the daylight streaming in from the high windows had yet to reach them. The woman was lying motionless, her face turned towards the wall. The man had obviously been stooped over her in the labour of massage, though not any more. Now he was standing at full height.

He appeared to be staring at Vita.

She froze. It was permissible for male slaves to accompany their *dominas* into the female baths, but they were not supposed to stare. Still, though the man's face remained in shadow, there was something familiar about him.

She studied his silhouette: a tall, thin figure with a broad chest and sinewy muscles. He looked very much like the man she had met outside her home yesterday at the banquet.

Her heart began to beat a little faster. She moved up the stairs and paused just before the edge of the pool, keeping her eyes on him.

The bumpy muscles of his arms seemed particularly familiar, as if they could have been the very muscles she had considered the afternoon of the banquet. They tapered down into strong hands that were slick with oil.

It was as if she could feel one of those hands brushing against her own. She felt herself flush.

He moved forward a little, as if he, too, wished to see her more clearly, and in that moment the sunlight reached his face.

Those eyes—she knew them instantly. They were not the eyes of a browbeaten slave, but of a man of dignity and intelligence, a warrior tucked inside a stony façade, quietly smouldering.

Her heart felt fit to burst. He was the man she had bumped into for certain. No other man could have made her feel the way she was feeling right now.

'Ven, you are useless today,' muttered the man's *domina*. The woman rolled over suddenly and gasped. 'Vita? Is that you?'

Vita, thought Ven. So that was her name. *Life*, it meant. She stood unmoving at the edge of the pool, naked but for her soaked loincloth. She reminded Ven of a deer that had just been spotted by a hunter.

'Well met, Lollia,' Vita said, folding her arms over her breasts.

'Well met indeed. I confess I did not expect to see you here,' said his *domina*, who seemed strangely unnerved as well.

'I was just leaving,' Vita said. She turned back towards the pool.

'Do not go,' said Lollia, sitting up. 'At least not until I may apologise.'

Ven sensed the other bathers listening closely. Vita turned back to Lollia and shook her head. 'There is no need to apologise.'

'Of course there is,' said Lollia, and Ven wondered what exactly the two women were speaking about.

'What I mean is that I am…accustomed to apologies,' said Vita. 'I no longer find them necessary.'

'I see,' said Lollia, brightening. 'In that case, will you not join me for a while? Let us chat and exchange a bit of gossip.'

Vita refolded her arms nervously, her eyes darting about. Ven still could not tell if they were brown or green, though there was no question of their beauty. Such eyes! They gave her otherwise regal-looking visage a twinge of wildness that was only enhanced by her lips, which reminded him of the petals of wild flowers. She was the loveliest woman he had ever seen.

'There is no need to be shy, darling,' said Lollia. 'It is just women here. And, of course, there is Ven, but he does not count.' Lollia turned to Ven. 'Get Vita a drying cloth, would you?'

Ven retrieved a drying cloth from a bag of supplies and crossed to where Vita stood. Keeping his gaze respectfully averted, he handed her the cloth.

'Gratitude,' Vita said to him. 'Ven.'

It was as if she had kissed his very cheek. He bowed and returned to his *domina*, his heart beating. Meanwhile, Vita wrapped the drying cloth around her chest and crossed to a nearby bench.

Lollia propped her head on her arm and studied Vita closely. 'It is a lovely morning, is it not, dear?'

'It is,' replied Vita. 'A bit warmer than expected.'

There was a long silence. 'I have heard that you have recently divorced,' said Lollia.

Ven pressed his thumbs into the bottoms of his *domina*'s feet. The audacity of such a statement! Did his *domina* have no discretion at all? Ven was so angered by her rudeness that he barely registered her words.

When he finally did, a strange lightness seemed to invade his limbs.

Divorced? Was Vita Sabina no longer the *vigile*'s wife?

'Yes, I have divorced,' Vita whispered, studying the floor. 'Just last night, in fact.'

'You need not whisper, dear. It is just a divorce,' said Lollia. 'I have had two of them already and another surely coming soon. I confess that I prefer my father's household to any husband's.'

He saw Vita press her lips together, as if fighting her emotion.

'Ven? Why do you pause?' asked Lollia. 'Rub me!'

'Ah, yes, Domina.'

Ven returned to Lollia's foot, but it was not long before he was stealing glances at Vita again. Vita's face was even lovelier at close range, but also sadder. Her noble round cheeks seemed shaped by a divine hand, yet one of them was redder than the other, as if it had been bruised. Her heavy lids were at once sensual and weary.

'Tell me, Vita, why do I never see you here? You do bathe, do you not?' asked Lollia.

Vita's laugh was thready. 'Of course I bathe. I just never have the time to make the trek.'

'But these baths cannot be more than a twenty-minute walk from your home.'

Vita folded and refolded her hands in her lap. 'I pass most of my free time sewing.'

'Sewing?' replied Lollia. 'What a strange hobby.'

'It is not a hobby. I earn coin by it.'

Lollia sucked in a breath. 'You engage in trade?' She pronounced the word *trade* as if uttering a curse.

'I have been earning money from my sewing for nearly ten years now,' Vita added.

'Ten years?' Lollia said. 'Well, you must have married very late indeed.'

'I married at the age of fifteen.'

Lollia gasped. 'Married at fifteen and ten years of marriage?' Lollia held out her hands and began to count.

'I turned twenty-five on the *kalends* of last month.'

'Ack! What a horror for you! I married at the customary age of twelve, of course,' Lollia offered, 'but with the ascension of Emperor Hadrian, my father was able to find a better match for me. And now an even better one in Lepidus Severus.'

'You make a lovely couple.'

'He is as wrinkled as an old piece of lettuce,' Lollia said. 'And old enough to be my grandfather! When he is on top of me, his prickly jowls graze my skin!'

Lollia burst into laughter, drawing the attention of the other loungers. 'Of course, the reason my father sought our union was for Lepidus's connection to Emperor Hadrian. He will be the Emperor's lead architect in the north, you know.'

'I have heard about the prestigious appointment. Congratulations to you both,' said Vita.

Lollia made a face. 'The post will require us to spend many years in the frigid wilds of Britannia among those wretched Britons.' She lifted her leg for Ven to rub beneath it. 'No offence, Ven,' she added.

'None taken, Domina,' Ven said, feeling nothing. He rubbed and rubbed.

'I would love nothing better than to behold the fabled lands of the north,' Vita said.

'If only you could go in my place!' exclaimed Lollia. 'But perhaps I will become pregnant and unable to make the trip.' Lollia glanced down at her stomach and Ven wondered if it had not grown a little thicker. 'On the bright side, Lepidus has promised to purchase me as many slaves as I would like once we arrive. They say the slaves of Britannia are particularly hard working. Tell me, Vita, why do you not own any slaves?'

'I, ah, I have never found myself in need of any aid,' said Vita.

'A slave or two might have helped you last night. My backside, Ven!' Ven started in on his *domina*'s wretched bottom, though there was rather little dough to knead. 'Really, Vita, what is your aversion to slaves? Can you not see the benefits?'

Lollia opened her mouth suddenly, as if struck by a thought. 'By Juno, I am brilliant!' She brushed Ven aside, swung her legs in front of her and sat up.

'What is the matter?' Vita asked.

'I just realised how I will convince you of the benefits of owning slaves.' She crossed to Vita and took her by the hands. 'Come, dear Vita. Lie in my place.'

Vita felt as if she was being coaxed into a spider's web. 'You wish for me to occupy the massage bench?'

'Trust me,' Lollia said. 'The only way to understand the benefits of owning a slave is to experience them directly. Besides, I feel I owe you a bit of pleasure.'

'You owe me nothing, really,' said Vita, but Lollia's grin was more like a snarl and, as she took Vita's hands and guided her to the bench, Vita felt helpless to contradict her.

'You must remove the drying cloth around your chest,' said Lollia.

'What?'

'Your modesty is excessive, Vita. Come, we are not Vestal Virgins here!'

There was a small chuckle from someone in the pool. Meanwhile, several new loungers had taken up residence on the benches around them. It seemed that Lollia was making Vita into the morning's entertainment.

'You will be lying on your stomach. Nothing will be exposed,' Lollia explained.

Vita forced a grin and tried to relax. Lollia was right. She should not be so modest. There were all kinds of women enjoying the baths. They walked around freely, as naked as nymphs.

'I know why you are worried,' Lollia added. 'It is because your breasts and backside are so large,' Lollia mused. 'I understand. But you must know that it is just women here. We do not judge.'

Vita continued to grin, though her teeth were beginning to ache. She glanced at Ven, who was carefully studying the floor. *Do not despair,* she thought. *All will be well.*

She undid her drying cloth and lay down on her stomach.

'That is the spirit,' said Lollia.

She sensed several large drops of oil being dribbled on to her back and she felt vaguely like a cow being seasoned for roasting.

'First her shoulders,' Lollia told Ven. 'Work your way down from there and use plenty of oil. Do not be lazy! We must convince Vita of the benefits of owning a skilled slave.'

The thought made Vita vaguely ill. It was Ven who deserved the massage, not she. It was too late to protest, however, for now his hands were upon her. She jerked slightly as he gently squeezed her shoulders, giving her a chance to become accustomed to his touch.

Waves of sensation pulsed through her and she wondered how long it had been since her shoulders had been touched. Surely not since she was a child, for it was as if his hands were coaxing a long-dormant part of her back to life. She filled with unexpected emotion.

She turned her head away from Lollia, for the flood of sensation seemed to be transforming itself into joyous tears.

She certainly could not remember experiencing anything more wondrous than what Ven was doing right now: gently rubbing the back of her neck. He worked his way downwards and she felt like a rope becoming slowly unwound.

She felt the tiny hairs on her neck stand at attention as they took notice of his breath. Other parts of her appeared to be taking notice, too. The skin of her arms, for example—it had gone to gooseflesh. The tips of her toes tingled, as well, and strange spirits seemed to stir deep inside her belly.

'It feels good, does it not?' asked Lollia. She had stretched out on a nearby bench and closed her eyes.

Good? That did not seem a sufficient description of the riot of pleasure taking place within her.

'Yes, very good,' Vita managed to say as Ven's thumbs gently pressed against the backs of her shoulders—parts of her she was now certain had never been touched by human hands.

Though the hands touching them now could not possibly be human. They were those of a god—a divinity incarnate who had materialised in her life and now seemed intent on rubbing all her troubles away.

She prayed the massage would not end. *Do not cease*, she thought. *Please. Ever.*

And then his hands were gone.

Vita lay still. So that was it. A lifetime's worth of pleasure packed into a few short moments. It would have to be enough.

'That was marvellous,' she pronounced, discreetly wiping her eyes. She pushed herself on to her arms and moved to stand, then felt the gentle pressure of two fingers against the small of her back.

'Not yet,' said a deep, sensual voice.

'Not yet?' she muttered, as if they were not the two most wonderful words she had ever heard in all her life. She nearly laughed aloud.

Not yet. She was a reasonable woman. She could accept those terms. She would rise from the bench and express her eternal gratitude when it was time to do so, but certainly not yet.

'That was just the shoulders,' Lollia observed, yawning. 'There is much more to come. You must try to relax.'

Vita sensed large drops of oil dribbling down her back. She was trying to relax, but the anticipation of his hands once again visiting her skin was causing her to tense.

And then there they were again: her newest, greatest friends, sprawling across her back and pressing gently downwards. Not a gentle reintroduction to bliss, then, but a full immersion.

'Ah,' she breathed as he squeezed her flanks. His grip was unwaveringly strong, as if his muscles had formed over thousands of years.

She felt totally beneath his control as he dragged his large thumbs down either side of her spine with an almost unbearable slowness. Tiny waves of pleasure resounded through her body.

Vita reminded herself to breathe as he arrived at her lower back and paused, then returned to the top of her spine for another pass.

She felt like a piece of clay. He was gathering her up and pressing her into a newer, better form. He made several successive passes up and down her spine, each time varying his movement slightly so as to reach some new cache of muscles.

She wondered how long Lollia would allow the massage to go on. She prayed the young woman would go for a dip in the pool and forget about Vita entirely. For her part, Vita felt dangerously close to forgetting herself. She closed her eyes.

'Hardd,' Ven muttered.

Her heart nearly stopped beating. It was a word from the ancient tongue—her mother's beloved Celtic. Or had she only imagined he had said it?

'Did you just speak in the tongue of the north?' Vita asked.

He gave no reply, but she sensed his silent affirmation. *Yes, I did.*

He was from Britannia for certain. She had suspected as much from the moment she had heard him speak. His Latin was too laboured to be native and too lilting to be German. It sounded just like her own mother's Latin— like a ribbon being tied into a loop.

Still, that was not what had stopped her heart. It was what he had called her in her mother's tongue: *hardd.* It meant *beautiful.*

'Pa lwyth?' she repeated in their shared tongue. *What tribe?*

His breathing ceased. 'The Brigantes,' he said at length. His fingers were only barely touching her now. It was as if her body were a lute he was unsure of what to play next. 'And you?' he whispered. *'A chi?'*

'My mother was of the Caledonii,' Vita admitted in their shared tongue. 'In the far north.'

'The Brigantes and the Caledonii are ancient enemies,' he observed.

'Does that make us enemies?' she asked.

She could not feel his fingers at all any more. She feared she had said too much.

In her youth, her mother had often spoken of the people of Britannia. They were separated into many different tribes that often fought. Their best men were raised to be warriors who placed honour above all else. Vita sensed that Ven was such a man. She had no idea what his honour might compel him to think of her now.

'You are very good at massage,' Vita offered in Latin, trying to change the subject.

'You say that, yet you have no idea,' he whispered.

She could not read his tone. Had she offended him somehow? Did his enmity for her mother's tribe spill over on to her? Or did he mean something else entirely? She was utterly confused. Her throat felt dry.

She sensed him stepping away from her and turned to find him disappearing from her line of sight. She had offended him, then. She had stirred an ancient hatred that compelled him to distance himself. She should never have mentioned her Caledonii blood.

She nearly shrieked when she felt the cool trickle of oil drops once again upon her back. She turned her head in the other direction and saw him standing at eye level, his strong, bulging thighs filling her vision.

He lay his hands on her shoulders. Slick with oil, they plunged downwards in a grand sweeping motion that seemed fuelled by something beyond duty. The gesture continued into the small of her back, then followed the swerve of her waist to its conclusion at her hips. He brushed the top of her loincloth.

She felt the heat of yet another blush threatening as she envisioned what he was seeing. Now there was not even the pretension of modesty. He was staring down

the length of her, the bump of her backside surely occupying most of his view.

She might have been mortified. The size of her backside was larger than other women's and she had always
felt ashamed of it. But there was something in the way
that he was touching her that made her feel uninhib-
ited. It was as if he were trying to communicate something to her.

He certainly seemed more enthusiastic, though she
would not flatter herself by thinking that he was enjoying himself. He was a slave, after all. Whatever enjoy-
ment she perceived in him was certainly a projection
of her own hopes. To him, this was an obligation, nothing more.

And yet there was nothing obliging about the way he
was touching her. He seemed to be using all the weight
of his body against the flanks of her back. Each stroke
brought with it an immense relief. It was as if he were
pressing all his goodwill into her.

He repeated the motion several times—long, ener-
getic swooping motions down the length of her back—
and she felt another wave of gratitude cresting inside her.

He gave her shoulders one last squeeze and paused.
'We are not enemies,' he whispered.

In that moment, Lollia yawned and opened her eyes.

'Ven, why have you ceased?' She turned to Vita. 'Has
he done your legs yet?'

'No, but that will not be necessary,' said Vita. 'You
have already been so generous with his time.'

She already felt another embarrassing blush creep-
ing up her neck.

'Have I at least convinced you to purchase a few
slaves of your own?' asked Lollia.

Just as Vita was opening her mouth to reply, a woman's voice echoed through the marbled chamber. 'Lollia, darling, is that you?'

A well-coiffed patrician woman was stepping into the other end of the pool amid a bevy of female slaves.

'Domitia Publia, what a lovely surprise!' squealed Lollia. She turned to Vita in a panic. 'Do you know who that is? It is the Emperor's wife's sister's mother-in-law! Gods, how is my hair?'

Not waiting for an answer, Lollia turned and waved at the woman a second time, then nearly dived into the pool, and in seconds Vita and Ven were on their own.

'What are you doing to me?' Vita whispered in Celtic.

'What are you doing to *me*?' Ven returned in the same tongue.

'I am just lying here. I am doing nothing to you.'

'You are trying to bewitch me,' he said.

She boosted herself up on her elbows and twisted to face him. 'What in Hades do you mean?'

He shook his head and silently went to work massaging her feet.

'Why will you not answer me?' she whispered.

Her lips had grown redder in the course of the massage, as had her blush. He observed that her eyes appeared more green than brown against that ruddy canvas, which was framed by the sandy brown of her hair. She was as lovely as a rainbow, yet she seemed to have no notion of her own beauty.

'Ven?' she asked in a voice made of silk.

He avoided her gaze as he worried each of her tiny toes between his fingers.

'Oh, sweet Juno,' she moaned. 'Why does that feel so good?'

'Do not moan like that.'

'Then do not rub my toes.'

'Then do not look at me'

'Do not look at you?'

'Return to your stomach, please,' he said. 'I will not succumb to the sorcery of your gaze.'

She tugged her foot away. 'And I will not succumb to your endlessly pleasurable touch!'

Finally, their eyes met and Ven watched a smile begin to split her lips.

This was truly a problem. He glanced across the pool. Thankfully, his *domina* remained deep in conversation.

Ven shook his head and tried to beat back his alarming good humour. 'You must not look at me that way. Now return to your stomach.'

'I will do no such thing,' she said.

'My *domina* will be gossiping about you soon. Eventually, she will turn to point you out. We cannot be gazing into each other's eyes in that moment, do you understand? I must be performing a task.'

Vita sighed. 'I understand. Just, please, do not rub my feet.'

'Your legs, then?'

'That will be even worse.'

Ven smiled to himself. 'You mean better.' He watched a blush creep up her neck and felt his own lust stir. This was no good at all. 'Where, then?' he demanded.

'My lower back.'

'Not your lower back.'

'Why not?'

'Because that creates a problem for me.'

She frowned at him and her eyes slid down his chest. 'Stop that,' he said.

She returned to her stomach with a huff. 'This is all highly unusual,' she grumbled.

'I do not disagree.'

'Rub my ankles,' she said after some thought. 'And the backs of my knees.'

He stroked the knob of her ankle with his thumb. 'Were you able to sleep last night?' he asked.

'Just a little. You?'

'Not at all.'

'Perhaps we suffer from the same affliction,' she whispered.

He said nothing. Her ankles were small and shapely. His hands could fit around them. 'Who are you?' he murmured.

'I am Vita of *gens* Sabinius, daughter of Senovara of the Caledonii.'

'And your father?' he asked.

'My father disowned me at the time of my marriage,' she replied. 'He has since deceased.'

'And your mother?'

'She died just before I was married.'

'Ah, so your mother—' Ven stopped himself. 'Apologies, I speak without thinking.'

'You may speak freely with me,' she said. 'Go on.'

Ven hesitated. How many times had a Roman woman urged such familiarity, only to scold him later for lack of respect? Still, this woman seemed less Roman every minute.

'So your mother was a slave. That is why your father married you off so soon after she died. You were not a legitimate child.'

She frowned and gazed at the floor.

'Apologies, I did not mean to give offence.'

She shook her head. 'How could you give offence by stating the truth? You have guessed my secret and rather quickly, I fear. My father was a high-ranking patrician and my illegitimacy harmed his reputation. I was fortunate that he endowed me well before giving me to Magnus.'

'That is well. A healthy dowry will sustain you until you are able to marry again.'

'I do not plan to marry again. And I will not be retaining any of my dowry.'

Ven moved to her other ankle. 'I do not understand. Do you have other kin, then? A brother or sister who has offered you a place?'

'I am afraid I have no one.'

'Savings? Money you have put away for this eventuality?'

Vita exhaled. 'You are working wonders on my ankles.'

'I see,' Ven said.

Gods, she had nothing at all. He envisioned Vita alone in a room inside one of Rome's crumbling high rises, scraping her meal from a pot. Rome's wretched *insulae* were notorious for fires and fevers and terrible crime. The vision sent an unwelcome ache into his heart.

'Why will you not retain your dowry?' he asked, instantly regretting his words, for there was only one reason. 'I see,' he whispered.

She twisted around once again and caught his gaze. 'I have never betrayed my husband! On the contrary, he has betrayed me. For many years. He betrayed me even last night—with a married woman, no less!'

She returned to her stomach, visibly upset, and he pictured the terrible scene. A memory struck. 'That woman did not happen to be Lollia Flamma?'

Vita gasped. 'How did you know?'

'Because she sneaked away from our home late last night and then returned without a sound.' Ven moved to the back of one of her knees and gently began to rub.

'She left her loincloth on Magnus's desk,' Vita confessed. 'Her initials are woven into the cloth.'

'She is careless even in her cheating.'

'She is young,' said Vita. 'She does not know what it means to suffer or to cause suffering in others.'

But Ven did not wish to discuss his spoiled *domina*. 'Your husband owes you the full value of your dowry,' he stated. 'You must seek its return.'

'Our marriage contract gives Magnus full *potestas* over me, I am afraid. He will never return it.'

'Not even a portion?'

'That would be impossible, for my dowry is our house itself.'

The house itself. Now it all made sense. When Magnus had married Vita, he had acquired the kind of home that would impress his superiors and help him rise through the ranks. A man like that would never give up such a symbol of status.

Ven's voice was barely a whisper. 'If you can prove your husband's adultery before a magistrate, your husband will have no choice but to return your dowry. That is the law. The loincloth is your evidence.'

'I would not dream of doing that.'

'Why not?'

'It would destroy Lollia's marriage and her reputation. She would never be able to marry again. She would be ruined.'

Ven paused. 'You would sacrifice your own dowry to protect Lollia?'

'I would never wish to be the cause of another's ruin.'

Who was this strange woman? In his twenty years in Rome, he had never encountered such an honourable heart. Ven wondered who would protect her in the bleak future that lay ahead of her. She was obviously too gentle and good for Rome's wicked streets.

'Tell me, was an *aestimatio* included as part of the marriage contract?' he asked.

'I believe that it was. My father was always keen on calculating the value of things.'

'If you can get hold of the marriage contract and the attached *aestimatio* and take it to a magistrate, it is possible he will rule in your favour, even without evidence of Magnus's betrayal.' He moved his hand to her arm, kneading it in such a way as to coax her bravery.

'How do you know all this?' she asked.

'I have served as Lepidus's legal clerk for many years and have read a great deal on such matters. The law is on your side in this. You must not be afraid to use it.'

There was a long pause. Ven thought he heard the sound of sniffling. He saw her hand move to her eyes, as if to wipe away tears. 'I would never dream of it.'

'Why not? It is your dowry. It belongs to you.'

Vita waved her hand in the air, as if swatting the idea away. 'You are very kind to offer your advice. Tell me, sir, why do you help me?'

Ven ceased his rubbing. Really, he had no idea why he was trying to help her. He should not have been speaking with her at all.

Nor should he have been admiring her curves, or considering her qualities, or enjoying how her skin felt beneath his touch.

Perhaps he was being tested by the gods. They were tempting him once again, showing him something beautiful and true, trying to see if they could goad him into doing something foolish. But he was not a fool. 'I am not trying to help you,' he replied to Vita at last. 'I am just trying to pass the time.'

He finished rubbing her other arm. There was nothing left for him to massage, so he stepped away from her and started towards his place at the corner of the bath.

Still, he could not stop thinking about that word. She had said it once again and it resounded in his head like the call of a siren.

Sir.

Chapter Four

After the baths that morning, Vita returned to her bed-chamber and counted her savings. Twenty-two *sesterces*. It was not much, but she felt certain it would buy her a month of time in an apartment somewhere in the city.

She ventured out on to the streets, determined to find that somewhere, and walked all the way to the Caelian Hill before realising that she was not thinking about shelter at all. She was thinking about Ven: his probing eyes, his sharp words and all the ways that he had touched her.

The massage. She could still feel its effects resounding through her body, making her feel lighter on her feet somehow. Her strides were longer, her breaths deeper, and she did not try to conceal the movement of her hips as she usually did. Her muscles tingled with awareness as she traversed the city streets, delighting in every step. It was as if she had become more comfortable in her skin.

She had never been touched in such a way by a man. In the early days of their marriage, Magnus had touched her as part of their coupling, but it was a rough, clumsy kind of contact that seemed to betray his uninterest. And though she had felt rejected when Magnus had finally stopped visiting her bed, she had also been relieved. She had always felt rather nameless beneath his groping hands.

Ven's touch, on the other hand, seemed to convey a kind of worship. She had felt instantly becalmed by his fingers' gentle probing against her back, which had grown stronger and more assured with each of her encouraging sighs.

He had played her like a lute, adjusting to her vibrations, anticipating her needs, increasing his intensity until his swooping, well-oiled strokes had transformed her placid calm into something more like amazement.

She was still amazed, though not just by his hands. She had also been touched by his words. His lilting Celtic had awakened a part of her that she had long ago laid to rest. *Hardd*, he had said, and it was as if he were channelling her mother's very spirit. A flood of reassurance had inundated her heart.

Still, there was nothing reassuring about what he had said to her next. He had advised her to seek the return of her dowry—dangerous advice that could lead to perilous acts.

He had no reason to help her in truth. He was a slave; his life was not his own. Indeed, he risked his own safety by speaking to her in such a way, a sad truth that he had seemed to remember when he had told her he was just passing the time.

His words had stung, but she was glad for them. If he had pressed her any further, she might have become convinced of his argument, which might have compelled her to do something foolish.

Magnus would kill her before giving up the house and she did not wish to consider the matter further. Her dowry was of no consequence. It was more important to make a clean, safe break with Magnus. As long as she could find a safe place to live and do her sewing, she would be able to survive.

Which was why she found it puzzling that she had arrived at the base of the Caelian Hill without having yet considered the problem of her situation. She had been walking for at least an hour, had passed many a towering *insula* without even seeing it. She was supposed to be looking for a place to live, not dreaming of a man she barely knew.

She gazed up at the large *insula* apartment building rising before her now: a titan she was determined to tame. She walked towards the entrance.

A handful of minutes later, she was walking away from the entrance, telling herself not to lose her spirit. Of course, there were no vacancies. She should have expected as much. Rome was full to brimming. It was the reason emperors often gave for their unrelenting expansion of Rome's borders. There was simply not enough space to accommodate its million souls.

Still, Vita would not be deterred. She said a small prayer to Diana and kept going up the hill. The next *insula* was the same and also the next. Full and fuller. At the top of the hill, the manager of a small, well-kept *insula* had an attractive room available with a view of the Tiber, but he required six months of rent in advance—a small fortune.

Another landlord was offering several rooms on the top floor of a five-storey building that did not yet have its roof. In another building, a grandmotherly manager escorted Vita to a room with a variety of droppings on the floor. 'You would not happen to own a cat?' she asked.

On a whim, Vita wandered to the area of Capitoline Hill and gazed up at what was considered to be the best *insula* in the city. She did not even knock on the door. Even if she could afford a room in such a dwelling, she knew she would not have been allowed to rent it. Renting to an unmarried woman was forbidden anywhere near Rome's sacred heart.

Discouraged, Vita returned to her home and began to clean up the atrium flood. By the time Magnus returned from his work, the house was sparkling clean.

'Where is my dinner?' he asked.

'Apologies, Magnus, I did not think you would be wanting one.' *Now that we are divorced.*

'Why not? You are still living here, are you not?' he said. 'At least for another three days?'

Vita nodded.

'In that case I will have the rest of the oysters in a stew with fish sauce and onions.'

Vita turned towards the kitchen.

'And bring me bread. I am famished.'

Vita sliced into a loaf of bread, unsure of how to feel. On the one hand, she was grateful as to how cheerfully Magnus seemed to accept the situation. He appeared genuinely glad that she was leaving him, though she should not have been surprised. It was not as if his life was going to change.

He certainly was not going to miss her. He had made that abundantly clear, though she wondered if he would miss the food she purchased and the expenses she regularly covered on his behalf. Perhaps he loathed her enough to be able to overlook those contributions or perhaps he had never even noticed them at all.

She served him his dinner in the *triclinium*. 'Is this all that remains of the honey?' he asked, holding up an empty clay pot.

'I believe it is.'

'You must get more tomorrow in that case,' he said. 'Since you are still living in this house.'

'If you wish,' said Vita.

'And my toga needs to be picked up from the fuller,' he added.

'Very well.'

He took one sip of the soup and frowned. 'After you are gone, I believe I will purchase a slave,' he said. 'One who can cook.'

He could not have stung her worse with an actual whip. Now that she was leaving, it seemed that he would use his savings to simply purchase her replacement: savings that he had been able to acquire thanks to her. No wonder he seemed so carefree. Her departure would leave him with the house, his freedom and tastier stews.

She retired to her bedroom and counted up her savings for a second time. It remained only twenty-two *sesterces*—less than half the cost of the room she had found in the Caelian that day.

She would have to look elsewhere, in a cheaper part of the city.

At the baths the day before, several matrons had mentioned the affordability of the Subura neighbourhood, though it was not recommended. 'So many fires and crumbling cement!' one matron had warned.

'You would be safer living inside a mine,' another had said.

Vita and Avidia had converged in the *caldarium* and decided to pool their resources. The prospect of having a roommate was a comfort to Vita, though she doubted Avidia would be able to contribute much in the way of rent.

Vita smiled sadly. Over the years, she must have sold over a hundred capes, some for over twenty *sesterces* each. What had become of all that coin? She looked up and spied a place in the ceiling that she had recently paid to have patched. She lay back upon her new pillows. She had bought them only a month ago so that she and Magnus might rest more comfortably in their respective beds.

She had made many similar purchases over the years—too many to count. Her life with Magnus had been rather grey and she had spent many of the proceeds from her sewing towards making it brighter. She had lived in the present instead of the future. She had been a fool.

Now she had only twenty-two *sesterces* to her name and a husband who wanted her out in three days.

Vita closed her eyes and pictured herself on the massage bench once again, lying beneath Ven's reassuring touch. *Do not despair,* she thought. *All will be well.*

She wanted to believe him, but how could she? Nothing would be well at all if she could not find a safe place to sleep at night. Rome's streets were dangerous for unaccompanied women, no matter what their station. Surely that was the reason Ven had urged her to recover her dowry—he did not wish for her to become destitute. He had wanted the best for her, as if she were worthy of such a thing.

Perhaps she *was* worthy.

His words echoed in her mind. *'You are owed the full value of your dowry.'* She wondered what exactly that might be. She guessed that the house was worth at least forty thousand *sesterces,* possibly more. Just a fraction of that sum could keep her in a Capitoline apartment for the rest of her life. It could even enable her to purchase a dwelling of her own. A sewing shop!

'The law is on your side in this. You must not be afraid to use it.'

The words were like honeybees. They swirled around in her mind, not allowing it to rest. Vita feared Magnus, but she was beginning to fear her destitution more. What was the purpose of a dowry if not to support a woman when her husband no longer would?

That was what she was thinking as she sneaked into Magnus's *tablinium* late that night and slowly pulled open the top desk drawer. She lifted her oil lamp above the shallow box and studied its contents. There were several scrolls inside, but none had anything to do with their marriage.

She glanced down at the deeper drawer running along the right side of the desk. Where did Magnus keep the key?

She was crouching beneath the desk, feeling along the wood for any crevices or secret compartments, when she heard his booming voice. 'Vita? Is that you?'

She jerked upwards, slamming her head against the top of the desk. 'Oh!' she yelped, then sank back down on to the floor.

'What are you doing, Vita?'

The pain was so intense that she could not answer him at first. 'Nothing. I—ah... Hello, Magnus. I was just—um—looking for my citizenship papers.'

'Your citizenship papers? Beneath my desk?'

'I did not know where you kept them,' she replied lamely.

She could barely see his expression amid the shadows, but his voice seemed plugged with a false cheer. 'I believe you keep your citizenship papers with your things, do you not? You should check.'

'All right, I will do that.'

Slowly, Vita stood. She felt dizzy and afraid. She

lifted her lamp and watched Magnus disappear silently back into the house. She made her way back to her bed-chamber, scolding herself. Why had she listened to Ven's advice? Now Magnus would be suspicious. If the marriage contract was in the desk as she suspected, he would surely remove it—or simply hide the key.

She touched the growing bump on her head—surely a sign from the gods. She could not afford to let herself be influenced by the opinions of others any more—no matter how well meaning. She was her own woman now and needed to keep her own counsel.

She was going to find an inexpensive place to rent, move out of the house, then get to work sewing the most magnificent capes in all the Empire. That was how she would survive.

She sat on her bed and laid out all her coin. Twenty-two *sesterces*.

She pulled one *sesterce* out of the pile and set it aside, for she would need it tomorrow to purchase honey and to pay the fuller.

The third bell of evening chimed and she counted up her *sesterces* again. Now there were twenty-one.

That evening after dinner, Ven stood outside his master's *tablinium* as the third bell chimed, then pushed open the door. 'Good evening, Dominus, I—'

Ven bit his tongue. His *dominus* sat upon his chair as usual, but his legs were sprawled wide, creating a space for the woman between them. She was pleasuring Lepidus with her mouth.

Ven lunged out of the room, pulling the door closed behind him.

It was not the first time he had caught his master enjoying a female slave, though he had hoped the old man would leave the Dacian woman alone for a bit longer. He closed his eyes and said a silent prayer for the woman, a captive from the previous Emperor's war. She did not deserve such a fate. No woman did.

'Come in, Ven,' his master said at last. 'We are done now.'

Ven stepped inside the chamber. The woman was fumbling to tie her hair and he saw the wetness of tears on her cheeks.

A rare grin stretched across his master's face. 'There is something about the look of terror in their eyes.' Lepidus said. 'She will improve with time.'

Ven bit his own tongue. He knew that it was customary for a *paterfamilias* to take liberties with his slaves. It was his right, after all, by Roman law. Still, Ven could not help the anger that welled up inside him, seeing the look on the filthy old man's face.

Gods, what was wrong with him? First Vita's safety and now his master's sins. He was allowing his emotions free rein and no good could come of it. He reminded himself that his life was not his own, nor was his will. Besides, he deserved his wretched fate. He had chosen it the winter that he had failed to save his mother's life.

It was the autumn of Ven's twelfth year, and throughout Brigante territory the grain harvest had failed—cursed by an early frost. The heads of wheat lay empty and bent in the fields and, as the days passed, the people of Ven's tribe grew empty and bent as well.

The Samhain feast was cancelled and it was determined there was not enough grain for the scattered Brigante settlements to survive the winter.

Livestock was slaughtered, plants gathered; sacrifices made. Requests for aid were discreetly sent to allied tribes, all of whom had experienced the same frost. Finally the tribal elders determined that there was no other choice but to appeal to the Romans.

The Roman soldiers stationed in Brigante territory were loved by none. They regularly extracted tribute from the Brigantes in exchange for 'protection', though it was never clear what that protection entailed.

Nor was it just grain they took from the Brigantes. The Romans took deer from their forests and fish from their streams and cows from their wide-ranging herds. They seduced their Brigante women, promising them better lives, and offered their ablest young men careers in the Roman army. They took and took and took.

That year, however, the Brigantes had nothing left to give. An envoy of northern Brigante leaders, including Ven's father, had travelled to the Roman fort at Vindolanda to request a deferral of their tribute requirements. The visit did not go well.

Days later, Ven and his mother watched from the doorway of their roundhouse as a cohort of Roman soldiers opened the underground grain cache and removed their settlement's remaining stores.

Throughout Brigante territory it was the same. The Roman soldiers visited every Brigante settlement there was, including the three hill forts. They came, saw and took, and by the time they were through the Brigantes had no more grain.

They had no choice but to attempt to take it back.

On the eve of their planned raid on the Roman fort, Ven sat on the floor of their roundhouse, sharpening his father's dagger.

'Let me go with you, Father,' he begged. 'I am already a fine hunter. You told me yourself. I am talented with the bow.'

'Hunting is different than raiding,' his father said, casting his mother a glance. 'Besides, I need you here. If I die, you will become the man of the house. In a few years, perhaps you will become a leader of our settlement.'

Ven's mother added a log to the fire and nodded at Ven's father. 'Will you serve our people, Ven?' his father asked him. 'If I die, will you help them stand up to the Romans?'

'I will, sir,' said Ven.

'And will you protect your mother and keep her safe?'

'I will,' Ven replied. He lowered his head. It was as if his father were already speaking from the grave.

'Promise me, Son. Protect your mother, whatever you do.'

Dread pressed down upon Ven's shoulders. 'I promise.'

They were the last words he ever said to his father.

The next day, his father and a dozen other warriors left their settlement to join the largest contingent of Brigante raiders ever gathered. By evening, the raid on the Roman grain stores had failed and only three of the warriors returned. Ven's father was not among them.

The winter came on swift feet. There was no grain and very little other food left. Ven's mother ate little, giving all of her extra food to Ven.

'Father died trying to keep us alive,' Ven told her. 'You must not give up now.' But she shook her head and sighed—sick with a broken heart.

Ven spent his days in the forest, hunting for prey. If he could just land a deer, he told himself, he could show his mother that hope was alive, that Father was watching over them. It was the reason he was so far away from the settlement the day the raiders came.

They were Parisi—an enemy tribe from the south. They swept through the weakened Brigante settlements, killing their remaining warriors and enslaving the rest. By the time Ven smelled the smoke from the fires it was too late.

He rushed back to his settlement and discovered everything—and everyone—to be gone.

Not a single soul had escaped the raiders.

The cold nipped at his ears, his face. He tried to follow the raiders' tracks, but it began to rain and then the rain turned to snow. He rushed back to his small roundhouse—one of the few that had survived the Parisi's destruction—and lit a fire. He stayed there all night, staring into the flames.

The next morning, he set out for the lands of the Parisi once again, but after only a few hours, his toes grew so numb he could hardly walk. He returned to his home, opened his family's cellar and stared at the stack of dry wood inside. It was enough to survive a winter.

Day after day, he set out to rescue his mother and, day after day, the cold would not let him do it. He brought tinder into the forest and tried to nurture a blaze, but the kindling was too wet to keep it going for long. He sharpened his arrows and assured himself that there would be good hunting where he was going, but the further he got from his home, the less certain he felt. He knew not where Parisi lands lay, only that they were far.

Fortunately, he knew the forests around his settlement well. He knew where the winter birds clustered and where the fish and rabbits hid, and, when his stomach began to ache with hunger, he set about finding food.

When he shot his first pheasant out of the sky, he

shouted with joy, forgetting for a moment that his mother lay somewhere in chains, waiting for him to save her.

Forgetting for a moment that he was a coward.

Each passing moment was proof of his own failure. Every day that went by, he betrayed his mother more. He was surviving, but in disgrace. He did not deserve to feel joy.

The days passed like admonitions. He caught his first fish, but he forbade himself from enjoying the meat. He should have been looking for his mother, braving the cold and the unknown, risking all to bring her home.

But he could not bring himself to do it, for he was afraid of what he did not know.

Thus every time the warmth of happiness crept into his heart, he stealthily blocked its path. He cowered inside his childhood home, stoking his fire and waiting for spring to come.

When it finally did, he sensed a strange loss. He gazed up at the sky one morning and found that it did not contain a single cloud. His stomach felt empty, though he was well fed. He searched his mind for his mother and could not find her.

He set off for the lands of the Parisi and found their hill fort in a handful of days. He lurked outside its timber-spiked walls, peering through the crevices to discover his Brigante brethren enslaved inside.

By day Ven searched for his mother, hoping to find her among them. By night he slept outside the walls and prayed for a miracle.

At last he was able to sneak into an open stable where one of his fellow tribesmen slept. 'Greetings, Uncle,' he whispered to the old man. 'I have come to rescue my mother from servitude.'

'Your mother?' The man squinted at Ven beneath the

moonlight. 'Ah, yes, you are the son of Enica. She said that you were coming for her.'

'She did?' Relief flooded into Ven's heart. 'But where is she? And how may we rescue her and the others?'

The man's expression was full of pity. 'You are brave to come, son of Enica, but I am afraid we cannot be rescued. Our animals are stolen and our homes are burned. There is nowhere for us to go.'

'We can go to the forest,' answered Ven.

'There are too many of us and not enough deer. We must be content with our lives here now. To dream of more would be foolish. Go now, dear boy, save yourself.'

'I am not a boy. I am the man of my household and I have come to rescue my mother. For whom does she labour?'

'For no man, son. Not any more.'

'What?' Ven felt ill. He put his hands against his ears, not wishing to hear.

'I am sorry, son of Enica. You mother died just days ago. It is too late.'

Ven lay down in the dirt, letting the cold invade his limbs. He could not move. He could barely even breathe. He had failed in the worst way a son could fail. He felt as if he had killed his mother himself.

When he was discovered the following morning, he did not even try to run. He accepted the collar around his neck and embraced his new life of servitude. And days later, when the Romans invaded the Parisi hill fort and captured everyone—Parisi and Brigante alike—Ven gave no resistance.

The Romans won. They always won. They took and took and took and then kept taking. They starved their allies and captured their foes. Land, grain and now the Britons themselves—it did not matter whether Parisi or

Brigante. Wherever the Romans went, they plundered. They made a desert and called it peace.

Ven and hundreds of other captives were marched to Londinium where they were loaded on to the deck of a ship. They huddled together in their furs, hungry and afraid, trying to stay warm as they were ferried across an endless sea.

Ven ignored his misery, for certainly he deserved his wretched fate. He no longer cared for food or warmth. He wanted nothing at all.

He had earned his punishment and would endure it like a warrior. He was young, but he was old. He was full of life, yet he was bone tired. The Roman sun shone down from above, warming his skin, but he felt nothing at all, for his heart had finally turned to ice.

Now Lepidus grunted a laugh as the Dacian woman rose to her feet. Ven reached out an arm to help her, but she did not take it. Nor did she even look at Ven as she rushed past him through the door.

Ven took a deep breath, willing away the dull ache inside his chest. She was not the first slave of Lepidus's whom he had failed to protect. She would not be the last.

Still, a wave of self-loathing overtook him as he re-trieved the stylus from a nearby shelf. He willed that away, as well and took his seat in front of Lepidus's desk.

'You wish for me to take down a letter, Dominus?'

'An invitation,' replied Lepidus. 'One which you will deliver yourself tomorrow morning.'

'After I accompany Domina to the baths, or before?'

'During that time,' said Lepidus. Ven looked up from his stylus in confusion. 'Your *domina* will not miss you. She is planning to meet her lover at the baths tomorrow.'

'Dominus?'

'My wife betrays me,' Lepidus replied, 'though I do not expect that you would have noticed such a thing.'

Ven shaped his expression to indicate surprise. On some level he *was* surprised—that Lepidus had managed to identify his wife's affair so quickly.

Lepidus pulled his stylus pen from its holder and studied it and Ven wondered how many lashes young Lollia would have to endure for her indiscretion. *It does not matter*, he told himself. He was just a slave after all. The suffering of others was not his concern.

'You look as if you have swallowed a bad oyster, Ven. What is the matter?'

'I am impressed by your cleverness, Dominus. How did you discover it?'

'My wife's whoring? I have suspected it for a long time. But when she accepted the invitation to the *vigile*'s banquet, I knew something was wrong. Lollia would never normally attend a banquet of people so far beneath us in rank.'

'Ah.'

'She tells me you conversed with the *vigile*'s wife yesterday at the baths. Tell me, what did you learn about her, Ven?'

'Dominus?'

'What do you know of the *vigile*'s wife?'

Why was Lepidus asking about the *vigile*'s wife? 'Ah, her name is Vita.'

'I know that, idiot. What else?'

Ven paused. Did Lepidus mean to approach her? But why? To do her some kind of harm? Gods, no. Ven would kill the man first.

'Ven?'

'She is no longer the *vigile*'s wife, Dominus. She has recently divorced him.'

'And?'

Ven felt as if he were being put to a test. 'She rarely goes to the baths, Dominus. She is uncomfortable there.' *Though she seemed to enjoy swimming.* 'In truth, I hardly know her.'

Lepidus twisted the hairs of his beard. 'Lollia reports that you massaged the woman for nearly an hour and that you spoke together in the tongue of the north. Do not tell me that you do not know her.'

'She did not say very much, Dominus,' Ven lied. 'She is a modest woman and rather shy.' At least that was the truth. Still, Ven could not help but feel as if he was describing Persephone to Hades.

'Tell me something I do not know about her, Ven, lest I begin to believe you are lying.' There was menace in Lepidus's voice. It tickled the scars on Ven's back.

'She learned the northern tongue from her mother, I believe.'

'And her father?'

'Deceased. She was disowned by him at the time of her marriage.'

Lepidus rolled the stylus pen between his hands thoughtfully. 'Does she know that my wife is her husband's lover?'

Ven swallowed hard. 'She does, Dominus.'

'Does she plan to sue for the return of her dowry?'

'No, Dominus. She does not wish to subject your wife's reputation to ruin.'

Lepidus rubbed his bald head. 'An honourable woman. I expected as much.'

'Yes, she is, Dominus.'

Ven noticed the Dacian woman's hair tie on the floor beside Lepidus's feet. It occurred to him how different the world was for women than it was for men.

'You seem to have a well-formed opinion about her,' said Lepidus. 'I thought you said you knew her scarcely.'

Was it hot inside Lepidus's office? Why did it seem as if there was no more air? 'I think well of her effort to protect Lollia's reputation, Dominus, for it is the reputation of this very house.'

Lepidus slid the stylus pen across the desk to Ven. 'I am ready to dictate the letter.'

Ven had never been less ready to receive a dictation. Still, he opened the stylus and held the metal pen over the wax.

'Good Vita Sabina,' Lepidus began, 'I am writing to entreat you to pay me an audience. The matter is urgent—your discretion, essential. Please call on me at my Esquiline Hill home tomorrow afternoon at the latest and in the meantime please accept this offering. Yours, Gaius Lepidus Severus.'

Ven wiped the pen clean against his tunic and tried to appear calm. 'Offering, Dominus?'

'I want you to take her an amphora of our good Massilian,' Lepidus stated. 'Give her the wine, along with my best wishes, and nothing more. Do not even think to speak to her in that barbarian tongue of yours.'

Ven struggled to keep his thoughts in order. 'If I am to bring the Massilian with me, I will not be able to accompany Domina Lollia to the baths.'

The old man leaned back in his chair. 'Then do it afterwards. Take the Scythian with you and get back as soon as possible. We must finish our drawings of Hadrian's Wall tomorrow. I wish them to be completed before we depart for Britannia.'

'When will that be, Dominus, so that I may plan for it?' Ven asked, but Lepidus had closed his eyes and at length appeared to fall asleep. Ven placed the stylus pen on his desk and turned to leave.

'Where are you going, Ven?' Lepidus grunted. 'I have not dismissed you.'

Ven turned and caught a glimpse of his master's coal-black eyes. They did not seem to reflect any light.

'You say that the *vigile*'s wife—the *vigile*'s ex-wife—has northern blood. I am wondering if it is true that women with northern blood make fiery lovers.'

Fiery lovers? What sort of question was that?

'Well?' Lepidus prodded. 'You must have some knowledge of the subject.'

Ven felt pressure against the backs of his eyes. Surely the old man was trying to provoke him. Either that, or... Ven could not even think of the other reason.

'I am not certain, Dominus.'

'Ah well, I suppose I shall soon find out.'

Ven blinked. He tried to breathe. Everything around him seemed to take on a slightly crimson hue. Did he mean to suggest that he desired Vita? Impossible. He would never want a kind, thoughtful woman like Vita. He was a man of thoughtless, primal appetites. He saw women as all alike—and the younger the better.

'Poor Vita,' Lepidus continued. 'To think that she sacrificed her dowry to protect a woman like Lollia, a woman who would shame her own husband. But I will be the winner in the end, Ven, and do you know why?'

Ven clenched his teeth, reminding himself that he was just a slave. He was nobody. His thoughts meant nothing. His feelings meant even less.

'Why, Dominus?'

'Because Vita is a desperate woman now and des-perate women do desperate things.' He flashed Ven a yellow-toothed grin. 'We leave the day after Vulcanalia, to answer your question. Without Lollia.'

Ven gazed at the tiles of the floor, but he could no longer distinguish them. 'And Vita Sabina, Dominus?'

'I will make her mine, Ven. Just watch me.'

Chapter Five

'It does not appear as terrible as it may feel,' said Avidia, regarding Vita's bruise-blackened eye. 'It rather looks like you had a night of poor sleep.'

'In one eye?'

It was the fifth hour of the morning and Avidia stood outside Vita's doorway in her best tunic and sandals, ready for a day of apartment hunting.

'Maybe it is slightly terrible, but only in the light,' said Avidia. 'Come, I have an idea.'

Avidia lead Vita into the kitchen where she moistened a rag and dipped it into the ashes of the hearth fire. 'Close your eyes while I turn you into a goddess,' Avidia said. 'And stop fidgeting.'

'I am not fidgeting.'

'You are always fidgeting. Now take a breath.' Vita did as she was told. 'Good,' said Avidia. 'Now hold it.'

Vita raised a brow, wondering how long she could last without breathing. She imagined it would take Avidia quite a long time to make her bruise-blackened eye look normal.

Magnus had gifted her the bruise that morning to go

with the bump on her head. 'If I ever see you in my *tablinium* again, I will kill you,' he had threatened.

Now Vita exhaled. 'I am useless at holding my breath.'

'Better than being useless at breathing,' Avidia said, then stepped back to behold her work. 'Now it does not look as if you have a blackened eye at all, it merely appears as if you have not slept for days.' Avidia grinned wickedly. 'I fear I have made you into the Goddess of Too Little Sleep.'

'That will do, though I wish you could have made me in to the Goddess of Too Much Coin. Speaking of which, how much coin did you bring with you?'

'Five *sesterces*—my life savings.'

At least it was something. With twenty-six *sesterces* between them, Vita hoped that they might be able to find something in the area of Aventine Hill. It was the ideal location, for it was near to the marketplace where Vita sold her capes and also to the tavern where Avidia worked.

Vita imagined the two women living together and watching out for each other. Avidia would work in the tavern by night and occupy the apartment by day, and Vita would do the reverse. It would be the perfect convivial arrangement—if only they could afford it.

'Have you ever been to a sibyl, Avidia?'

'A seer? I could never afford such a thing.'

'In the early days of my marriage, I visited one. I asked if happiness lay in my future.'

'And what did she say?'

'She told me that it was a useless question, that happiness was pointless—as ephemeral as a cloud—and that I should not aspire to it.'

'What did she recommend you aspire to then? Fame?' asked Avidia.

'No.'

'Love?'

'Guess again.'

'Perfectly cooked dumplings?'

Vita grinned. 'She told me to aspire to freedom.'

'Freedom? But you are a Roman citizen. Are you not already free?'

'That is what I asked the sibyl. She replied that there are many kinds of prisons, most of them invisible, and that most people spend all their lives trapped inside them. "Seek your freedom first," she told me, "and everything else will come."'

'A wise woman,' Avidia observed.

'Wise, indeed, but I was too young to see it. I stood in her stuffy office and told her I cared nothing for freedom. I begged her to tell me if happiness would ever be known to me and she agreed to cast my horoscope. A few moments later, she was foretelling my life.'

'Mercy of Juno! What did she tell you?'

'That I would find the happiness I sought, but only after a long while and many trials, and that it would come as a surprise—like a knock on the door in the middle of the day.'

'She gave you no other details?'

'Only this: that the gods had a wicked sense of humour and, because I was so intent on happiness and so eager to dismiss her own good advice, that one day I would have to choose between the two.'

'Between happiness and freedom?'

'Yes.'

'That is all she said?'

'She said I must pay her three *denariis*, or I would have neither,' said Vita.

Avidia laughed. 'Not just a messenger of the gods, but also a thief!'

'But perhaps she was right, Avidia. For all these years I have tried and failed to find the happiness of a wife and keeper of a home. The only time I ever feel happy is when I am making and selling my capes. The rest of the time I am miserable...or at least, have been miserable, until very recently.'

Vita imagined Ven staring down at her, his eyes beaconing to her in a way that made her stomach feel strange. Every time she thought of him, her spirit felt light.

But that was wrong, was it not? For that was happiness and not to be trusted, at least, not according to the sibyl. Freedom was the prize, not happiness.

She closed her eyes and pictured herself free and alone. She was living in a tiny room in one of the squalid *insulae* that crowded Rome's neighbourhoods. Still, she had her capes around her, along with plenty of fabric and thread. She was alone, but she could do what she wanted. Her money was her own, to spend as she liked. She could come and go as she pleased, answering to no one.

'Perhaps freedom is more important than happiness,' Vita mused.

'But you have been pursuing your freedom for years,' said Avidia, 'in the form of your capes. You earn steady coin by them, do you not?'

'I do.'

'That is freedom. You have taken the old sybil's advice without even knowing it.'

'But if that is the case, then so have you, Avidia.'

'In what way?'

'You can cook.'

'Everyone can cook.'

'Senators cannot cook.'

'Senators do not have to cook!'

'Soldiers cannot cook.'

'Well, I suppose that is true.'

'I cannot cook. I can barely make a stew.'

'That is sadly, and utterly, true,' Avidia said with a grin.

Vita studied her unlikely friend. The woman's nose was red, her teeth stained brown from too much drink. The lids of her eyes lay heavy upon her face, as if she had exhausted herself. 'I think that we both must overcome what enslaves us,' Vita said. 'Lest we die without ever having lived.'

A tear cascaded down Avidia's cheek. 'I pray to the gods that I might find the will one day,' she said. Slowly, she brightened. 'Come, let us go find a place to live.'

The two women gathered their things and were nearing the door when they heard the knocking of a fist against it.

Tap, tap.

'Who is there?' asked Vita, and the sound of her voice sent his heart racing.

'It is I, Ven.'

I have come to pretend that I do not think of you, that there is nothing between us, that I wish to do my duty and nothing more.

'I am the slave of your friend, Lollia Flamma,' he clarified, for it was possible that she had forgotten his name. 'I served you at the baths yesterday. Do you remember me?'

Do you remember me? What a foolish thing to ask.

'Of course I remember you!' she shouted.

Ven glanced back at the Scythian guard standing just behind him. 'I have come to read you a message from my master. An invitation.'

'An invitation? To a banquet?' she chirped. 'Just a moment.'

He could hear her fumbling with the lock inside the door. Even the clanking of metal seemed full of her enthusiasm.

Ven glanced behind him at his blond-haired companion. He stood not two paces away, as still as a statue. His gaze was stony, his expression, blank. He was holding out the amphora of Massilian as if it were a baby that disgusted him.

Ven knew better than to mistake the man's detachment for uninterest, however. He was watching and listening carefully, for that was what he was paid to do. He would report everything that transpired back to Lepidus. If Lepidus did not like what he heard, Ven would pay in lashes.

The door swung open and Ven heard Vita gasp. 'Oh, Ven!'

There she was, the woman who haunted his thoughts. She was as lovely as he remembered, though there were shadows around her eyes—and one eye in particular. By the gods, what had Magnus done to her now?

She stepped forward as if to embrace him, but he shook his head subtly and stepped backwards in an effort to deter her.

'I feared I would not see you again,' she said. Her warm grin nearly melted his bones. 'And now here you are. The gods are kind.'

He averted his gaze to the ground. 'Greetings, Domina.'

'Domina?' She studied his face. 'Is everything well, Ven?'

'Everything is well, Domina,' he said. 'I have come with my Scythian *associate*.' He glanced back at the Scythian, trying to make her understand. 'We wish to deliver you a message from my master, Lepidus Severus.'

Ah, she seemed to say.

'Would you like me to read the message aloud, Domina?'

'I believe I can read it myself,' she said. She plucked the wax tablet from his hands, then glanced behind her. 'Come, Avidia, let us read together.'

A tall, curly-haired woman stepped behind Vita and flashed Ven a wink. The two studied the text for a long time. 'I do not understand,' Vita said. 'Lepidus requests an audience with *me*?'

Ven nodded. 'He insisted that it should take place today if possible, or tomorrow at the latest.'

'But why?' Vita asked. 'Why would he wish to meet with me alone? And in such a hurry?' She was searching Ven's eyes, pleading for more information, but the Scythian was listening and Ven did not know how to proceed. How could Ven convey the depths of Lepidus's wickedness in a single look?

'I do not know, Domina, but he has also asked me to deliver you this amphora of Massilian wine, as a token of his goodwill.' Ven gestured behind him.

Avidia gasped. 'That is the size of a shipping amphora!'

Vita studied the expensive gift with suspicion. 'What is this about?' she whispered in Celtic.

Ven bit his tongue. Hard. So hard, in fact, that he

could feel warm blood filling his mouth. He knew that if he uttered a single word in the Celtic tongue, the Scythian would report it to Lepidus.

'Apologies, Domina, I do not understand,' he said. He glanced behind him at the Scythian. 'Please accept the wine along with my master's ardent desire for you to call on him as soon as you possibly may.'

Vita's eyes flashed and she returned to Latin. 'Please thank your master for this most generous expression and tell him I will call on him this afternoon on one condition.'

'Yes, Domina?'

A small, sly smile streaked across her lips. 'That you be there to answer the door.'

Later that afternoon, Vita stood outside Lepidus Severus's large home in one of Rome's most illustrious neighbourhoods, feeling meek. Towering above her were four columns supporting an imposing triangular pediment carved with the muses.

Vita closed her eyes and pictured the world inside. She saw a grand atrium flanked by rooms populated with slaves at work. Beyond them lay the well-appointed *tablinium* in which their master received his clients.

She envisioned the spacious office giving way to the garden at its far end—a paradisiacal realm of fruit trees, fountains and life-size statues in various stages of repose. The garden was surrounded by a shaded peristyle walkway along with more rooms for the master's wife and children. Every morning the lucky inhabitants awoke to the sound of birdsong and the soft trickle of water that never ceased to flow.

An island of tranquillity amid Rome's dirty streets.

Vita pictured all this because she had grown up in

a home much like the one she beheld and her heart swooned with the memory of it. As a girl she had gone about her days as a spoiled patrician daughter, with tutors and social calls and endless hours of weaving.

But in the end she was not a patrician at all, for Vita's father, a senator of Rome, had fallen in love with Vita's mother on the day he had purchased her.

By law, they could never marry, nor could her father dignify the partnership in any way. They could not be even be seen in public together, lest her father's reputation suffer. Like the tattoo on her mother's neck, the stigma of her mother's enslavement remained until her dying day.

Soon after her mother's death from fever, Vita's father had married and his new wife would not accept Vita's presence in their home. Vita was a Roman citizen, but she was not respectably born and so her father had sent Vita away as best he could.

Still, the home he had endowed her with had never been her own. It had always belonged to Magnus.

Now Vita wiped her cheeks and tried to arrange her hair. She did not blame her father for what he had done. He had loved Vita and had tried to secure her future. How could he have known that he was marrying her to a man who had been twisted by his own greed?

It was no use dwelling on the past, or so she had finally learned. Besides, she would be seeing Ven soon—the only reason she had agreed to this meeting at all.

In seconds, he would answer the door and, for a fleeting moment, their eyes would meet and she would feel that strange, excited feeling inside her stomach. It was possible that without thinking he might utter a word or two in their shared tongue. He had done it before, after all, had accidentally called her beautiful, and for that possibility alone she wanted to look her best.

Still, she feared her appearance was not what it could have been. It was stiflingly hot and the coal dust that Avidia had so carefully applied to Vita's eyes that morning had been running down her cheeks all afternoon.

She imagined she looked something like a Gorgon after a long day in the Underworld and supposed that in some sense she was. She and Avidia had traversed the squalid Subura neighbourhood all that morning, reaching for a dream they could not seem to grasp. They simply could not produce enough coin for a place of their own, even in the most affordable part of Rome.

'The Massilian wine!' Avidia had exclaimed on their way back to the Aventine. 'I can sell it in the tavern and pocket the profits. It will make up for our shortfall and soon we can try again.'

It had been a clever, risky idea, to which Vita had agreed instantly, though she doubted she would ever see her unlikely friend again.

Freedom is the prize, she told herself now and scolded herself for her vanity. She should not have agreed to this silly social call. She should be pounding the paving stones while it was still light, searching for a place of her own.

She lifted her fist to the door and tried to conjure her most sociable grin. 'Greetings, Good Lepidus,' she would say. 'It is an honour to be invited into your lovely home. You would not have an extra room to rent?'

Surely he had summoned her here to confront her about his wife's affair. *Yes, your wife is having an affair with my ex-husband.* That was what Lepidus expected her to tell him and then he would ask her to supply him with all the sordid details.

She had long since resolved to tell him nothing. How could she? After learning what his wife was doing, the old man was likely to divorce her instantly and, by law, the poor woman would not be able to marry again.

No, Vita would not say a word. She would delicately dance around the subject, explaining that her divorce with Magnus had been a long time in coming and she knew nothing about any affair with Lollia.

She would thank him for the wine and take her leave, and thus could return to more urgent matters—such as survival itself.

She lifted her hand and knocked upon the door.

Tap, tap.

Slowly, it creaked open and all at once she was glad she came. There was Ven, looking tall and strong and unmercifully handsome. She moved towards him for the traditional greeting—a kiss on the cheek—then remembered how inappropriate that would be.

'Welcome, Domina,' he said, stepping backwards.

'Hello, Ven.'

She followed him through the entryway past a well-muscled guard seated beside a litter. Apparently, Lepidus was rich enough to employ men to carry him around Rome and a glance at Ven's muscular physique suggested that he was often one of those men.

Now he ushered her into a spacious *tablinium* where Lepidus appeared to be extracting himself from his desk chair. Behind him stood several busts atop pillars, along with a rather lifelike statue of some broad-chested personage.

Except that it was not a statue. It was a perfectly motionless man—the same man who had accompanied Ven to her house the day before. The Scythian. Ven fell into place beside him while Lepidus finally rose to standing. The ageing equestrian managed a polite bow.

'Vita Sabina, thank you for coming. Please, sit.'

He motioned to the chair in front of his desk. As she took her seat, she stole a glance at Ven, but he did not meet her eyes.

Lepidus folded himself back into his own chair and sent her a thin-lipped grin. 'I trust you had no trouble finding the house?'

'None at all,' replied Vita. 'The Domus Severus is well known. A splendid abode.'

'Very kind of you to say. And I trust that your husband does not know of this visit?'

'He is my ex-husband now, I am afraid, and, no, he does not.'

'You must forgive the secrecy. It is just that it is a matter of a rather delicate nature, and you know how small the city is.'

'Over a million souls,' said Vita with a half-hearted grin, 'yet it often feels as if there are only a hundred.'

'Ha!' croaked Lepidus. 'Clever woman. Well, I will get right to it then. My new wife is having an affair with your husband and has been for some time. I believe she is trysting with him right now, behind the laundress at the Forum Boarium.'

Incredible, thought Vita. Lepidus wasted no time and apparently employed very skilled informants. 'I must admit that I am not surprised.'

'That is not the worst of it, I fear,' Lepidus continued. 'It appears that now Lollia is pregnant with your husband's child.'

Vita blinked. 'Well, that *is* a surprise.'

'I doubt she has told him yet,' said Lepidus. Vita caught the slightest tremble in his lower lip. 'They plan to meet again tomorrow during the Vulcanalia festival, at the bonfire outside the Temple of Vulcan.'

'Forgive me,' said Vita, 'but how do you know all this?'

'I am a resourceful man.'

Lepidus leaned back in his chair and glanced up at the fair-haired Scythian. 'And my wife is a careless woman—though the way that she and your husband carried on at your banquet was nearly proof enough.'

'I confess I did not see it,' Vita admitted. 'Not at first.'

'Well, perhaps you are too quick to see the good in people. Your husband, for example. I take no delight in telling you this, but I once heard him called the Virile Vigile of Rome.'

Vita nearly laughed. 'I have known of my husband's dalliances for a long while.'

'Surely you must have thought of divorcing him before now.'

'I have, but ours was a *cum manu* contract.'

'Ah! How very quaint. So your father's household will not take you back?'

'My father is deceased.' She heard a tremble in her voice and sucked in a breath. Strange. It was no longer Magnus's betrayal that brought her near to tears, but this—her imminent destitution.

'And Magnus will not return your dowry, I suspect?'

'He will not.'

'Then I believe our predicaments are rather alike, for I cannot divorce my wife either—not without sending my career into ruin.'

'I am sorry to hear that.'

He took a thread of his beard between his fingers. 'Do you know why I grew this beard, Vita?'

Vita shook her head. Just behind the old man she

could see Ven's long, muscular legs. If only she could follow those legs to his torso and then up his chest to his face so that she could look into his eyes and feel their comfort.

'I grew this beard in honour of our illustrious Princeps, Emperor Hadrian.'

'A wonderful way to honour him,' she replied.

'When Emperor Hadrian took the purple, I knew that there was a kindred spirit at the helm,' Lepidus continued. 'You are an uneducated, unworldly woman and cannot truly appreciate the significance of what I am about to tell you, but I will say it anyway.' Lepidus lowered his voice to a whisper. 'Our intrepid Emperor harbours the passions of the Greeks—that genius civilisation. He loves everything Greek: philosophy and rhetoric, art and theatre, and most especially architecture.'

Vita feigned surprised interest, though, of course, she already knew everything that Lepidus had just told her. It was widely known that Hadrian was a Homer-loving Grecophile with a penchant for hunting and beautiful men. By whispering it like a secret, Lepidus revealed his own lack of worldliness.

Now the old man tilted his eyes to the heavens. 'All my life, I have followed my passion for designing strong, lasting things. I do not wish to brag, but I am a great architect, perhaps one of the greatest that Rome has ever seen.' Lepidus blinked and appeared to wipe away a tear.

'I have been divinely inspired to participate in the construction of countless temples, bridges and roads. You cannot glance around the Forum without seeing one of the great works that my brilliant mind has helped bring to fruition. After my father died, my mother once suggested to me that I had in fact been sired by a god.'

Sired by a god? Now Vita really could not look away.

'I do not think it an accident of the gods that I was born to live during the reign of Hadrian. By wearing this beard, I am signalling my part in his great works to come. It is also why I married Lollia.'

'For her father's connection to Hadrian?' Vita asked.

'Indeed, and that connection has already borne fruit, for I have been promoted to Chief Military Architect in the north. Very soon I shall be setting sail for Britannia to help build a wall nearly a hundred miles in length, the greatest wall the world has ever known.'

Vita vanquished a grin. It seemed that anything Lepidus touched would be the greatest the world had ever known, though one of Vita's tutors had once told her of another, much longer wall somewhere in the mysterious east. 'A great honour,' she said.

'It will be a long trip to Britannia,' he continued. 'Seven days by ship to Narbo, in Gaul, then ten more days over land and several more by sea to Londinium. Finally I will make the long trek north to the Roman fort at Coria, where I will reside for a minimum of five years overseeing construction. And that is why I have asked you here today. I would like you to come with me.'

Vita blinked and sat up in her chair. Behind Lepidus's head, she saw Ven's legs tense.

'While I cannot divorce for reasons we have discussed,' Lepidus continued, 'I would like to offer you a concubinage.'

Vita nearly gasped. It was the most ridiculous thing she had ever heard. 'I am sorry, I do not understand.'

'You are a noble woman, Vita Sabina. I have watched you put others before yourself, endure suffering and public shame, and act honourably and discreetly, like a good Roman woman should. Just look at you there, sitting so stiffly and properly in your chair. In some ways you remind me of a soldier—always working for the dignity and good of Rome.'

Vita opened her mouth to speak, but no words came.

'Perhaps you are not skilled in the arts of entertaining,' Lepidus continued. 'Perhaps you are not high ranking or well educated or even close to the physical ideal, but I am willing to overlook those things. You speak the language and that will go far in helping me interact with the barbarians at Coria.'

'Coria?'

'It is not a beautiful woman that I will need in that place, but a loyal, uncomplaining Roman protectress with thick, strong arms and a barbarian tongue. That is you.'

Vita nearly laughed aloud. No matter how many ways she had imagined the purpose of this meeting, she never would have guessed it to be this: a recruitment.

'I do not know what to say—' she said, but Lepidus would not let her finish.

'I confess that when Lollia told me that she overheard you speaking to Ven in the tongue of the north, I nearly jumped. It is as if the gods have brought us together to achieve the important purpose with which I have been tasked. Please, will you not demonstrate for me?'

Vita frowned. She felt as if the room were spinning.

'Say something to Ven in the tongue of the north,' Lepidus goaded. 'I only wish to hear that repulsive accent.'

Finally, she could look at Ven, only now she barely wished to. She had just been insulted in a dozen different ways and felt a familiar blush of shame invading her cheeks.

But then Ven bent his head and somehow caught

her gaze and she felt instantly anchored to the ground. 'Um…hello, how are you?' she asked him in Celtic.

In a cheerful tone, Ven replied, 'Lepidus is a dangerous man. Do not accept his proposal.' He nodded his head, as if he had just wished her a good morning.

'Wondrous,' Lepidus mused. 'How well does she speak it, Ven?'

'Well, Dominus, but with a strong Caledonian accent.'

'Are the Caledonii your tribe?' Lepidus asked.

'They were the tribe of my mother,' said Vita. She turned to Ven and switched to Celtic. 'I would not become this man's concubine if my life depended on it.'

Ven gave an interested nod. 'Tomorrow morning at the baths,' he said. 'I will meet you below in the hypocaust. I have something to give you. It will help you survive.'

Vita gave a businesslike nod and suppressed the joy blossoming within her. She did not trust her ears, but what he had said sounded a lot like hope.

'And what did you say just now?' asked Lepidus.

Vita searched her mind. 'I told Ven that my mother's clan was based far in the north. He reminded me that the Brigantes and the Caledonii are ancient enemies.' Ancient enemies who sometimes banded together to help each other survive.

'Indeed? Is that why your accents are different?'

'It is,' said Vita. Now her smile had become genuine. *'I have something to give you,'* he had said. He was going to help her. Perhaps she would not be lost.

'It will be an advantage to have representatives of two different tribes in my entourage,' Lepidus mused. 'But your real value will be as a loyal representative and keeper of my household.' He untied a scroll and let it unfurl towards Vita.

'As a concubine, you would be expected to perform the services of a wife as needed, though I will be bringing along a slave, as well. The rest of my slaves I will acquire in Coria. You would help with that, along with the selection of furnishings for our household and the like.'

'Of course,' Vita said, pretending to study the scroll.

'It would be a term of five years and at its conclusion I will provide you with between ten and fifteen thousand *sesterces*, depending on the quality of your service.'

Vita blinked. Her pretence disappeared. 'Fifteen thousand *sesterces*?'

'How could I expect you to come with me if I cannot offer you something worthwhile in return?'

She looked down at the contract unfurled before her—a carpet for Vita to walk upon if she chose.

'Read through the details and tell me your answer by tomorrow,' said Lepidus. 'I leave the day after tomorrow from the port of Ostia.'

'The day after tomorrow? May I ask why you are leaving so soon?'

Lepidus sighed. 'I do not wish to be further humiliated by my trollop of a wife.'

Vita stood and bowed. 'Of course.' She rolled up the contract and took it in her hands. 'By tomorrow, then.'

'Come with me and be my concubine, Vita. After only a few years you will be able to make whatever life you choose. You will finally have—'

'Freedom?'

She could feel Ven's eyes on her now. They were burning through her, telling her not to be a fool. 'Good Lepidus, may I ask you a professional question?'

'Of course, my dear. Anything.'

'What is the purpose of building a wall so far north?

Is it really to separate the Romans from the barbarians as they say?'

'You are curious for a woman,' replied Lepidus. 'The answer is no. It is not being built to separate the Romans from the barbarians. There are barbarians on both sides of the wall, by the gods. People are so foolish.'

'Then why?' asked Vita.

Lepidus started to reply, then stopped himself. 'Accept my offer, my stout little Vita, and then I shall tell you the real reason for the wall. I think you will be surprised by my answer.'

Chapter Six

On the penultimate morning she would ever spend in her own bed, Vita awoke, feeling proud of herself.

The evening before, she had ripped up Lepidus's contract and burned it in her brazier. Now she gathered up the black ashes and placed them in a bowl.

She would not go with Lepidus, no matter how much coin he offered her. She would not go with him if he were the god of abundance himself! She had finally learned her lesson about contracts and men, and she would never again enter into another. Freedom was the path and, yesterday in Lepidus's *tablinium*, she had successfully resisted a temptation to stray from it.

She stood and dressed, then took a look around her bedchamber, vowing not to miss it. She had already done most of her packing, had culled through her belongings until they fit into a sack that she could carry without aid.

Soon her life would be her own and that was all that mattered. It did not matter that she did not have a place to live—she would find one eventually. In the meantime she would find some small unnoticed corner of Rome in which to sleep.

By day, she would sew and sew. She would sell so

many capes that she would quickly grow rich. Some day soon, she would have enough coin for the grandest apartment in Rome. She would have time to go to the baths whenever she liked. She would eat in fine taverns and attend lovely banquets. She would meet up with Lollia and exchange gossip every *ides*.

And who was to say she could not continue her acquaintance with Ven? As an independent woman, she would be able to do what she liked. There would be no one to condemn her for exchanging words with him in public. There would be no consequence for her to accept a massage or other service, as long as his *domina* agreed.

Perhaps she could arrange to see him more often somehow. Perhaps their friendship could bloom. Just the idea sent a flush of excitement through her.

And it was all ahead of her—a life of her own. She could not wait to begin it.

She went about her morning duties with so much good cheer that when she went to the *tablinium* to pour Magnus more *posca*, he looked up from his porridge to ask her what was wrong.

'I am happy for the change of weather,' she said.

'The weather has not changed.'

'Perhaps I am looking forward to the Vulcanalia tomorrow.'

'You are looking forward to a sky full of smoke?'

'We must placate the god Vulcan, lest he burn the harvest.'

Magnus shot her a mighty frown. 'Where will you live?'

The question took her by surprise and she laughed. 'I have not yet found a place.'

'No place, yet you laugh like a fool.'

'Fools are the beloved of the gods.'

'This bread is stale.'

'I took our wheat ration to the baker yesterday.'

'But this bread is stale today.'

In the past, Vita might have apologised profusely, then spent the rest of the morning silently berating herself for the error. Alternatively, she might have plunged headlong into the creation of a new cape and tried to make herself feel useful again. Not any more.

'You may pick your loaves up from the baker after work,' Vita stated. 'Or tomorrow. Or never. It is up to you.' She held her breath.

Magnus jumped to his feet suddenly and swiped his bowl of porridge off his desk. 'Useless woman!' he shouted. He pushed Vita to the floor as he stormed out of the chamber and she heard the hard slam the front door behind him.

She waited for the tears to come. She held her breath in anticipation of the pain of humiliation, which had become so familiar over the years that it was nearly a comfort. But the pain never came, nor did the tears.

She expelled all her breath. It was a miracle. His anger had not harmed her. His words—it seemed they no longer mattered to her at all. It seemed that she had made her heart into ice.

She jumped to her feet and skipped back upstairs as if she were the winged messenger himself. She had known in her mind that divorcing Magnus was the right decision. Now she knew it in her gut. She did not need this house, this life, him. She was nearly free.

All that remained was to find a place to lay her head and she had the whole day in which to look. She gazed out the window of her bedchamber, finding the air fresh and filled with hope. She would find a place to live today for certain and tomorrow she would march out of the door and never look back.

But first she had a meeting to attend to.

And now, with Magnus gone early, she had plenty of time to prepare for it. She started off by combing her hair, securing half of it with a pin atop her head. She had never been fussy about her appearance before, but she wanted to look her best for Ven.

She swirled a bit of henna powder with water and stirred the mixture with a stick. Perhaps that was the true reason for her happiness. She was going to see Ven. For the first time since they had met outside her doorway, they would be alone, for he wished to meet in the hypocaust. Together beneath the baths, they could do and say whatever they wished.

She imagined giving him a proper greeting: a kiss on the cheek. She wondered if she could achieve it without blushing. She would tell him about her day ahead and ask him about his own, making certain to find out the next time he planned to accompany his *domina* to the baths.

She paused and felt suddenly as if she were falling from a height. She realised that she had been mistaken. Ven would not be accompanying his *domina* to the baths—not this day, or ever again.

For Ven was going north with Lepidus.

'No!' she shouted. She began to pace. How had she overlooked such a terrible truth? Ven was Lepidus's most valuable slave. Of course he would take him north. She remembered now how Lepidus had remarked at the benefit of having both Ven and Vita with him in Britannia. But Vita was not going to Britannia, which meant that, after today, she was probably never going to see Ven again.

Vita checked her small copper mirror, then added

more powder to the paste and continued to stir. She would need really need the paste now, for she sensed all the colour had drained from her cheeks. She dipped in a finger and began to rub.

Her preparations had suddenly acquired a new gravity. How long had Lepidus said he planned to stay in Britannia? Five years? She could wait for five years, though there was no guaranteeing his return. More likely, he would find a way to escape Lepidus and remain in the lands of his kin. In that case, this was likely to be the last time she would ever see him. She wondered whether she would be able to conceal her feelings from him.

Vita bit her bottom lip, just like her mother used to do before applying paint. The deep crimson would draw Ven's attention to her lips and everything she had to say. 'May Mercury speed your journey,' she would tell him. 'You will be missed.'

It was too impersonal. 'I am grateful for all you have done for me,' she would say. 'I will pray to the gods for you.'

It did not seem to be enough. No words were. In only a few days, she had come to care deeply for the man, though she knew him poorly. There was so much she wished to learn about him. Who were his family and how did he lose them? How did he learn to read and what were his favourite texts? What made him sad? What brought him joy?

And why was it that when she looked into his eyes a private Vulcanalia took place inside her?

Now she would never know.

She dabbed more paste on her cheeks, feeling suddenly as if the whole world had lost its colour. She wished she had had more time with him. They had spoken only briefly, but she sensed they could have conversed for days. And just the thought of his hands upon her bare skin made her beg Juno for equanimity.

Gods forgive her, she thought of him that way—like a woman thought of a man. She yearned for him.

It felt good to finally admit it to herself. Indeed, the feeling was so overwhelming that she had momentarily considered accepting Lepidus's offer, if only to be close to Ven.

Of course, she would never do it. She would never again be a man's wife, let alone his concubine. Never again would she bind herself to another, no matter how rich the reward. Freedom was the prize and she could not allow herself to forget it.

She dribbled a bit of water into the ashes of Lepidus's burnt contract and stirred them into a paste. She painted the black mixture around her eyes, praying that when he looked into them, he would see how she really felt.

'I will miss you,' she would say. 'So very much.'

Suddenly there they were—her missing tears. How very strange! Where had they come from and why would they not cease? They were streaking the black liner and the red that she had just finished applying to her cheeks.

This would not do at all. She dug in her travel sack for a drying cloth, then began to reapply the pastes. She needed to look her best for the one man in the world who found her worthy. One last, good impression before they said farewell.

'Ouch, Ven! You just pinched me!' shouted Lollia. Ven had not noticed his *domina* turn on her side. Instead of squeezing her shoulders, he had inadvertently pinched her arm.

'Apologies, Domina,' Ven said. He had not been able

to concentrate all morning. Even now, after over an hour massaging his *domina*'s limbs, his mind raced.

At any moment, they were going to be robbed.

Ven knew because he had arranged for it himself. Instead of waiting for his *domina* outside the dressing room that morning, he had doubled back to the entrance to the baths and apprehended the toughest-looking street urchin he could find.

'I wish for you to enter the *tepidarium* in one hour and rob me of this bag.' Ven held up his *domina*'s bag of supplies. 'Then meet me in the hypocaust.' He poured a half a dozen *asses* into the boy's hand.

'You are paying me to rob you?' the boy had asked in puzzlement.

'Yes, and if you do it successfully I will give you this.' Ven had held up a bronze *sesterce*.

The boy raised an interested brow.

'Will you do it or not?'

The boy had nodded vigorously, but now Ven feared he would not fulfil his promise. Ven pictured Vita waiting for him patiently below the *tepidarium*, wondering why he had not yet appeared.

'I received some wondrous news from my husband last night,' said Lollia.

'Indeed?' echoed Ven, trying to sound interested.

Why had he asked Vita to meet him beneath the *tepidarium* in the first place? It was the deepest part of August, by the gods. Why not the *frigidarium*, where she would at least be able to keep cool?

'I shall not be accompanying Lepidus to Britannia after all, it seems,' said Lollia.

'That *is* wondrous news!' he replied, trying to sound surprised. 'I know that you were dreading the winters.'

He pictured Vita standing at the entrance to the hypocaust, trying to withstand the heat. How long would she last before she simply gave up?

'It appears that Lepidus is leaving me here in Rome to do as I like,' Lollia continued. 'Ha! Imagine that! Has he told you when he plans to leave, Ven?'

'No, Domina,' Ven lied, for Lepidus had sworn him to secrecy.

'Well, I imagine it will be soon. It is a long trip to that remote island—thirty days at least to reach his post. Of course you already know that, for you made the trip yourself once.'

It was a cruel thing for her to say—to remind Ven of his enslavement—though it did not bother Ven in the least. He was accustomed to his *domina's* stabs and could easily endure them. After all, his heart was made of ice.

Still, in moments like these, when Vita was near, it seemed to melt just a little.

Vita stood at the bottom of the stairwell and leaned against the wall, trying to keep away from the worst of the hot air. She gazed through the forest of clay columns at the large brick oven at the other end of the hypocaust. Every twenty minutes a slave would arrive with an armful of wood to feed the flickering beast. Since she had arrived, she had already seen four of them come and go.

The air was unnervingly hot. As she breathed it in, it seemed to heat her very lungs. She knew that the longer she waited, the sooner he would be there, for he would not leave her waiting here for ever. In just a few moments she was going to see Ven and they would share a private moment together.

She would breathe in his scent and feel excitement ball up in her stomach. Perhaps they would exchange a few words in their sacred tongue. Maybe he would squeeze her hand.

After Magnus had rejected her so long ago, she never thought she would long for a man again. But now, standing in the sprawling hypocaust, yearning for just a glimpse of his dazzling grin, she felt wholly changed.

It did not matter if Ven did not feel the same. It was enough that he had ignited the flame of her lust—a flame she had believed long dead. He had made her feel alive again.

Now she realised the real reason why she had really been feeling so happy lately. It was not her decision to divorce Magnus as she had at first believed. In a sense, she had been divorced from Magnus for years. The real reason for her happiness was Ven.

She had met him only four days ago, yet it was as if she had always known him. Or perhaps he simply fitted the description of the man that she had conjured inside her heart long ago—the kind, noble man who somehow also desired her. She had been so alone for so many years—invisible to the world. Now she finally felt seen. Beautiful, even.

It was all because of him. Even when she was not thinking of him, he was part of her awareness. Every moment seemed full of him and everything was funny, or lovely, or worthy of praise. Sloshing buckets of water pouring joyously across the tiles. Cups of tart *posca* and bites of salty bread. The glimmer of the stars through the atrium roof. The colours of dawn.

It was Ven. He was the reason.

She lifted her hair off her shoulders, letting the sweat drip down her neck. Where was he? Surely he would be here soon. Sweat poured down her back. She gazed up the stairs at the blue sky above. She wondered if the gods were smiling or laughing.

'Tell me, Ven, are you not eager to journey to your homeland with Lepidus?' asked Lollia, obviously glad to have avoided such a fate herself.

'I am eager to continue to serve him, Domina.'

A lie. There was only one thing Ven was eager for: to see Vita.

'Come now, I know you wish for some things.' His *domina* rolled over on to her back and gingerly arranged her breasts. She was watching him closely, waiting for him to look at her, but today he could not falsify his admiration as he usually did.

'I wish for nothing, Domina,' he repeated and began to rub her feet.

Lollia sighed wistfully. 'I wish for something, Ven. Do you know what it is?'

Power? he thought wickedly. *Diversion? Desire?* 'Cooler weather, Domina?'

'I wish for love.'

Not again, thought Ven.

A more conscientious slave would have assured his *domina* that her husband loved her, or that her husband's love for her would develop with time, or some other vague placation, but Ven and Lollia were far beyond such fictions. 'Then you shall find it,' he said. 'Some day.'

'I believe I may already have found it, but I am not certain it is reciprocated.'

It was an unexpected response. 'You are in love with him, then?' Ven asked boldly. 'The man with whom you have been trysting?'

Lollia's eyes flashed. 'Ven, how dare you?' She raised her hand to slap him, but before she could, the blessed street urchin arrived. He breezed past the massage bench, swept up Lollia's bag and skipped off running. Glory of Jove.

Ven turned to his *domina*, trying not to betray his joy. 'Domina, did you see—?'

'That boy just stole my bag, Ven!' she shrieked. 'Get him!'

The boy rushed down the stairway so quickly that he nearly knocked Vita to the floor. 'Who are you?' he demanded.

'Who are *you*?' she returned. She glanced at the bag he held tightly in his grasp and the answer became clear all at once. 'He paid you well, I hope?' she asked.

'Six *asses* already,' said the boy, 'and a *sesterce* at the end.'

'A *sesterce*?' said Vita. 'You will be eating fish cakes for days!'

The boy's grin was nearly too large for his face, yet somehow it became bigger as Ven came running down the stairs after him. Vita caught Ven's eye and her heart nearly stopped.

'Well done, young man!' he said, turning to the boy, who handed Ven the bag and bowed.

Ven dug inside the bag and held out two *sesterces*. The boy gazed at the two shiny coins, then gingerly pulled one from Ven's grasp.

'I hold out two coins, but you take only one?'

'Our agreement was for one, sir,' said the boy.

'Would you look at that, Vita? It appears we have just encountered a rarity in Rome—a truly honest man.'

The boy's chest seemed to fill with air and Vita felt her own chest expanding along with it.

She felt unreasonably happy. Not only would she soon

be alone with her favourite person in the world, that person had for the first time said her name.

'Take the second coin, son,' said Ven. 'As a reward for your integrity.'

The boy studied Ven's eyes, as if searching for the trick in them. 'Do you not believe me?' asked Ven. He gestured to Vita. 'Look what you have done. You have united me with a goddess! Do you not think I would be grateful?'

The boy glanced at Vita, nodded, then took the second coin. He gave Ven a deep bow. 'Gratitude, sir,' he said and in an instant he was gone.

Vita laughed. 'He reminded me a little of Cupid,' she remarked. 'A good omen.'

'You are a good omen,' said Ven. His smile was like the sun behind the clouds. It burst out in a rush of warmth and she lifted her face to it and basked.

'How much time do we have?' she asked.

'Ten minutes? Five? She will come looking for me soon.' He reached beneath the hem of his short tunic and held out a gold *aureus*, the equivalent of one hundred *sesterces*.

He gestured for her to take it. 'This is for you—to help you find a place to live.' She gazed at the sparkling gold coin. It was enough to rent a room for many months. 'It is not much, but it is something. Please, take it,' he urged.

She stepped back. 'Ven, I cannot accept coin from you. I would never even dream of it.'

'That is why you must take it.'

Vita blinked free a tear. She had promised herself she would not cry.

'You are a good woman, Vita. You are worthy of this.'

She knew she should just accept it, for she did not

wish to fight him. She only wished to fall into his arms and let him gather up all her pieces. This man, this beautiful man, wished to give her all he had, though all she really wanted was him.

'I am so sorry, Ven, but I cannot accept this generous gift. One day, when Lepidus frees you, you will need—'

'Lepidus will never free me.'

She drew a breath. 'One day, when you escape, you will—'

'I will not escape, Vita,' said Ven.

'But why not? You will soon be far from Rome. Can you not choose your moment?'

'Vita, you are looking, but not seeing.'

He bowed his head and there before her was the reason, written in ink on flesh. *FGV. Fugitivus*. Runaway.

She had stopped seeing the tattoo the moment after they had first met.

'Romans patrol constantly in the lands of my kin,' Ven said. 'They fear another uprising.'

'So the rumours are true?' asked Vita. 'About another Brigante rebellion?'

'I think so,' said Ven. 'There is another Roman legion being deployed to Britannia right now. The Romans will soon be patrolling Brigante lands, searching for rebels. There is no sanctuary for me among the Brigantes or the Romans, Vita. Not with this tattoo. I will never be free again.'

He could not continue. To say more would be to burden her unnecessarily. The truth was that since he had met her, he had felt a dangerous stirring inside him. It was the same disquiet that had plagued him before his attempts at escape, with one difference: he wished to take her with him.

'You must not let yourself become defeated!' she

cried. 'When you arrive in Britannia, you must attempt to get yourself free. Promise me you will try.'

'I cannot make a promise that I do not intend to keep.'

'But why? You will have five years in Britannia. You must only wait for the right moment to present itself. All you need is patience and determination…and the will. Gather it, Ven. Do not allow your own mind to enslave you!'

She was breathing too hard and he saw the moisture of tears on her cheeks. 'Do not weep,' he whispered. It seemed strange that thoughts of his escape might provoke her tears.

He gently took her hand and let his fingers weave with hers. She gazed down at their joined hands and he pulled her towards him. She pressed her head against the contours of his chest and sighed as he surrounded her with his arms.

'I will miss you,' she said. 'So very much.'

Then come with me, he thought. Her soft breaths against his chest were like tiny caresses and a strange sense of peace enveloped him. If he could just remember this feeling for the rest of his days, he knew he could survive.

'I failed to find the marriage contract,' she whispered. 'There was a lock on the drawer and I could not find the key.'

'That is all? A lock without a key?'

'It does not matter,' she replied.

He buried his head in her hair and breathed in her scent—a mystic alchemy of loneliness and sunshine and that wondrous substance of his youth: soap. He took in many breaths of her.

'We must both be strong now,' she whispered. 'You

must not give up your fight and I will not give up mine. You must escape Lepidus. Freedom is the prize.'

He knew he should not speak, but he could not help himself any more. His heart's meltwaters had finally become a flood.

'You are the prize, Vita,' he whispered back. 'You.'

There was no time to respond to him. She looked up and there were his lips. They pressed down upon hers in a crush of breath and heat. 'Ven,' she breathed.

'I do not sleep,' he told her. 'I barely eat. I suffer fevers. I only think of you.' He brushed her hair to the side and touched her cheek with a trembling hand.

'I am plagued by similar maladies,' she said, but she could not say more, for he was kissing her again and she did not want him to cease.

He swept his tongue into her mouth and she replied with a sensual sweep of her own. She had never felt so bold in all her life. It was as if she could not get close enough to him.

He bit her lower lip gently and pulled at it. She giggled and he paused to look around. He must have been assuring himself they had no witnesses, for what he did next was surely against the law. He took her just-bitten lower lip between his own lips and sucked it. Long and hard.

Her giggle became a moan.

She had met him only days ago, yet it was as if she had always known him. He was the man she had conjured inside her heart long ago—the kind, noble protector who somehow also desired her. She had been so alone for so many years—invisible to the world. Now she felt seen. Beautiful, even.

His arms were like wings, they enveloped her completely. She relaxed into them and sighed, then inhaled. He smelled like everything she wanted, a strange, musky elixir that wafted into her nose and somehow made her heart feel light.

She was dizzy and reckless and probably quite mad, yet nothing could worry her now. She was safe in Ven's arms and all would be well.

'I have wished for this from the moment I first saw you,' he said. He leaned back and studied her face.

'I confess that have wished for the same,' she said. 'I never believed such a wish would come true.'

'Your eyes,' he said. 'They seem to change colour with your mood. They remind me of…' He paused and looked up as if searching for a memory buried deep.

'What colour are they now?' she asked.

'Deep brown—like two mature acorns. Perhaps they are brown when you are happy.'

Vita smiled. She had never heard anything so amusing. She stood on her toes to get a better look at him and he slid his hand around the back of her neck. 'Vita?'

'Ven, I—' she began saying, but there was a sudden clang of metal against stone. Across the forest of columns, a slave was poking at the fire inside the furnace once again. Was it possible that twenty minutes had passed?

'Ven!' shouted a woman's voice from above.

Ven gasped, then stepped back. 'That is Lollia. I must go.' He pressed the gold coin into Vita's palm. 'Take it.'

She closed her hand around it and looked deeply into his eyes. 'We will meet again,' she said. 'Thank you.'

He grinned, but his smile was so hopeless that it nearly broke her heart. 'Until we meet again, then,' he said.

'Ven!' cried Lollia. Her voice was closer now, but Ven was not moving. He appeared to be plucking the hairpin out of Vita's own hair.

'Ven, you must go now, before Lollia sees you down here.'

He held the metal object before Vita. 'This pin will open the lock to Magnus's desk drawer. All you need is patience and determination…and the will. Promise me you will try.'

'I promise,' said Vita. 'Now go!'

Chapter Seven

On the morning of the Vulcanalia feast, Vita awoke feeling bleak. She should have been joyous. This was the first day of her freedom after all. Her new life was about to begin. And now, thanks to Ven's selfless generosity, her problem was solved. She would finally be able to find a place to live.

The gold coin he had given her was more than enough to pay for a room somewhere. Indeed, with such full pockets, she would have her choice of places. She would have a room in which to live and rest in privacy and safety. A place to do her sewing and begin a life. A starting point for happiness.

Still, she could not help but think that her happiness was leaving her—walking out of Rome on two long legs. Ven would be gone for five years and possibly longer, depending on the duration of Lepidus's post, though if Ven took her advice and made his escape, he would not return at all.

She hoped he would escape. She hoped he would never have to return to Rome, for no one deserved to suffer a life in bonds. Freedom was more important than happiness. Vita understood that now. Still, she could not help but feel that some essential part of her life was slipping away.

The bell for the second hour of the morning sounded. On a normal day, she would be late in preparing Magnus's breakfast. Today, however, there was no rush. During the festival of the Vulcanalia, Magnus did not have patrol duties, for the festivities were overseen by the Praetorian Guard.

Vita made her way to the kitchen, pausing to give her final offering of grain to the household Lar. 'Protect all inside this house,' Vita begged the divine icon, adding, 'On this day in particular.'

She assembled Magnus's breakfast and headed to the *tablinium* with his tray, but he was not sitting at his desk as usual. She padded into the *triclinium* and discovered him lounging on one of the sofas. He was petting one of the feral tomcats that regularly invaded their home.

She set down his breakfast on the table beside him. 'Happy Vulcanalia, Magnus. I imagine we will soon begin to smell the smoke of the bonfires,' she said.

'Have you found a place to live?' asked Magnus, reaching for a slice of cucumber.

'I have not.'

'You must be gone from this house today. You realise that, do you not?'

'I do.'

'Lollia said she saw you at the baths.'

'When did she tell you that?'

'When I made love to her behind the laundress yesterday,' said Magnus. He spread a scoop of olive paste over a cucumber and took a bite. 'Did you not pick up the bread from the baker?'

Vita's throat felt dry. Did he mean to rub his betrayal in her face?

'Well?' asked Magnus. 'Did you pick up the bread or not? I have heard that when a woman is with child she needs plenty of bread.' He skewered a sardine and fed it to the cat. 'Lollia is with child, you see. It is my child, Vita. An heir of my own. A son to inherit this beautiful house.' He glanced around the *triclinium*.

'Why do you say such things, Magnus? Are you trying to hurt me?'

'Hurt you? How could I hurt you when you are divorcing me? Imagine that—the Virile Vigile of Rome. Divorced by his ridiculous, portly wife. Ha!'

Finally she understood the source of his anger. She had somehow humiliated him. 'But, Magnus, it is you who—'

'Lollia said that you did not know what to do with yourself at the baths,' he interrupted. 'She mentioned that her slave gave you a massage. That is rather unlike you—to accept service from a slave.'

Vita's heart froze. 'Lollia insisted on it. She said that she wished for me to understand all the benefits of ownership.'

'Do you understand them now?' he asked. Was Vita mistaken, or was there a threat inside his voice?

She lowered her tray. 'No, to be honest, I do not.'

She waited as the moments slid past. Married or not, if Magnus even suspected her relationship with Ven, she was going to receive a terrible beating. She breathed in, imagining Ven beside her, and a strange calm overtook her.

'I have never supported slavery,' she stated.

'And I have suffered as a result,' Magnus said.

Vita gestured around their well-appointed *triclinium*. 'You have wanted for nothing.'

'Except for a woman to warm my bed. Any attractive

woman would do—even a slave—but you have always resisted purchasing one. It is why I must seek my pleasure elsewhere, you understand? You have caused this.'

'If you are trying to upset me, you will not succeed,' said Vita. 'You have dishonoured me with your adultery and thus have dishonoured yourself. And you are mistaken about my appearance. I am not unattractive.'

He shook his head and stood. She had never spoken to him so boldly and feared what he might do next. Still, she would not diminish her words by running from him now.

He started towards her, but in that instant the tomcat jumped up on the table and began to feast on Magnus's scraps. Distracted, Magnus kicked the tray to the floor, then pushed Vita aside and headed for the entrance.

'If you are not gone from this house by the time I am back,' he cried, 'you will regret it.'

The door swung shut and Vita took a breath. Her heart pounding, she rushed upstairs and placed Ven's gold coin inside a small purse with the rest of her *sesterces*. She tied the purse tightly to the belt of her tunic, lifted her sack full of belongings, and speeded back downstairs.

She crossed the atrium, realising that this was the last moment she would ever see the house that had sheltered her for so long. Her house. Her patrimony.

Her father would never have wanted it to be this way. If only he had been alive, perhaps she could have appealed to him. He had been a strong man, a noble man, and had endowed her with the house so she would be secure throughout her life. She knew she was dishonouring him by leaving it so willingly to Magnus. She had not even put up a fight.

She glanced into the *tablinium* and caught sight of Magnus's desk.

Ven's words echoed in her mind. *'Patience and determination...and the will.'* It was possible the marriage contract was still inside the drawer. She had to try.

She dropped her sack in the atrium and crossed into the *tablinium*, pulling the pin from her hair. She slid the tiny metal rod easily into the keyhole of Magnus's desk drawer and moved it in the lock, hearing the soft clang of metal as she probed.

She pulled at the drawer, feeling a slight give when she moved the rod in a certain direction. She pulled again and the drawer opened a little more. She moved the hairpin again, then heard a tiny click. She pulled drawer open wide.

'You wicked, treacherous woman!' Magnus shouted. He was standing in the doorway, an unsheathed *gladius* sword in his hand.

'Magnus, please.' She stepped backwards and put her hands up.

'What did I tell you I would do if I caught you in here again?' His voice was like cool metal.

'Kill me,' she whispered.

'What did you say?'

'You said you would kill me,' she cried. His eyes looked lifeless. His jaw was slack. She felt certain that he really did mean to kill her. She glanced behind her at the back doorway of the *tablinium*. It led into their enclosed garden.

'If I do not kill you now, I will kill you later,' Magnus said. 'So you can run into the garden now and let me hunt you down, or you can stay and die with the shred of honour you have left.'

He was no longer enraged. His words were as calm as if he were describing a day at the chariot races. 'The house is mine now and you can never take it back. I am a *vigile* of Rome, after all, and you are nothing.'

He lunged across the room towards Vita, slashing the *gladius* in the air, but instead of escaping into the garden, she dived underneath his swing. She slid out on to the floor of the atrium and jumped to her feet.

She ran towards the entrance to the house, catching sight of him out of the corner of her eye. He was closing the distance between them. She could practically feel his sharp blade pushing into her back.

She swung the door open just as he caught up to her. He grasped the skirt of her tunic as she moved through the doorway, tearing it. She turned to push the door closed, but his hand pushed back. It reached at her body, searching for something to grasp, and took hold of her coin purse, pulling it free.

She could hear the coins spilling upon the ground as she thrust the door hard against his hand. 'Ow!' he screamed and she dashed off across the plaza.

When she finally turned around, she saw him holding his injured hand against his chest, still chasing her. He was already halfway across the plaza, quickly closing the distance between them. She could not outrun him. She needed to confuse him somehow.

She turned in the direction of the tavern where Avidia worked, then thought better. She turned up one road and down another, tracing a circuitous route back to the table-lined storefront. By the time she reached the tavern, there was no sign of Magnus.

Vita stepped inside the tavern, immediately drawing looks from the half-dozen customers occupying the space. 'Avidia the waitress?' she asked.

A man pointed towards the back of the tavern and Vita rushed into the small kitchen where another man stood stirring a pot over a fire. He looked at Vita's torn tunic and sweaty brow. 'We do not serve your kind in here. Please leave.'

'I am looking for a woman named Avidia. I am in danger and I need her help.'

The man frowned, then glanced at the floor.

There on the tiles lay Avidia, sprawled in a drunken slumber, the red of the Massillian staining her lips. 'It is the second time in two days,' he said.

Vita crouched by Avidia's side, trying to wake her. 'Avidia, please! I need your help. Wake up!' Her friend only continued to snore.

'She owes me nine *sesterces*!' shouted the man. 'Did you come to pay the debt?'

'No, sir. I am afraid I have no money at all,' Vita said. Not any more. 'A wicked man is trying to find me. I am in fear for my life.'

'Then get out of here and take this useless woman with you!'

Vita cringed. *Useless woman.*

'She is not useless,' Vita growled. 'She is just... trapped.'

She placed her arms beneath Avidia's arms and attempted to lift. 'Come along, Avidia,' she said. 'Time to get going.' Avidia let out a lavish snore.

Vita did not know what to do. Avidia was drunk, Ven was gone and Magnus was hunting her like a deer.

'Get out!' shouted the man. He lifted his spoon as if to punish her with it and she ran out of the tavern and back into the street.

She glanced around for Magnus. He was probably canvasing the neighbourhoods right now, advising his fellow *vigiles* to keep their eyes out for her: a short, round, green-eyed woman going somewhere in a hurry.

How could she possibly escape him?

Lepidus. If today was the Vulcanalia, then the old man would be setting out on his journey to Britannia tomorrow morning. If she could reach the port of Ostia by that time she could join him.

Him and Ven.

It was her only choice. She had lost all her coins and all the rest of her belongings. She had no family to turn to and nobody to help her. All she had was the will to survive and her own two feet. Slowly, they began to move on their own—in the direction of the river.

Soon she was running as fast as her legs could take her. River barges travelled regularly between the city and the port and she was certain she could sneak her way on to one.

She had to try to reach Lepidus. It was the only way she could survive. Without her sewing, she could not support herself. She would be alone on the dangerous streets, without any possibility for better. Meanwhile, Magnus and the other *vigiles* would be hunting her.

She did not even have her identity. She had packed all of her official documents in the sack she had left in the atrium, including the proof of her citizenship. Magnus would surely destroy those documents as soon as he could. He would have his own little Vulcanalia celebration that very night. First he would burn her clothes, then her documents, and finally her sewing. There would be nothing left of her.

It was what Magnus would want. If he could not find her himself, he would simply destroy her existence. Without her proof of citizenship, she could easily become enslaved.

At least with Lepidus she would be safe. She would have to endure more hard years and keep as far away from Ven as she possibly could, but in the end there would be coin…and freedom. There was no more to think about, she needed to get to Ostia.

Arriving at the Emporium warehouse area beside the river, she could hardly believe her eyes. The large river port was normally a hive of activity, but today it was all but empty.

She gazed out at the docks and saw a number of barges anchored, but no captain or crew member in sight. Vita jogged past the long line of offices, but they were all locked, and the oxen that pulled the barges were no-where in sight.

She spied a dock worker coiling a rope near one of the smaller barges.

'Excuse me, sir, will you be taking that barge back downriver soon?'

'Sorry, madam, no barges today in or out of the city. The priests have forbidden it.'

She gazed out at the empty river. Not a single fishing boat was plying its quiet waters and, for the first time all day, she noticed the heat. The sun god beat down on the parched city without mercy and sweat poured down Vita's neck.

The bonfires that had begun to burn on each of Rome's seven hills seemed only to add to the heat, as did the ominous layer of black smoke that was already gathering in the sky. The god of fire expected his due, lest he burn all the harvest.

She should have guessed that the Emporium would be closed on this day: it was only the largest grain storage area in all of Rome. Still, she feared the fourteen-mile road to the Ostia port, which was regularly patrolled by *vigiles*.

She gazed out at the river once again. Her mother had

taught Vita to swim in these waters when she was just a girl. They stayed remarkably cool in the summer—much cooler than the baths—or so her mother always told her father in order to justify their outings.

The truth was that her mother was happiest when she was near the river. 'It is the wildest thing in Rome besides the cats,' she always said. Other mothers would teach their children to swim at the baths, or in the comfort of their own villas, but Vita's mother had preferred the river. As a result, Vita had quickly become the strongest swimmer she knew.

Now that Vita stood on its sacred banks once again she saw that nothing had changed. Its waters ran swift and true and they could deliver her to the sea in only a few short hours.

She took several steps into the river, sensing the three Fates watching her from above, weaving their merciless threads. Her life had almost been hers. For a handful of days she had seized it, without the help of any man.

She had even made a friend. Her dear Avidia would have been a perfect companion, if only Vita could have woken her up. Like Vita, Avidia had unlocked the door to freedom, but had not been able to step through it.

Vita gazed down at the swirling water. She knew that if she took another step, she would belong to the current, the waters of which would either drown her or deliver her into another prison. Still, she could not see another way.

If only she had not been proud. If only she had walked out the door and never looked back. Freedom was more important than happiness and now she would have neither.

That was not entirely true. She would have Ven. She would not be able to kiss him or touch him or even speak with him, but he would be there none the less. Her quiet sentinel, ever vigilant, the only man she could trust. She took one final step and let the current sweep her up.

Chapter Eight

'Well, there you are, Vita!' gasped Lepidus. The bald, grey-bearded equestrian looked genuinely surprised as she hailed him the next morning. She started across the plaza towards him, hoping he would not notice her ragged tunic and tangled hair. When she stood before him, he frowned. 'You look like Medusa herself.'

She bowed and forced a smile. 'Apologies for my appearance and for my tardiness, Lepidus.'

'Tardiness? I did not think you were coming at all. This is a happy development,' he said, though still he frowned. He plucked an oak leaf from her hair.

'I was just taking some shade,' she lied. In truth, she had spent the night beneath a stand of trees outside the docks, curled against the chill. 'Then your proposal still stands?' she asked.

'It does. Do you have the contract?'

'I am afraid it was lost.'

'And your baggage?'

'Also lost.' His expression was confused. 'It was my ex-husband Magnus,' she explained. 'He was…upset when I left him.'

She held her breath, hoping Lepidus would not compel her to further explanation. Thankfully, he did not.

'Well, in that case we will need to get you a new tunic. We cannot have my concubine looking like a tavern woman now, can we?'

Vita nodded gravely, reminding herself to be careful. Lepidus might have seemed cheerful and kind, but he was the same man who had delivered Ven his scars.

Ven. She had thought of him all night, despite herself. She knew that she would have to distance herself from him, for she certainly could not betray Lepidus. A contract was a contract and Vita was an honourable woman.

Still, she looked around the plaza, hoping to catch sight of Ven. Instead she caught the eye of the stone-faced Scythian standing several paces away. She nodded politely at the thick-chested man, but he did not nod back.

'Is this our vessel?' Vita asked Lepidus. She eyed the long, thin merchant ship roped to nearest dock. Its name was painted on the side of its bow in a waxy crimson hue: *Europa*.

'It is the only vessel departing today, I am afraid.' He glanced around the plaza with a look of mild disgust. 'A throng of plebs and not a single cabin available to rent. I fear it will be a tiresome, crowded journey.'

Vita was relieved that there was no cabin, for it meant that Lepidus could not expect her to perform her contracted duties right away. He would expect her cooperation eventually, though, and she dreaded the day.

'It will be a handful of days up the coast to Narbo in Gaul,' Lepidus explained, 'then overland by carriage to the port of Burdigala in Aquitania. From there we sail north to the mouth of the Tamesis and Londinium, then on to the fort at Coria.'

Vita opened her mouth to speak, but Lepidus continued. 'If you are like my wife, you are probably wondering about accommodations for our journey. I assure you that everything will be of the highest standards. I carry a letter from the offices of the Emperor guaranteeing us a room in any government *mansion* we encounter. You will stay with me, of course, and the Dacian outside our door.'

'The Dacian?'

He motioned to a small blonde-haired woman approaching them, her arms filled with provisions. 'That is my Dacian slave,' he said. 'I purchased her over a year ago and have trained her well. She will teach you much about how to please me.'

Vita nodded, trying to keep up her good cheer. Lepidus had owned the woman for a year and had not even learned her name?

'Hello, I am Vita,' she said to the woman. 'And you are?'

'Zia, Domina.'

She had managed to place all the goods she had purchased in one hand so as to free her other hand to lift Lepidus's massive travel bag.

'I have chosen to travel light,' Lepidus explained. 'The army will provide for our needs at the fort and I shall purchase more slaves as well, but first we must get there!'

'Let me help you with that,' Vita told Zia and the two women were attempting to lift the bag together when Vita caught sight of Ven. He was striding across the plaza towards them, carrying a bagful of coal and the carcases of several plucked chickens.

She could not help but notice him. His gait was smooth, yet so different from other men's. Because of his unusual height, his strides seemed to tread the very air. It was as if he were floating above the people he passed—a towering god wandering amid the mortals.

'This is my bodyguard,' Lepidus was saying. He gestured to the Scythian standing behind him. 'And there is Ven whom you already know.'

Vita returned her attention to Ven, who was now only paces away from them. He wore his short tunic as usual, along with sandals whose straps wound up the twin pillars of his legs. Beyond them lay his narrow waist and the vast, hilly terrain of his chest. She remembered the moment when she had rested her head against it.

She gathered her courage and looked at his face. It struck her as so handsome it did not seem to be real. Did no one else notice his remarkable good looks? Or did his status as a slave somehow diminish them? His eyes alone were a marvel of the gods. Instead of reflecting the light from without, they seemed to be repressing it from within, with varying degrees of success.

Just then, for instance, they seemed bursting with intensity and, when they locked with her own eyes, she feared she might simply turn to dust.

In an effort to defend herself against his smouldering beauty, Vita closed her eyes. It was her only recourse, for she should not have been admiring Ven at all. She should not have even been thinking about him. She was a claimed woman now, a concubine, and there was only one man to whom she owed her attention.

She turned to Lepidus and smiled tightly, trying to erase what she had just seen. It was impossible. Ven's image remained in her mind as if it had been branded there. Worse, her heart was filled to brimming.

'Excuse me, Vita, but are you well?' asked Lepidus.

'You look very flushed.' Vita nodded, then fixed her gaze upon the concrete beneath her feet.

'It is just the sun,' she told Lepidus. 'Do you not find it rather warm?'

At that moment, the ship's captain and crew appeared on the deck and all the passengers who had gathered on the dock went silent. The nine men stepped before a shrine of Jupiter and kneeled.

'Bless our journey, mighty Jupiter,' the captain entreated the icon, 'and spirit us to the port of Narbo's safe bosom.' One of the crew handed him an amphora of wine, some of which he poured over the shrine. He tossed the rest into the sea. 'All aboard!'

Soon the crew was at oars and the long, square-sailed *phaselus* began to glide northwards on a light breeze. Vita stood quietly at the stern, trying to find her bearings. There was something final about floating out to sea and, as she gazed out at the shore, it was as if she was not simply bidding farewell to the ground, but to her old life.

She should have been relieved. She had managed to reach Lepidus—and just in time to join him. She had not been killed or injured, nor was she wandering the countryside searching for work among unscrupulous landowners.

Thanks to Lepidus's offer, she would enjoy a comfortable life—a life of safety and good wine and fine accommodations. The years of her concubinage would pass quickly. All would be well.

She should have been grateful, but all she could think of was Ven. How would she manage to forget him now? She had tried and failed to swallow her heartbreak when they had said goodbye in Rome. What would she do now that she had to dismiss him every single day?

She had no choice but to forget him completely: her very survival depended on it. If Lepidus found out about her feelings for Ven, he would destroy her contract and leave her in the cold. Or worse.

Ignore him, she told herself. *Erase him from your mind.*

Perhaps she could make him into her enemy. She could offend him somehow, say something cruel, make him hate her enough to prevent him from looking at her in that way that turned her insides into porridge.

It would be perhaps the greatest test she would ever have to face. She feared she would have to destroy some vital part of herself, or bury it so deep that she would never be able to retrieve it again.

Several of the crew hoisted the sails while the others drew in the oars. Meanwhile, the passengers were laying down mats and settling on to the deck for the journey up the coast to the next port.

Lepidus was not among the deck dwellers, which meant he had gone below. The others had surely joined him there as well, having no choice in the matter.

It had always seemed strange to Vita that travellers would huddle inside the hull of a ship when the great wide world spread out before them. Still, she would need to join Lepidus soon, lest he think her already shirking her duty.

She gave the craggy shoreline one last look, then turned to leave, crashing face first into a familiar wall of flesh. Her joy leapt up, but she beat it back down. 'You should not have come here,' she said.

'I will not let him touch you.'

She turned back around and stared at the shore. 'He will touch me and soon. I agreed to it. This was my decision and now I must live with it.'

'Will you not even look at me?' he asked.

'I cannot look at you. You know I cannot. This thing between us, it can no longer be.'

He was shaking his head, having none of it. 'When I saw you standing beside Lepidus, I nearly shouted with happiness.'

And so did I. She shook her head. 'Happiness is fleeting. Freedom is the prize.'

'Vita…' His hand grazed hers, but she pulled it away. Curses, it was still there. The heat.

'You must understand that I am doing this to survive,' said Vita. 'Magnus tried to kill me yesterday.'

'What?'

'I barely escaped Rome with my life.'

She saw his hands squeezing the wood of the rail, his fingers white with anger. His voice dropped to a whisper. 'It was my fault.'

She shook her head. 'That is not true.'

'He caught you trying to pick the lock. Tell me if I am wrong.'

Vita said nothing, but she sensed the heaviness of his regret. 'Please do not blame yourself, Ven.'

'Why not, if it is my fault?'

'I would not have tried to pick the lock if I had not wished to,' she told him. 'It was my choice.'

He shook his head and closed his eyes. 'I do not deserve you.'

'And you do not have me,' said Vita. 'I belong to Lepidus now. We must not speak alone again. Do you understand?'

Ven nodded, but she sensed his resistance.

'My contract with Lepidus is the only hope I have for survival now,' she explained. 'I have lost everything. I am a desperate woman and have therefore made a difficult promise.'

'You will not even converse with me, then?'

'I must lie with him, Ven. Do you know how trying that will be? To lie with another man, when all I can think about is...'

'Is what?'

She shook her head. 'Nothing. It does not matter. The time is past. You must go now and leave me alone. Always.'

They were the hardest words she had ever had to say. But there was only Lepidus now and the next five years of life her life stretching out before her like the never-ending sea.

'Please, Ven, just go.'

Soon after their ship had departed Ostia, the wind had come up from the north and the heavily loaded vessel had spent hours tacking against its teeth. Instead of taking a few hours to reach the port of Centumcellae a few miles up the coast, it had taken many and, by the time they arrived, it was too late to find lodgings.

Most of the passengers slept on the deck that night, the collective hum of their snores blending with the rhythmic whispers of the waves.

Thankfully, Lepidus did not ask Vita to join him on his sleeping mat below deck. He slept alongside the Scythian while Ven and Zia joined the other slaves in a small area beside the galley.

Lying on deck beneath the stars, Vita was able to finally relax and was seized by a deep, dreamless sleep.

When she awoke the next morning, the ship was already pulling away from its port. Heading for the stairs, she nearly crashed into Zia carrying Lepidus's chamber pot. Vita plucked the chamber pot from the woman's arms and emptied it over the deck herself.

'Gratitude, Domina,' said Zia.

Vita cringed. 'Please do not call me Domina.' She glanced about the deck. 'At least not when we are alone.'

But they were not alone. There was Ven, only steps away, watching them.

'Excuse me, women,' he said, addressing both Vita and Zia at once. 'I wonder if either of you knows where I may find a metal brazier for cooking?' Ven made a gesture with his hands for Zia's benefit, but Vita knew that his question was all for her.

'I believe I saw one among a family near the bow,' Vita said, nodding in that direction.

She moved to go below deck, but Ven gestured for her to stop. 'Would you mind leading me to them? It is just that Lepidus has requested a roasted chicken for his breakfast and I must prepare the fire quickly, lest he grow angry.'

Vita bit her lip. He had outmanoeuvred her, the clever fox. She had no choice but to lead the way.

'I apologise for this,' Ven said as they walked together towards the bow. 'I believe I know how you may avoid Lepidus's bed.'

'The brazier is just there,' Vita said, pointing to the small metal container. She stepped around him to leave and as she passed by his side, she whispered. 'How?'

'Tell him you lost the contract.'

'I did lose the contract. I burned it.'

A rare smile traversed his lips. 'Tell him that you insist that another be drawn up and that it be properly signed and witnessed. Tell him it is a matter of honour.'

There was no time for another word and soon Vita

was below the deck, making her morning salutation to Lepidus. 'Can you not bring me a cup of water, Vita? My throat is parched.'

'Of course,' said Vita. She found the fresh-water amphorae in the rear of the hull and filled his cup, returning with it. 'My shoulders are rather sore,' he said, drinking down the liquid. 'Can you rub them for me?'

'Yes.' While Vita went to work rubbing his shoulders, the old man motioned to Zia, who was soon rubbing his feet.

He laughed bitterly. 'Just look at me—a *paterfamilias* of equestrian rank, receiving his morning massage on the floor. I should have stayed in Ostia and waited for a larger ship.'

'The time will pass quickly,' Vita reassured him.

Lepidus snorted. 'I have a weak stomach. No time passes quickly for me aboard a ship. It is the reason I must pass most of my time below deck.' He rubbed his bald head as if to consult it. 'But as soon as we reach the port of Narbo, we shall consummate our arrangement in the comfort of a proper bed.'

Vita drew a breath. 'Good Lepidus, before I can perform the task I have committed to, I must ensure that our arrangement is legal. Without a contract, signed and properly witnessed, my reputation would be in question, you see. I am sure you understand the need for the formality.'

Several moments passed and Vita was not sure if Lepidus was thinking or waiting for the right moment to throw her overboard.

'Of course,' said Lepidus at last.

'I apologise for the inconvenience,' she said.

'I admire your chastity. It is the primary reason I selected you after all.' He spouted a laugh. 'It was certainly not for your good looks and slender figure!'

Vita leaned into her work, wondering at how little his insult had hurt her. Perhaps it was enough consolation to know that there was one man in the world who did desire her. It only happened that she could not look that man in the eyes ever again.

'Lower,' Lepidus commanded and Vita rubbed down his back.

'I should like to know what kind of weather is expected today,' continued Lepidus, 'and at which ports we will be stopping. I am also wondering if any of the other passengers might be in possession of an extra pillow. Could you find out?' asked Lepidus. 'I would ask Ven, but the two of us will be busy with work all day and this Dacian of mine is useless with Latin.'

Zia made no response, though surely she could understand that she had just been insulted.

'Of course, Lepidus,' said Vita, a vision of her future flashing inside her mind—an endless stream of work and criticism. Had she really expected anything different? She stood to leave.

'Where are you going?' asked Lepidus.

'To find out the information you requested.'

'Not yet, stupid woman! First finish rubbing my back.'

Vita obeyed—what choice did she have?—and soon Ven appeared carrying several scrolls.

'Are those the milecastle drawings?' asked Lepidus.

'Yes, Dominus,' Ven said. 'Shall I leave them with you?'

'I would prefer that we go over them together,' replied Lepidus. 'Vita, will you light our oil lamp?'

* * *

Thus the first leg of their journey passed in a blur of activity as Zia and Vita took turns fetching Lepidus's water and preparing his food, rubbing his limbs and then washing them, emptying his bedpan, cleaning his dishes and accompanying him in strolls on deck.

Meanwhile, Ven went about serving Lepidus in other ways, including many hours spent poring over scrolls. Whatever architectural work was being done, Ven seemed to be doing the bulk of it.

This left Lepidus with more time on his hands than Vita would have liked, for in his spare moments he seemed compelled to point out Vita's faults.

'You are too slow in your movements.'

'You have not washed my tunic properly.'

'You have incorrectly peeled this grape.'

The man was an exacting taskmaster, yet it seemed he could do nothing on his own. Vita's only solace was that she was not alone, for she had Zia.

A shared language was not necessary—she and Zia recognised that they were fighting the same enemy: misery. The battle plan they developed was simple: one would attend to Lepidus while the other rested and attended to her own needs, then they would switch places.

Still, because Zia could not speak Latin, it fell to Vita to keep Lepidus's mind stimulated when he was not working—a formidable task, since the man did not seem capable of a moment's repose.

'This boat was constructed with interlocking timbers. You probably did not notice that, did you, Vita?'

'Why do you wear your hair in such a mess?'

'We must get you a new tunic.'

'Those clouds obviously portend rain. Do you know why?'

He salted his diatribes with unanswerable questions.

'Why do the days grow shorter?'

'Why is the sky blue?'

'Why are some sails made of linen and others of hide?'

When Vita would attempt answers, he would shoot them down like a birds from the sky.

'You obviously know very little. Then again, you are just an uneducated woman.'

'How well can you read, Vita?' he asked one afternoon as they strolled about the deck.

'Passably well, I would say. Why do you ask?'

She spent the rest of the journey reading to him from Pollio's four-hundred-page treatise *De Architectura*, the leatherbound copy of which Lepidus apparently kept with him at all times. By the time they arrived in the port of Narbo, Vita knew more about pediment styles, raised foundations, and decorative plasterwork than she ever could have hoped.

As they readied themselves to disembark, Ven leaped off the boat ahead of their party, intent on hailing a carriage for them.

The loading plank was lowered, and Zia was the first to travel down it, carrying the largest of Lepidus's bags. Vita and Lepidus went next, walking arm in arm down the platform, while the Scythian followed like a shadow behind them.

'You must count yourself rather fortunate, Vita,' Lepidus mused. 'It has not been a *nundinum* since we set out on this journey and already you have acquired much of the knowledge necessary to assist a great man.'

Vita nodded in agreement, though she was rather distracted by the small struggle in which Zia was currently engaged further down the dock. She had briefly stopped to rest and now was attempting to hoist Lepidus's large travel bag upon her back once again. The exhausted woman could not seem to clear her own knees.

Reaching the dock, Vita ran to Zia's aid at the same moment that Ven appeared at the other end of the dock and did the same. The three converged at once, and Vita and Ven nearly crashed into each other as they each seized a handle of the bag.

Zia laughed, then so did Vita and finally so did Ven. Glancing back at Lepidus, Vita released the handle she held, but not before the flash of Ven's smiling eyes sent a lightning bolt of longing into her stomach.

She nearly fell backwards into the water and, as she turned to join Lepidus, she had to feign frustration as an excuse for her rising blush.

'You are quite a helpful woman, Vita,' observed Lepidus.

'Gratitude, Lepidus. I try to be.'

'It was not meant as a compliment.'

Already accustomed to Lepidus's criticisms, Vita bowed her head in contrition. 'Please tell me how I did wrong.'

'You act as if you are a slave yourself. You are not a slave, however. Your function here is to serve as my companion and feminine representative. You are the Gaia to my Gaius, dear, not a penniless pleb.'

'Yes, of course, Lepidus. My apologies.'

'I know that you count yourself fortunate to be with

me—any woman would—but you must not let that transform you into an obsequious little hen. Remember your dignity.'

Vita nodded. She did count herself fortunate, though not for the reasons Lepidus believed. She felt fortunate for Zia and her wordless companionship, and for the food and transport Lepidus provided them. She felt fortunate for Ven who kept his distance, yet seemed to be looking out for her at every second. She also felt fortunate that she had not yet been obliged to share Lepidus's bed.

Still, she marvelled at how quickly she had grown accustomed to her life with Lepidus, which was essentially no different from her life with Magnus. She wondered if it was human nature to see the good in things. It seemed to be an important skill—a means of survival— yet it was that same stubborn good cheer that could trap a person in the wrong kind of life.

'I look forward to guiding you in the fine art of pleasing me tonight,' Lepidus remarked as they approached Zia at the end of the dock. 'The Roman *mansion* here in Narbo is said to be rather luxurious.'

'I look forward to fulfilling the terms of our contract,' said Vita, 'but I must remind you that it is not yet signed.'

Lepidus's eyes flared, but he quickly veiled his anger. 'In that case, I will use the Dacian to fulfil my needs tonight. I will have the matter of the contract seen to tomorrow.'

Vita saw Zia's lips purse with alarm. The woman had understood everything. She lifted her hand to adjust her grip on Lepidus's bag and Vita saw that it was trembling. It was then that Vita truly understood the weight of the woman's load.

'It is not necessary to call upon Zia tonight, Lepidus,' Vita blurted. 'I am certain we can find some compromise to meet your needs. It is my duty, after all, and I would hate to neglect it.'

Vita swallowed back the bile in her throat. The thought of giving herself to Lepidus was appalling, but she knew she did not have a choice. It was the price of her passage—of any woman's passage—in this man's world in which they lived.

Chapter Nine

That evening Vita sat on the edge of the bed in her freshly cleaned tunic and listened patiently as Lepidus laid out his expectations.

'I should tell you that I do not kiss,' he said, removing his own tunic. He glanced at her lap. 'And I shall require you to keep yourself shaved in the manner of the Egyptians.'

'The Egyptians?' she answered. 'Have you been to Egypt?'

'I have, in my younger days.'

'The land of Egypt fascinates me. Is it true that there are pyramids so high that they scrape the sky?'

'Three very large ones and hundreds of a smaller variety, yes. I studied them for a time.'

'You studied the pyramids?' Vita gasped. She clapped her hands together. 'Lepidus, you never cease to surprise me! Tell me, what are they like?'

Vita listened in rapt attention as Lepidus dived into a detailed description of the pyramids, which had never seemed so truly wondrous to Vita as they did just then, as the moments swept past. His description lasted for the better part of an hour.

'Pardon me if I am prying, but how is it that you were able to travel to Egypt at all?' Vita asked, summoning all her energy.

'Well, that is a story,' said Lepidus, diving headlong into another long explanation of his illustrious education and the apprenticeship that landed him in Alexandria and later Thebes.

Vita congratulated herself as she feigned her fascination. It seemed that she had discovered Lepidus's Achilles heel: talking about his own illustrious past. 'You must have been quite talented to have been selected for such a journey.'

'Very talented indeed,' he waxed. 'Have I told you that Mother once said that I was sired by a god…?'

On and on he continued until after many hours he became exhausted, and the two lay down together on the thin mattress and swiftly went to sleep.

The next day, Lepidus had Vita's contract drawn up as promised—two copies, following her request—and they signed the documents in the presence of a local magistrate.

Soon they were journeying overland in a small carriage along the Via Aquitania, an old provincial road that lead to Burdigala on the northern coast of Gaul. The long idle hours gave Vita time to contrive an array of excuses and by that evening she had settled on her best hope.

'I am afraid that my courses have arrived,' she informed him.

'There are other ways I may take my pleasure,' he replied.

'To take pleasure with a woman during the time of her courses invites the wrath of Juno, did you not know?'

Lepidus shook his head in frustration. 'In that case send the Dacian in.'

'I am afraid Zia is experiencing her courses as well,' explained Vita. 'It is something that happens frequently when women travel together.'

Lepidus narrowed his eyes. 'This is growing rather tedious, Vita.'

'My deepest apologies, Lepidus,' she said. 'I must say that I feel selfish and not just for this small inconvenience. In many ways I am a greedy, insatiable woman.'

'Why do you say that?'

'Because I am burning to know about your time in Greece. Did you not say you learned a new technique for raising columns?'

Thus during the second leg of their journey northwards through Gaul, Vita managed to avoid misery of a certain kind and for that she was eternally grateful.

What she could not seem to avoid was another kind of misery. It came in the form of Ven, who sat exactly across from her in the carriage throughout the journey. For hours each day, he and Lepidus studied drawings and discussed architecture together, during which time Vita had to keep her eyes averted, lest she accidentally catch Ven's eye.

The problem was not just Ven's proximity, which functioned as a kind of magnet for her attention. It was also that the men's discussions were interesting and she yearned to take part in them. They spoke of a wall that would stretch over seventy miles from coast to coast. In the east it would be constructed of stone and in the west of turf and timber, to be replaced with stone over time.

Why? she wondered. Perhaps it had something to do

with the availability of materials, or some urgent need for a barrier.

It would be a formidable barrier indeed. Lepidus had designed the eastern wall to be fifteen feet tall and ten feet wide with a deep earthen ditch dug along its northern side: a sizeable obstacle for any foe. Vita wondered who the foe was exactly. Did the Brigantes not hold territory on both sides of the wall?

The men spent much time speaking of the design of the wall's towers, which would be constructed at every third of a mile. At every mile there would be a small castle and gateway that would allow for the passage of travellers.

Why build a wall at all if you were going to place so many passageways through it? Vita wondered. *And what is the purpose of so many towers so close?*

She wondered fervently as the men spoke, sometimes biting her own tongue.

She gazed out at the passing landscape until her neck became tired, then stared down at her hands as if they could give her the answers she craved.

Sometimes she would indulge in wishful fantasies. She imagined the cabin of the carriage lurching suddenly, causing her to lunge forward and fall into Ven's lap. It was not so very unlikely a scenario, especially given the deteriorating quality of the Via Aquitania.

All it would take was a small bump to result in an accidental touch and she found herself imagining such a happy accident in a thousand different ways, knowing all the while that she was flirting with danger.

The more she thought of Ven, the more she could not stop thinking about him. She had observed him now for many days—his quiet competence and strong, serious manner. He seemed to be always a step ahead of everyone else: anticipating needs, solving problems, shouldering burdens. She had never met a more capable man.

He was the perfect companion for Lepidus, who unfortunately displayed none of those talents. On the other hand, Lepidus did seem to have a special gift for making complaints and his protestations over the quality of the road gradually morphed into grievances about his aching back. At the end of each day the old man was interested in little more than a solid meal and a good sleep and Vita was saved once again by circumstance.

When they finally arrived in the port of Burdigala on the estuary of the Garonne River, Lepidus announced that they would stay a few days to recover before continuing on their journey.

'I want nothing as much as a bath,' Lepidus pronounced on the afternoon of their arrival and soon they found themselves inside a bathing complex to rival any of those in Rome.

'I will meet you outside the baths at sunset,' Lepidus told Vita, making his way to the men's large entryway. 'Do not forget to shave in the manner of the Egyptians. And, by the gods, oil yourself clean. You look a mess and stink of the road.'

Vita nodded obediently, then watched in wonder as Ven, Zia and the Scythian followed dutifully behind Lepidus, leaving Vita utterly alone. She glanced around the spacious entrance hall, wondering if it was all a dream. After over a month of travel, she found herself suddenly and gloriously on her own.

She sighed, wishing that Zia could join her. It seemed that she would be performing Lepidus's massage today all on her own, for slaves were the only women allowed inside the men's baths. Vita vowed to make it up to her Dacian friend somehow, then set off across the hall.

The women's section of the bath complex was much smaller than the men's, of course, but Vita could not complain. In many Roman baths, women had full run of the facilities, but they were allowed to enjoy them only in the mornings and for a limited time.

Here in Burdigala, there was an entire area reserved just for women, including a fine *caldarium* with a hot pool and a smattering of massage benches, and a *frigidarium* with a small plunge pool and sitting area.

They were no Baths of Trajan, but they were more than Vita could have hoped for in this northern outpost.

Still, she could not completely enjoy the unexpected treat. Later that night, fresh from his bathing, Lepidus would surely call on Vita to perform her duties. It was the true reason they were here, she feared. He was expecting her to prepare for their first encounter.

Vita purchased a vial of oil and drying cloth and tried to keep her spirits up. She stepped into the dressing room and removed her tunic and sandals, but kept her loincloth tied. She knew that the Romans of Gaul had different customs than those of Rome and she did not know who she would find inside.

To her surprise, when she stepped into the steamy *caldarium*, she found not a single soul. She placed her drying cloth on a massage bench and lay down on her stomach, feeling instantly relaxed. Sunlight poured in from one of the high windows and she reassured herself that there was still much time before the unsavoury part of her day began. She closed her eyes.

She must have dozed off, because when she opened her eyes again the light was lower and she found she was no longer alone. A long shadow passed by her side. Before she could look up to see who it was, she felt two strong, familiar hands gently squeezing her shoulders.

Her heart leaped and she moved to sit up, but those hands pressed downwards, keeping her in her place.

'What are you doing here?' she managed.

'Giving you a much-deserved massage.' His deep, familiar voice echoed against the walls, though there was a different quality to it—a kind of edge. He dug his fingers beneath her shoulder blades.

'You should not be here,' she said, stifling a moan of pleasure. 'You should leave right away.'

'As a slave, I am perfectly within my rights to be inside the women's baths.'

'I mean to honour my commitment to Lepidus.'

'I would expect nothing less.'

'Then what are you doing here?' she repeated, though there was no need to keep her voice so low. The two were truly alone.

'Lepidus fell asleep halfway through his massage,' said Ven. 'I had nothing to do.'

'You should return as soon as you can. Surely he will be up soon.'

'If I know him at all, he will sleep for some time.'

'How much time?'

How much time? It did not matter. There would never be enough. They had this moment and hopefully the moment after. They had whatever memories they could produce and whatever fantasies those memories could grow. They had this thing between them—this strange, forbidden thing that seemed larger than them somehow, as if it would always exist, had always existed.

'Perhaps an hour.'

'You risk too much,' Vita said.

'If he wakes early, Zia will tell him I have gone to the latrine.' Vita laughed softly as he rubbed his thumbs over the knobs of her spine. 'I understand you have been inventing some even better excuses lately.'

'Who told you that?'

'Lepidus himself. The one about your courses was impressive.'

'I fear that the time for excuses is over. The more I delay, the angrier he will become...and possibly the rougher.'

Ven clenched his teeth together. 'Just tell me what I can do to stop him and I will do it.'

'There is nothing you can do,' she said with a sigh. 'It is inevitable.'

He moved to the other side of the bench and watched with interest as she gathered her hair together and tucked it beside her neck. He wanted to kiss that neck so badly that it pained him.

'You think I am a fool,' she said.

'I think you are the bravest woman I have ever met.'

He dribbled oil on the exposed part of her neck, then began to rub it in gently. His lust rose like a serpent.

'Not there,' she said.

'Right.'

He dribbled oil on her arm, then lifted it as if raising a sacred blade. 'You are also the loveliest woman I have ever met.' He lowered the arm and began to knead.

She laughed. 'Such rhetoric!'

'Truth!'

'Tell me, where did you study?' she asked.

He crossed to her other arm and continued his work. 'Why do you ask?'

'Because only educated men know how to flatter so well.'

She was scolding him after all, it seemed, but for the grave sin of seeing her truly. He lowered his voice. 'I will not allow you to serve the misguided tale you tell yourself by discrediting my sincerity.'

'More rhetoric!'

Ignoring the slight, he folded his arms over his chest. 'There is none of you left to rub.'

Without driving one or the other of us mad.

'Then let us simply converse.'

'If someone walks in, I should be at work.'

'Then continue to work. You forgot the backs of my knees.'

He spied a *strigil* on a nearby bench. 'I should scrape you down instead. Did Lepidus not command an oiling?'

'Very well,' Vita said, 'but you are trying to avoid my question. Speak plainly, Brigante. Where did you study?'

Ven fetched a *strigil* and a drying cloth, then placed the curved blade of the instrument against the back of her thigh. 'Study?' He smiled to himself as he moved the strigil slowly over her well-oiled skin. He switched to his native tongue. 'I will tell you sincerely that I was educated in the wilds of the north. My father was my *grammaticus*. He taught me to fish in the roiling waters of the sea, stalk deer in the silent forests and sow wheat in the fields outside our small settlement.'

He arrived at her ankle and wiped the accumulation of oil from the blade, then moved to her other thigh. 'My father's mentorship was brief, however, for in my twelfth autumn, he was killed in a battle against our Roman occupiers.'

'I am sorry,' Vita whispered. 'May he rest for ever in the fields of paradise.'

Ven completed her other leg, cleaned his blade, then started on her back. 'After the battle, few men were left to defend our settlement. A rival tribe raided.' He paused, swallowing his grief. 'I was hunting in the forest during the raid. When I returned, there was nothing, and no one, left. They had enslaved everyone, including my mother. It was a difficult winter.'

'Did you not have anyone to look after you?'

'None. I was alone.'

She lay quiet as he moved the *strigil* down her back. 'Though in difficult times one often discovers the best of oneself, yes?'

'You were only twelve,' she whispered.

'Yes, and that is when I acquired new tutors: the hunger and the cold. They taught me how to coax a fire from wet branches and dig for roots deep beneath the snow. They taught me how to run, really run—in the simple effort to warm my bones. Hunger and cold were terrible task masters, but they taught me much. And yet...'

'And yet?'

'They taught me nothing of courage.'

'It sounds as if you displayed a good deal of courage,' Vita insisted. 'What more did you have to learn?'

'I am afraid we have run out of places to scrape clean,' Ven said in Latin.

'Will you not answer my question?' she returned in Celtic.

He drew a breath. What would she think of him if he told her the truth? What would she say when she realised that the man who stood before her was not a man, but a coward?

'Please, Ven, tell me what happened next.'

He would be a fool to go on, yet he yearned to. It was as if his sad story were made of clothing—layers of heavy furs that had burdened him for years. Telling it aloud made him feel as if he were finally shedding their weight.

'We must find me a new task,' he whispered in Celtic, 'lest someone enter and see us conversing like old friends.'

She leaned up on to her arms suddenly and twisted to the side, as if to address him. She did not stop there. In a blur of movement, she rolled on to her back.

He blinked, hardly believing what he was seeing. Now she lay before him facing up, bare-breasted and lovelier than any fantasy he could have ever conjured. Her generous breasts sprawled to the sides, just begging to be touched. Below them her shapely stomach moved with her breaths, tapering to gloriously curving hips swaddled in cloth. It was as if she were inviting him to consider that there were things in life beyond pain and survival.

'What did you learn next in your education?' she asked in Celtic. There was a waver in her voice and he could discern the pounding of her heart at the base of her throat. It occurred to him that she had just been quite brave and she had done it for him.

Humbled, he willed himself to continue.

'I learned how fear can twist the mind.'

He dribbled oil on to her leg, then poised the *strigil* at the top of her thigh and stared down at her flesh. He could not seem to decide what to do next. He felt the softness of her hand atop his own.

'You once told me not to despair,' she whispered, her fingers weaving with his. 'That all would be well. It has helped me more than you know.'

'I am glad of it.'

'But sometimes it is necessary to despair,' she said.

'Sometimes one must raise one's muzzle to the moon. Do you understand?'

Ven felt himself smile. 'You are an unusual woman.'

She frowned. 'If fear can twist the mind, then silence can twist the heart.' She squeezed his hand. 'Tell me, Ven. Tell me so that you can let it go.'

She was right. He needed to say it aloud, to confess to what he did. He needed her to see what lay within his wretched heart.

Ven took a breath. 'Before my father died, he made me promise him that I would keep my mother safe. But after she was taken, I did not keep her safe. I did not fulfil my promise. I could have rescued her, but I did not.'

'Why not?'

He scraped the *strigil* down her thigh and paused. 'I do not know. Ignorance. Fear. What would compel a young man to remain in his home when everything that made it a home was gone?'

'It was all that was known to you.'

'That is true.'

'Surely you feared to leave.'

'I did, for it was unusually cold that winter and there was nothing to eat. I was afraid that if I went looking for my mother, I would die myself.'

'That is not cowardly, Ven. That is human.'

'But I could have saved her. The Parisi hill fort where she was taken was not far from our settlement. In the spring when I finally set out, it took me only a handful of days to reach her, but by then she was already gone. I failed her.'

'Did you know the Parisi hill fort was near?'

'Of course not.'

'Then how can you blame yourself? As you said, you feared death.'

'I made a promise to my own father. I told him I would put my mother's safety first. I failed them both. I failed myself.'

She said nothing more and he was grateful. It was enough to say the words and know she heard them, to release them into the hot, steamy air. Surely she was judging him now, condemning him, as he deserved. He pulled his hand away from hers and dribbled oil down her other thigh.

'Please, continue your story,' she said at last. 'How did you arrive in Rome?'

'I was enslaved by the Parisi. I took up the very position that had been occupied by my late mother. The Parisi were enemies of the Romans and it was not long before the Romans invaded their hill fort.' Ven laughed bitterly. 'Then we were all enslaved together—Parisi and Brigante alike. Our tribal divisions meant nothing to the Romans. We were all just barbarians to them.'

'You were brought to Rome on a ship then?'

'Thankfully, yes. There were others who were forced to walk across Gaul, but because of my age I was placed on a vessel and in less than a month I was standing on the auction block at the Roman Emporium being sold alongside several tons of grain. I was barely thirteen.'

There was a long silence and he could sense her emotion. 'My own mother once shared a similar fate,' she whispered. 'But you already know of that.'

'I can only imagine her suffering,' said Ven. 'What the Romans have done here, to our beautiful Albion, to us...' He stopped himself, surprised. He did not usually indulge in such piteous talk.

'Your education did not end on the auction block, however,' she said. 'I know that for certain.'

'In Rome I began a new stage of my education,' continued Ven. 'It happened the day my master tossed me on to the floor of his *tablinium* and gave me my first beating. After that, pain and humiliation became my mentors. They taught me how to survive in the wilderness of Rome.'

'How did you learn to read and write?'

'Mostly in secret. I was tall even as a young man and my masters made a sport of beating me. I noticed that the educated slaves were treated better, so I educated myself. By day I carried my masters' litters and cleaned their chamber pots; by night I read Plato.'

'A resourceful young man.'

'I did what I had to do to survive.'

Vita sat up suddenly and braced herself on her arms. 'What did you just say?'

Ven paused, confused. 'That I did what I had to do to survive.'

'And the winter before? When your father died and your mother was taken—what did you do then?'

'What do you mean?'

'When you remained at your settlement alone, did you not believe that you were doing what you had to do to survive?'

Her eyes searched his, but he could not determine what they sought. 'I could have survived and still saved my mother,' he said.

'That is not what I asked. I asked you what you believed. Did you believe that if you tried to find your mother, you would die?'

'Yes, I suppose I did believe that,' Ven said.

'Then why do you blame yourself for your mother's death?'

Ven blinked. 'Because...it was my fault.'

Vita shook her head. 'I stayed with Magnus for ten

years because I did not believe that I deserved better. I think that you have spent many years doing the same.'

Ven shook his head. 'That is not true. Twice I have tried to escape Rome.'

'But were you really trying to escape?'

Ven gasped at the suggestion. 'Of course I was.'

Memories flashed before his eyes, visions of himself running half-heartedly through the streets of Rome, stopping to ask which way was north. Really he had never expected to return to his home, for it did not exist any more. He had destroyed it.

She was watching him so steadily now; he feared to look away. 'When Lepidus gave you the scars on your back, did you weep?' she asked.

'What? No. Of course I did not weep. A real man does not weep beneath his punishment.'

'And when you received the tattoo across your forehead, how did you feel?'

'I felt nothing. Nothing at all.'

'Not even the terrible tapping of the needle against your skin?'

Of course, he remembered that. How could he ever forget? 'I did not care.'

'Why did you not care?'

'Because... I deserved it.'

Vita expelled a breath. There were tears in her eyes; they were making his own heart feel weak.

'Do you forgive me for contracting myself to Lepidus?' she asked suddenly. 'For binding myself to a man I abhor? For acting against all honour and the truth inside my own heart?'

'Of course I forgive you.'

'Why?'

'Because you did it to survive.'

'Then why can you not forgive yourself?'

'Apologies, I do not—'

'You have been punishing yourself for years for a crime you did not commit,' said Vita. 'You did not have a choice any more than I did. You believed that you would die trying to save your mother, just as I believed I would die if I did not escape Magnus's wrath. You were just trying to survive. Your mother's death—it was not your fault.'

She gave him one last, long look, then shook her head and lay back on the bench. He found himself gazing at nothing at all, for everything was blurry. *It was not your fault,* she had said. The words floated in the air all around him, insisting on his consideration. After everything he had told her, that was her conclusion? That it was not his fault?

He went over her argument in his mind, trying to find the holes in it. She had compared his decision to hers: as something inevitable. *'You were just trying to survive,'* she had said. He had never thought of it that way. Mostly, though, he had never even considered that his own fear might have been forgivable.

It was not your fault. The words were warm, like steam. For the first time since he could remember, he felt his heart rest.

She reached out her hand and he took it. Now the warmth that surrounded him seemed to pour into him through the vessels of her delicate fingers. This woman. This thoughtful, honourable, wondrous woman. What had he done to deserve her in his life?

'You are beautiful, do you know?' he said. 'In every possible way.'

And I love you, by the gods.

She smiled and shook her head dismissively. 'Rhetoric,' she whispered.

'Truth.'

Why would she never let him praise her? He gazed at her figure: her womanly breasts and her soft, forgiving flesh. The clean white loincloth wrapped about her gorgeous curves seemed to highlight their sensuous beauty. She was a goddess in every way. Divine.

'Why do you stare?' she asked. She pulled her hand away and squeezed her arms around her chest.

'Forgive me, but I love your body. Looking upon it is like looking upon a garden.'

She laughed. 'In that case, you are either desperate or mad,' she said. 'Or lying.'

Her smile was a mix of gratitude and regret, as if she were at once thanking him for his compliment and offering a silent apology.

It was altogether wrong. How could a woman as lovely as she feel it necessary to apologise for herself? 'I wish I could make you see yourself from where I am standing,' he said.

Now her uncertain smile became a true frown. 'I fear the sight.'

'Your body is everything my own body is not. You are round where I am straight, short where I am tall—'

'Fat where you are thin?' she interrupted. She laughed bitterly.

'Not fat,' he said. 'Lush.'

She turned her face to the side, her expression pained. 'You do not have to mollify me. I know that I am no Venus.'

Ten years with that beast of a man, thought Ven. How could he convince her of her own beauty?

An idea struck and he switched to Latin. 'I fear we

have not completed the discussion of my education.' He dribbled oil on to her stomach and gently ran the *strigil* down the length of it.

'Is that so?' She smiled. 'Well, in that case please go on.'

'My education did not end with reading and writing. After that, I went on to rhetoric.'

'Ah, so you did study rhetoric!'

'I did and confess that in the arts of rhetoric I had many teachers.'

There was only one part of her that had not yet been scraped clean. He dribbled several drops of oil on to her breasts and paused.

'From my Roman masters I learned how to speak in circles, to placate when appropriate, to confuse when necessary and, most especially, to lie. Lies are easy for me now: I have discovered that they are the true language of Rome.'

'I do not disagree,' she said.

He switched back to his native tongue. 'You accused me of flattery and suggested that I am a liar. I do not deny that I speak untruths, but I only do so in Latin. I could never speak a lie in my mother tongue. Little of me remains from my youth, but I will not soil one of the only things I have left of it—the language of my tribe.'

'The language of your innocence,' she muttered.

'If I speak to you in the language of the north, you can be certain that I speak only what is in my heart.'

He stood above her and looked deeply into her eyes. 'When I say you are a beautiful woman, it is not because I am trying to flatter you. You dishonour me by suggesting otherwise. Though you may not see that part of yourself, you must accept that I believe my own words.'

He was fully clothed, yet had somehow taken off all

of his furs. Though he wore a slave's short tunic and loincloth, he was in another sense utterly naked, just as she was. Each had been stripped bare by the other. Disrobed and scraped clean. Exposed.

She blinked, and he saw a tear roll down her cheek. 'What do you want from me?' she asked.

Chapter Ten

'I want nothing at all,' he whispered back. He glanced at her oiled breasts and handed her the *strigil*.

Vita felt shaken to her bones. She had never felt closer to a man in all her life. It terrified her. 'Nobody says such kind things without wanting something in return,' she said.

'I want nothing.'

Then why do you make me care for you? That was what she wished to ask.

'It is possible to serve someone without expecting anything in return,' he said. 'Did you want something in return from Lollia Flamma for choosing not to expose her adultery?'

'No, I suppose not.'

'It is enough to know that she will not suffer, yes? That she has avoided a terrible fate?'

She blinked up at him. She could see his spirit so clearly now. It was as strong and beautiful as the northern sea.

'I am grateful to you…beyond words,' she said.

For wanting me. For protecting me. For bringing me back to life.

'It is I who am grateful,' he said.

She laughed. 'For sparing your decadent *domina*?'

'For these moments we have together.'

She studied the *strigil* in her hands, then gave it back to him. 'I would not want you to leave the job unfinished.'

She lay back and told herself not to fear. It was just a *strigil* and there was nothing unusual about a servant cleaning a woman's breasts.

But he was not a servant and, as he gently placed the curved blade at the edge of her flesh and began to move it across her skin, her heart beat harder. He was touching one of the tenderest parts of her and he was doing so with more care and attention than she would have ever done for herself. It was as if she were not being cleaned, but worshipped.

'Lepidus does not deserve you,' he whispered.

'Rome does not deserve you,' she said.

'Such hyperbole.' He edged down the slope of her breast. At the boundary of her nipple, he wiped off the excess oil with the cloth. 'You speak like a true Roman.'

'I am a true Roman. At least—part of me is.'

He moved the *strigil* to the side and lifted the edge of her breast with reverent care, then moved the *strigil* along the tender flesh. Releasing her breast, he looked up at her. 'I am thinking of a kind of metal,' he began, 'a precious mix of silver and gold. They mine it in the province of Egypt. Do you know it?'

'Electrum?'

'You are as that strange metal. Roman and barbarian in equal parts. Rare and beautiful.'

'You accuse me of hyperbole, yet you speak like an enraptured poet! Surely you want something from me. Tell me, what is it?'

'I do not want anything from you, but I do want something *for* you.'

Vita smiled gamely. 'Please tell me what it is so that I may fulfil your wish.'

'I want you to find your freedom.'

In that moment, the sun ceased to stream in from the high windows and the *caldarium* grew ominously dark. It was as if time had suddenly resumed its passage. 'Go now,' she whispered. 'Return to Lepidus.'

Ven's voice was less than a whisper. 'You must escape him soon, before you share his bed. Before you have paid the cost.'

Vita closed her eyes. How was it possible for a man to know a woman so well? Though perhaps it was not a man knowing a woman, but one injured soul knowing another.

'I do not wish to speak of it further,' Vita said. 'My freedom will come five years from now. It is the only choice.'

'It is not the only choice. *"You must escape Lepidus."* You said that to me once, do you remember? Let us escape together, Vita. Let us find our freedom together.'

Her heart was pounding now. This was madness. 'But your scar. Did you not say it was an unacceptable risk?'

'No risk is too great—not any more.'

'I do not understand. What has changed?'

'Before I met you, Vita, I was…different. Each year, the seasons changed, but in my heart it was always winter.' He stared up at the painted ceiling, as if searching for the right words. 'That is how a slave survives, do you understand?'

'I understand,' she said. She thought of her mother. She could count on one hand the number of times Vita had seen her smile.

'Since I met you, there has been a change of season inside me,' Ven continued. 'I laugh with acquaintances and smile at strangers. I pity the helpless and grow angry at small injustices. I bite my own tongue and pace across floors. I see colours everywhere—the crimson of the sunset, the azure blue of the sky.' He gazed into her eyes. 'The colours of a woman's eyes.'

'I see them, too,' Vita whispered. 'The colours.'

'I do not know myself any more. Every time I imagine Lepidus touching you, I think of how I might kill the man. I see it so clearly in my mind—how easily I might wrap my hands around his fleshy throat. It is dangerous, this new season inside me. It is as if I grow weaker.'

'Not weaker,' she whispered. 'More alive.'

'Escape is the only way. Life is short and happiness shorter. We must seize it now, while it is in our hands. Together.'

He lifted her hand to his lips and kissed it, then placed it upon the bench.

'Tomorrow you must tell me your answer,' he said. 'We have nearly run out of time.'

And then he was gone.

That night, Lepidus's back was still too sore to ask anything of Vita and for that she thanked the gods. They returned to their room inside the large *mansion* and he instantly fell asleep on the wool-stuffed mattress. As soon as she heard his snores, Vita stretched out on the floor beside him and tried to arrange her thoughts.

Escape Lepidus? She had never even dreamed of it— perhaps because she knew she could never do it on her own. But the instant Ven had made the suggestion it had seemed inevitable, like the cry of a newborn babe.

Freedom. Suddenly it was within reach, and she

would not be alone in her effort to grasp it. She would have help; she would have Ven. He would be by her side—the strongest, ablest man she knew—and it seemed that he would not escape without her.

She opened her eyes and gazed up at the timbers. Despite her efforts to distance herself from Ven, she felt closer to him every day.

Still, she could not help but wonder if this was some new kind of test. She had bound herself to Lepidus because she had no choice, but if she escaped with Ven, she would be bound to him as well. It would be a welcome bond, of course, but a bond none the less, for she would owe him her very life. They would be making a contract between their hearts.

What would happen then? She wished the old sibyl were there to advise her. She cared for Ven—she feared that she loved him—but she did not trust her own emotions. She had loved Magnus long ago, had she not? How could she be sure that Ven would not come to loathe her just as Magnus had done?

'Seek your freedom first,' the wise old sibyl had said. *'Everything else will come.'*

If freedom was the prize, then would escaping with Ven be another grave error?

She had been up most of the night thinking of such things and slept in until well past the third hour. Thankfully, Lepidus slept in as well. When he finally awoke he was not eager to get out of bed.

'That wicked woman made my back feel worse!' he howled. 'Tell her to bring me some tea. And get me a hot towel and some willow-bark oil. From now on, there will be no other hands upon my flesh any more but yours, Vita. Where are my clean loincloths?'

Vita fetched Lepidus a clean loincloth, then opened the door to their chamber and gently coaxed Zia awake. It was customary for slaves to sleep outside their masters' chambers, but Vita still hated seeing Zia there—especially when Ven and the Scythian were always granted a servant's room.

'I will purchase the supplies if you can get the tea,' she whispered to Zia, making the motion for tea. 'Drink one yourself before you return.' Zia shot her a grin, then hurried off to the *mansio* kitchen while Vita set about her errands.

By the time Lepidus was dressed and ready for his day, it was already time for the midday meal. They strolled about the town for a while enjoying the breeze, then took a late lunch inside a large, well-provisioned tavern.

Day became night and they began drinking wine. 'This Gallic vintage is quite good,' Lepidus commented, adding that it seemed to help the aching in his back. Vita made sure to keep his cup full and, by the time they arrived back in their room, the old man was happily drunk. He collapsed upon the mattress just as he had done the night before and Vita took her place on the floor beside him. She fell into a deep sleep.

When she awoke the next morning, she opened the door to wake Zia, but the Dacian woman was not there. Believing her to be on some private errand, Vita returned to the bedchamber and waited another hour. When she opened the door again and still did not see her, Vita became worried. She searched the *mansio* and its surroundings; Zia was nowhere to be found.

When she finally returned to their bedchamber, Lepidus was sitting up in bed. He yawned absently. 'Where have you been, Vita?' he asked.

'Searching for Zia. She has disappeared.'

He did not seem worried by the news.

'Did you notice anything unusual last night?' Vita asked.

'Not really, though she may have been unhappy when I commanded her to pleasure me.'

Vita stared at Lepidus, who only shrugged. 'I took her in the hall so as not to disturb you. She was rather reluctant, I must say. I am afraid I had to be rough with her.'

Vita pressed her back against the wall, trying to keep her knees from buckling.

Lepidus swung his legs from the bed and motioned for his sandals. 'It is your own fault, Vita. If you had done your duty as a concubine, I would not have had to bother her. Now pack up my things and let us go find a ship. It seems my back has healed.'

Vita tried to make her heart into ice, but as she readied Lepidus for departure, her despair seemed to cook inside her, transforming into a barely controllable rage. 'I will not leave until we can find Zia,' she stated. 'We must ensure that she is well.'

'I would love to find that little whore myself,' replied Lepidus, 'but not to ensure she is well. The deserter deserves a good lashing and a nice big tattoo on her face.'

'How can you say such things?' cried Vita.

'Shut up,' Lepidus replied, then slapped her on the face.

Vita gathered up Lepidus's things without seeing them.

When they finally reached the docks, she was not sure if there were black clouds on the horizon or if she was merely witnessing the state of her own soul. 'Find out which ships are leaving for Britannia and when they plan to depart,' Lepidus commanded. 'And get a weather forecast—a good one.'

The old man must have seen the rebellion stirring in Vita's eyes, for he motioned to Ven to accompany her.

'Where is Zia?' Ven asked as they approached the nearest ship.

'Lepidus forced her to pleasure him late last night. This morning I could not find her anywhere. She is gone.'

'Gods, no.'

'It is my fault,' Vita said. 'If only I had awoken...'

'It is Lepidus's fault and no one else's,' Ven corrected. 'We must get you away from him as soon as we can.'

Vita gazed up at the large cargo ship tied before them. Its name was surrounded with decoration—a tangle of leaves and branches in garish yellow and green. *Pax*, it was called.

'It feels as if this journey will never end,' Vita said, aware of Lepidus's eyes upon them.

'It will not—unless we devise our own ending,' said Ven. He gazed at the horizon. 'Those clouds portend stormy seas. This will be the most difficult part of the journey so far—especially for Lepidus.'

'Good, I confess that I wish for him to suffer,' said Vita.

'Find me on our last night at sea,' said Ven, then he turned to herald one of the sailors. 'Tell me, sir, will this vessel be departing soon?'

They returned to Lepidus with good news: The cargo ship was leaving that morning, bound for the town of Gesoriacum in Belgic Gaul. There, it would take on more passengers and cross the channel overnight. In only ten days, if the gods and winds were favourable, they would be Britannia.

'What about the weather?' Lepidus asked.

'Smooth sailing,' Vita said.

The trip up the coast was wondrously tumultuous. The unsettled seas tossed the floating 'basket' as if it were a toy. It seemed that every time Vita went below deck, Lepidus had turned a new shade of green. She wondered if divine justice was at work.

On the ninth night of the journey, Vita waited until long after midnight to meet with Ven. After assuring herself that both Lepidus and the Scythian were well asleep, she stole over to the slave area and found Ven lying on the floor, wide awake. Saying nothing, she climbed the stairs to the deck and made her way towards the bow beneath the moonlight.

In minutes he was standing behind her, quiet as the breeze.

'You are still thinking about Zia,' he stated, reading Vita's mind. 'You fear the same fate.'

'I cannot imagine what he must have done to her.'

'She was fortunate. If she had been caught escaping, he would have whipped her to the edge of death.'

'Do you really believe that?'

'Believe it? I have lived it.'

Vita fell silent, remembering the web of scars across Ven's back. 'It seems I have bound myself to a madman.'

'So you have considered my proposal?'

Vita gripped the rails. She had done more than just consider it. 'If he catches us, it will be the same fate for us, will it not? We will be lucky to survive his wrath.'

'That is so.'

Vita took a breath. 'How will we do it? And when?'

He reached his hand and covered hers. 'You have just made me the happiest man in the world.'

'And you have just made me the most terrified woman in Gaul.'

'Not Gaul, Vita, Not any more.' He gazed out at the distant horizon. 'Britannia.'

Vita followed the moon path across the sea. Just beyond it she could discern the jagged profile of land: the land she had longed to see all her life. 'My mother's homeland,' she whispered. 'And yours.'

'And also yours,' said Ven. 'Tell me, how well can you swim?'

Early the next morning, Vita tipped the chamber pot over the deck and eyed the land of Britannia: a rocky coastline followed by endless grassy hills. It was as her mind had always pictured it. Her heart nearly burst.

She returned below deck and fetched Lepidus a glass of water, which he promptly vomited back into the chamber pot. 'We are nearing the coast now,' Vita reassured him. 'It will be over soon.'

In truth, she was reassuring herself. She fetched a wet rag for Lepidus, but instinctively dabbed it on her own brow. The wind remained diminished, but the seas still roiled beneath the ship. Soon she would be struggling beneath those riotous waves. She wondered how different they would be from the lazy currents of the Tiber.

'Oars!' shouted the captain and she could hear the whipping sound of the slackening sails. That was her cue.

She placed her hand over her mouth and feigned the heaves of sickness. 'Excuse me, Lepidus, I believe I will be ill.'

She rushed up the ladder as planned, taking one last

glance at Lepidus through the rails. He was lying on his mat as usual, heedless of her movements, but just beyond him the Scythian was wide awake. He caught her eye.

Curses, she thought, but there was no changing her course now. She quickly climbed the ladder and caught sight of Ven. There he was, just as they had planned— her tall, noble sentinel, ready to take her hand.

They barely acknowledged each other as they walked together slowly towards the bow of the ship. 'The Scythian saw me,' she muttered without turning her head.

'Follow the plan,' said Ven through his teeth. 'No matter what you do.'

She did not look up. She did not wish to. She knew the shore was near and the sea nearer, and that soon she would be contending with both.

Just as they were arriving at the bow, she caught movement out of the corner of her eye. A figure was running towards them from behind. The Scythian. She lifted her leg over the bow just as Ven did, then felt a hand gripping her ankle. She heard a loud splash.

She was pulled back on to the deck, deafened by the thud of her own head against the wooden planks. She struggled to keep her wits. 'Ven!' she shouted, but he had disappeared.

A fist plunged heavily into her gut. Pain shot through her. She curled into a ball, trying to catch her breath, and once again caught sight of the Scythian. He was climbing over the rail, preparing to jump. Then he was gone.

Her head throbbed and her stomach burned with pain. She could see someone approaching her from several paces away. It was one of the sailors attempting to come to her aid.

He would quickly identify her and Lepidus would be

alerted. *'Follow the plan,'* Ven had urged her, *'no matter what you do.'*

She forced herself to her feet. Coughing for breath, she lifted one foot over the rail.

'Stop that woman!' cried the sailor. He was running towards her now, reaching out his hands. She lifted her other foot.

She plunged beneath the waves, nearly paralysed by the cold. *Move!* she told herself. She fought for the surface, vaguely aware of a shadow moving above her, a great wooden sea monster, its belly full of grain.

It was the boat itself. It was moving directly over her head. She kicked downwards, somehow managing to stay submerged as the great ship passed above her.

She came to the surface in a riot of coughs. When she had finally cleared her lungs, the ship was already nearly half a mile away.

She searched the horizon for signs of Ven, catching sight of two splashing figures nearly as far away as the ship. The two men appeared to be swimming directly for the shore. Ven was ahead: Vita could see his long arms tearing through the water, but the Scythian's shorter, thicker arms were not far behind.

Vita tried to shout, but she had no strength in her belly to do it. Every breath she took was a labour and even kicking her legs seemed to pain her.

Still, she started towards the men, forcing herself to move her aching limbs. The more she swam, the further away the men seemed.

She tried to increase her pace, but her head throbbed and the blow to her stomach seemed to have sapped all her power. She was not really swimming, but treading through the undulating waves.

The ship was nearly out of view now and so were the

men. Her strokes grew weaker and the shore seemed even further away.

She fixed her gaze on the nearest rock outcropping she could find onshore. It was moving rapidly to the right of her vision. Soon she had to turn her head in order to see the object at all. She was caught in a current for certain. She was being swept out to sea.

Chapter Eleven

When Vita opened her eyes, she did not at first know where she was. She blinked up at the sky, its crimson hue suggesting sunrise, and heard the crashing of waves. Was this the country of death? A crimson sky and a windswept beach?

She tried to lift her head, but it throbbed painfully—a very reassuring sign—and when she laboured to lift her neck a stab of heat shot down her spine. Blessed Neptune, she had not been swallowed by the sea. She was miraculously, painfully alive!

Ven. Where was he? What had happened? She struggled to recall. She rolled to the side and felt an ache in her stomach. Her limbs were so numb with cold that she did at first sense that she was lying on a bed of hard stones. Looking up, she realised that she had landed on a beachful of them. They answered each heave of surf with their cackling applause.

It came back to her all at once. The ship. Ven. The Scythian. She had hit her head and then sustained the Scythian's fist deep in her gut. She had managed to throw herself overboard, but by then Ven and his pursuer were already halfway to the shore and Vita had been caught in a mighty current.

She remembered very little after that but fear. Then cold. Then, nothing.

She blinked up at the sky once again. Pushing hard against the pebbly ground, she managed to sit up. She touched her head. A bump the size of a plum had formed on top of it. She wrapped her arms around her stomach, which felt more tender still. Her whole body was shivering.

She willed herself to her feet. A road could not be far away. On the continent, all roads led to Rome, but here in the Empire's most distant province, all roads led to Londinium, or so her mother had told her once.

It was the reason she and Ven had decided on Londinium's main bathhouse for their meeting place. In case they got separated, they would seek one another at the baths. Whoever arrived first would wait for the other each day until seven days had passed.

After that time, if they still had not converged, they would assume the worst and they would never look back.

But surely they would find each other. Vita had no doubt that Ven had outswum the Scythian. And even if he had not, Ven could easily outrun the man on land, for his legs were nearly twice as long. It would be no contest at all.

Surely Ven was standing near Londinium's bathhouse right now, watching from some shadowy alley. If she could just walk inland for a distance, surely she would find a road to take her to the city. How far could it be?

She pulled herself to her feet, noticing that her whole body was shivering. She glanced at the sky. Was it possible that the sunrise was getting darker somehow— perhaps obscured by a cloud?

She looked east and saw no sign of the sun. Looking west, she spotted a few last rays shooting upward. Sweet Diana, it was not sunrise, but sunset! She was going to have to pass a night in this place. She looked around her, wondering what tribe's territory she had involuntarily invaded. Then again, she didn't know how far she was from Londinium, a thoroughly Roman city. Surely there was little danger.

She wondered where she might take shelter for the evening and how she might get herself warm. She spied a large stand of bushes growing at the base of a low cliff not a dozen paces up the beach. Perhaps she could gather some kindling from them and try to start a fire.

Starting towards the bushes, she was reminded once again of her injured stomach. She bent like an old woman as she walked, and when she reached the bushes she collapsed beneath them to rest. The sun dipped lower. She gathered together as many dead branches as she could and was searching for a good fire board when she heard voices above her.

Men's voices.

She dived beneath the bushes and attempted to cover herself with the branches.

She lay there for a long while, hearing her heart pound in her ears. Her stomach rumbled with hunger. Surely that was what had attracted the squirrel. It sneaked up beside her and began to chirp uncontrollably. 'Get out of my territory!' it seemed to say. 'Wicked Roman!'

'Shoo!' Vita said. 'Get out of here!' But the squirrel only chirped louder. The men were very close.

'Did you hear that?' a man said in Celtic.

'A woman's voice, no?' said another man. 'From beneath those bushes, I think.'

Vita buried her head beneath the leaves, but it was no use.

'Is that what I think it is?' asked the first man.

'It is…and she is ours.'

Was it Vita? He could not be sure. The woman was still too far away to see clearly and was further obscured by the pouring rain. He pulled the grain sack over his head and stole closer.

He had been waiting for Vita outside the busy bath complex for seven days now without a sign. He had slept very little and eaten not at all. He had hardly even moved. A shadowy alley with a view of the baths was where he lived and he had hardly moved from it.

Over the course of his vigil, his spirit had grown dimmer. Anger, impatience and doubt took turns commandeering his thoughts and, every day that passed, it grew harder to vanquish them. When he had awoken that final morning, he had nearly lost his hope. Now it was sunset.

But perhaps all was not lost. Ven watched as the woman stepped into the wide portico of the entrance. There was something so familiar about her. 'Vita?' he called to her, but she did not seem to hear him. He fell into step several paces behind her and soon was following her across the entry hall.

He pulled the grain sack from his head and kept his head down, trying to appear normal. She looked just like Vita from behind. She was short and curvy and walked with a lovely sway. She even wore her sandy brown hair in the same way—half-up and half-down, fixed with a pin.

The woman made her way towards the women's dressing room and his thoughts raced. How many short, round, Roman women with pinned brown hair were there in Londinium?

'Vita, is that you?' he called again, but still she did not respond. She had nearly reached the dressing room entrance when he planted himself before her, blocking her path.

'Ack!' the woman shrieked, and Ven beheld her terrified face. It was not Vita's.

'Ah, my apologies,' Ven sputtered, moving out of the woman's way, but he had already drawn the attention of everyone entering the baths. He raised his head and glanced around him, further displaying his slave's tattoo.

'You there,' someone said. 'Where is your master?'

Ven tried to find who had addressed him, but he could not discern the source. There were several men now staring at him with suspicion.

The reward for the return of a runaway slave was as high in Britannia as it was in Rome. That was his first thought. His second thought was that he was the tallest man in the chamber. And the only one wearing a slave's tattoo.

'Seize that man!' someone shouted.

Ven dashed out of the baths as fast as his legs would take him, forgetting that a running slave was a guilty slave—whether in the wilds of Britannia or in the heart of Rome. He managed to escape the men from the baths, but in so doing had acquired several new pursuers. The more he ran, the more men ran after him, until it seemed that all of Londinium wished to give chase.

Ven splashed through the muddy streets, heading for the river. There was no other choice. If he could not lose his pursuers by the time he reached the docks, then he would simply disappear into the turbid waters of the

Tamesis. It was how he had lost the Scythian in the end, after all. He had simply out-swum him.

But Ven's legs did not fail him, nor did the rain, which helpfully obscured his escape. By the time he reached the shipyards at the south-eastern edge of the city, his pursuers had all but disappeared. The rain was coming down in torrents, soaking Ven to the bone. He hardly cared. He slowed to a walk in a low-lying area full of boats in various stages of disrepair. They littered the rain-washed shoreline like broken promises.

He let sorrow overtake him. He had failed to reunite with Vita. More than seven days had passed and she had not come. Even now, he could hardly believe it and had spent many long hours wondering what might have happened to her. Had she been abducted by tribesmen? Had she been returned to Lepidus for a price? Had she simply died at sea?

Turning away from the cemetery of ships, he made his way eastwards towards the deep-water docks. He refused to believe that she had died.

She was alive—he was certain of it. She had definitely made it off the ship, for he had spotted her himself, and even if she had not been able to swim effectively, the sea would have eventually delivered her to shore.

There was no doubt in Ven's mind that she was alive. Somewhere, she was alive and waiting for him to come save her, just as his mother had done long ago. Even if she had been injured in their escape, she would have not given up easily. There was simply too much fire inside her heart.

He arrived at the deep-water docks and studied the giant cargo ships tethered in a long row. The *Pax* was among them and, as he neared its tall prow, he remembered his final moments with Vita. She had taken his hand without any hesitation, had trusted him to lead her in to a wondrous future.

He wondered if he should not dive into the river anyway and let it take him where it would. He had failed her, after all. He had promised her to keep her safe and had instead lost her.

He spied a broken jar at the end of the dock. Tiny black balls spilled out of it like marbles. They were black olives—probably shipped in from Spain. Days ago, he might have seized upon such a discovery, but he was long past hunger now. Instead he gazed up at the large 'basket' ship from which the tiny imports had come.

The ships docked here were full to brimming with trade goods. They moved up and down the river day and night, bringing the delicacies of Rome to Britannia's soldiers and settlers.

Roman immigrants to Britannia were not the only ones enjoying Roman goods. The Britons did, too. When Ven was a boy, he had known many men from his tribe who privately traded with the Romans. They grew bumper crops of grain in secret, just for the privilege of purchasing an amphora of fine Falernian or a jar of Spanish olive oil.

Indeed, most of the tribes here in the south had now made formal alliances with the Romans for the sole purpose of securing trade, their chieftains apparently believing that pungent fish sauce and sweet grape syrup was worth more than freedom.

It occurred to Ven that it was not legions that would ultimately conquer Britannia, but the contents of these hulking ships.

It was also the reason he needed to get out of here. There were *vigiles* in Londinium just as there were in

Rome and commercial docks such as these were regularly patrolled by them.

He made his way along an empty part of the river shoreline and concealed himself among some large boulders. The rain continued to fall and he opened his mouth, letting it quench his thirst.

She was alive. Somewhere, right now, she was alive. Perhaps she was even turning her mouth to the sky, welcoming the sweet liquid and praying for a miracle.

But there was no such thing as miracles. There was only patience and tenacity and endurance—the kinds of skills one needed in a hunt. And Ven was nothing if not a hunter.

His stomach rumbled, and he gazed down at its concavity. Even beneath the thick hemp of his tunic, he could see the bones of his ribs. In his long, desperate wait for her, he had let himself become weak, but no more.

No more waiting, no more hoping. Just doing. He would search all of Britannia for her—his Roman-Celtic princess with mystic eyes and a voice of soft silk. He feared neither cold nor privation—nor even the cursed legions themselves. He had failed his mother once, but he would not fail Vita. He would find her, or die trying.

The first fortnight was the hardest. Not because of her bonds—tight leather straps around her wrists. Nor due to the relentless travel by horse, which scrambled her thoughts and rattled her bones. Nor even because of the rain, which did not so much cease as ebb and flow like the tide.

It was because she knew he was waiting for her.

She imagined him standing outside Londinium's central baths, trying to keep himself concealed. Surely

Lepidus had sent out word of his disappearance. Every centurion and slave catcher in Britannia was probably on the hunt for him.

Every day she did not meet him at the baths, he faced greater danger.

Her heart ached with his absence. With each new sunrise, she felt sadder. With each hoofbeat, her heart broke more. There he was in her mind, lurking in the rain, searching every woman he saw. Waiting and waiting and waiting.

She did not ask her captors where they were taking her. She did not want to know. It was away from Ven— that was all that mattered. Away from freedom and a future worth having. Away from the man she loved.

The hours passed like days. Her captors offered bread, but she did not eat it. They offered water from their udder bags, but she drank without satisfaction. Each night they placed a fur over her to protect her from the cold, yet she failed to thank the gods for her good treatment.

Instead, she spent all her energy praying for Ven. In the mornings she prayed to the Roman gods. One by one she hailed them, willing them to hear her. By midday she had turned her attention to her mother's gods. She knew only a few by name, but she gazed up at the sky and brazenly asked for their aid.

By the evening she was praying to all of nature. *Protect him*, she thought, looking all around her. She entreated the trees and begged the brooks. *Keep him safe.*

Late one night, she rose to pray beneath a sacred oak. *Please, Grandfather*, she begged. *Keep him alive. Let him find his freedom.*

On the final day of their journey, they paused at the edge of a field. Beyond it lay a hill covered with buildings surrounded by a high wall. The men approached the settlement with reverence and, when they reached the entry gate, one sang out the news of their arrival.

Vita remained atop one of the horses as the men dismounted and led the beasts inside the busy hill fort. She could feel a hundred sets of eyes upon her as she was ushered down the main street. She buried her bound hands beneath the fabric of her tunic and tried to maintain her dignity as the people whispered and pointed.

Soon she was ducking beneath the low thatch of a steep-roofed roundhouse where she was presented to a man with a large red beard who was dressed in several layers of furs.

'For you, Chief Rennyt,' said one of the men. 'A gift.'

'For my wife, you mean,' the man said and motioned to a tall, red-haired young woman with two babes on her hips.

The woman handed Vita one of the children and grinned. 'I am Orla,' she said. 'And that is little Bodenius. This way.'

Carrying the heavy toddler, Vita followed the young woman into a smaller roundhouse filled with the scent of mushrooms.

'Change him,' she instructed and Vita did her best to clean the small child while the woman looked on. She took the babe back into her arms and motioned to the hearth fire, where a pot of mushroom soup sat boiling. 'Please keep the fire going until the soup is ready, then feed it to my grandmother here,' she said.

Vita turned to discover a grey-haired woman stretched out on a mattress behind her. 'This is a new slave, Grandmother,' said the young woman. 'They found her when they were in the south.'

'Hello, dear,' said the old woman.

'Hello, madam,' said Vita. She crouched next to the fire until the young woman departed. 'Excuse me, Grandmother,' Vita whispered, 'but where am I?'

'You are in the north,' replied the old woman.

'How far north?' asked Vita.

'North of where the Romans are building their cursed wall,' said the woman. 'But you are a captive so I cannot tell you more.'

'What tribe is this?' asked Vita.

'We are the northernmost band of the proud Brigantes.'

On the fourteenth day after his separation from Vita, Ven awoke to the crying of gulls. It was strange to see the coastal birds so far up the river. He assumed it was because the fishing was good. He jumped to his feet and canvased the shoreline, quickly discovering a tall stick and sharp stone with which to whittle it. As he began to shape his makeshift spear, he considered what he thought to be a logical plan.

He would begin his search for Vita along the southern shores of the island, starting with the area where she had likely landed. He would work his way up from there, canvasing the villages and interviewing any locals he might meet along the way.

He would continue his methodical sweep, and when he reached Londinium, he would enquire after Lepidus. By then the old man would have been well on his way north and Ven would find out if he travelled with a female. He would let that knowledge direct his path from Londinium.

There was only one problem: his tattoo. He could not allow it to be seen. He would have to purchase a hat and find something other than his slave's short tunic to wear. Where would he find the money for all of that?

But first there was the problem of his empty stomach. Spear in hand, Ven studied the silty waters of the river, then lunged with his spear. He killed his first fish with an almost mystic ease, then gazed up at the pale morning sky. Sometimes the gods were kind.

Testing his strange fortune, he quickly speared another fish, then another, and by sunrise he had a dozen fish skewered on a long branch.

It was just past dawn and the area around the docks was still mercifully empty of souls. Still, Ven could not risk discovery, so he started downriver to find a place to eat his breakfast in safety. Just as he was passing the last deep-water dock, he noticed a tall, thick-chested man standing at its end.

The man wore a thigh-length tunic and long linen trousers—a typical tribal costume. His hair was long and rather tangled and he sported a strange geometrical tattoo on his arm. Beside him lay a small pile of furs.

'Good day for a sail,' the man said in Latin. Ven nearly stopped in his tracks. There was not even a hint of a Celtic accent in the man's voice: his words were as crisp and learned as a senator's. 'Wind from the south, I mean,' clarified the man. He nodded down the river as if he considered it his own.

Ven silently chided himself for his poor judgement. Despite the man's strange appearance, he was clearly Roman.

'Good day for sailing,' Ven returned, noticing that the man carried a large, well-used leather backpack, as if he made his living through travel.

'Fish for sale?' asked the man.

'They can be,' replied Ven.

'How much?' The man dug in a pocket and emerged with a handful of coins.

Ven stood warily at the beginning of the dock. Slave catchers took many forms and the man could easily have been one in disguise. Still, a trade was a trade and Ven needed clothing. 'You can have them all for the trousers you wear,' Ven said.

The man grunted a laugh. 'These trousers are worth more than a hundred fish.'

'How about one of those furs, then?' asked Ven.

The man laughed at Ven's outrageous request. 'I will give you some coin for the fish,' he said.

Ven strode down the deck, figuring that if the man attempted to seize him, he could simply push him into the river—or dive in himself. Ven planted himself before the man and held out the fish. 'Three *sesterces*,' he said.

The man gave Ven a quick assessment, taking in his tattoo, his spear, even his sandals. He did not accept the fish immediately, but instead held out his arm. 'I am Titus,' he said.

'I am Ven,' said Ven, gripping the man's elbow in the customary Roman greeting.

'Ven? I have never heard of such a name.'

'It is short for Venator.'

'Hunter?'

The man glanced at the sky just as Ven had just done not moments before, as if in gratitude. There was a keenness in his eyes that suggested presence of mind. As he studied the pile of furs, the man's occupation came to Ven at once: he was a hunter, too.

'Can you hunt things besides fish?' he asked and Ven could not help but grin.

'What do you think?'

Chapter Twelve

Ven struck his flintstone against the iron bar and coaxed his blaze to life. Beside him Titus was clearing a place on the ground for a bed mat. He was taking a rather long time at the task, digging through several layers of earth before filling the small concavity with fallen leaves.

They had been travelling together for nearly a month, yet Ven still found it strange how long it took the Roman to make himself comfortable at night. For all his tough talk and rugged exterior, in many ways he was as picky as a patrician.

Ven smiled to himself. After twenty years of bondage to Romans, Ven had finally escaped, only to be enslaved to yet another nit-picking Roman. This time, however, it was all a ruse and bless the gods for that. Indeed, bless the gods for Titus.

The two men had struck a deal. Titus had agreed to claim Ven as his slave in exchange for Ven's services as a hunter. Proceeds from the sales of their furs would favour the men equally, giving Ven a chance to save a bit of coin. Even better, Ven would be allowed to dictate the direction of their hunt.

It had been a slow, thorough, zig-zagging journey north, with a brief respite in Londinium, and no sign of her.

Ven blew gently on the tinder, while his hunting partner stared into the flames. He was instinctively aware of his surroundings—the twitter of birds, the swish of a nearby stream, the song of twilight crickets. Here in the wilds of Britannia the world made sense. Here life was simple.

Yet things had changed.

That very day, he and Titus had visited the Roman *colonia* of Camulodunum to buy bread and enquire about the local hunting. An old Roman legionary fortress, the town had been converted into a settlement in which the locals of the Trinovante tribe held the same rights as Romans.

Fancying themselves Romans, some Trinovantes had gone as far as to renounce their own heritage. The Trinovante baker's wife had ignored Ven's perfectly good Celtic, for example, and instead had addressed Titus in her broken Latin.

'You will not find much game in the Forest of Camulus, sir,' she had explained to Titus. 'A group of Iceni chieftains and Roman tribunes hunt there regularly. I am afraid they have already taken the low-hanging fruit.'

Ven had been puzzled by the woman. Surely she had lost ancestors in the famous revolt of Queen Boudica against the Roman occupiers, yet there was no malice in her voice as she described the intermingling of her tribe's leaders with the Romans.

'We have no interest in low-hanging fruit,' said Ven in Celtic and the woman frowned.

'Your slave is rather bold,' she told Titus in Latin. 'Tell me, where are you staying tonight? We have a comfortable room above our ovens here for rent. Stays very warm at night.'

'Our lodgings are outside of town, I am afraid,' replied Ven on Titus's behalf. *Beneath the eternal stars.*

The woman's eyes flashed. Collecting herself, she smiled at Titus. 'You must not leave before trying out our new baths. They are just down the way—a gift from Governor Nepos.' She looked Ven up and down, barely concealing her disgust. 'Your slave, of course, is welcome to use the river.'

It was all Ven could do not to roll his eyes.

The tribes of southern Britannia were obviously not tribes any more; they had become 'populations'. They declared their loyalty to the divine Emperor and sacrificed cattle to his cult. They made their lives in Romanised towns, where they had mixed with the Roman occupiers so completely that Ven could barely tell who was Roman and who was not.

'I think we should head north tomorrow,' Titus said now. He had stretched out on his bed mat and was staring up at the orange-tinged sky. 'There will be a greater supply of animals and fewer vexing townsfolk.'

Ven stood to gather more firewood. 'A fine idea, though I should remind you that my journey ends when we reach Brigante territory.'

That was not entirely true. Ven planned to stay in the lands of his kin only long enough to gather information. His journey would not end until he found Vita.

'I have not forgotten about your impending departure,' said Titus, 'though Brigante territory is a long way off and there is a long winter ahead. Still, the thought troubles me constantly.'

'Clearly not enough to help me gather firewood,' called Ven.

'I am merely storing my energy to prepare our lavish meal.'

'And what do you plan for us tonight?'

'Boiled barley for the first course, flavoured with a bit of dust. That will be followed by shreds of salted venison and slices of apple from the sacred groves of... where are we again?'

'The Forest of Camulus.'

'The Forest of Camulus!'

Ven watched his companion stand and walk softly down to the river with his bronze pot. A twig snapped behind him and he stopped in his tracks. Ven chuckled as a tiny brown bird hopped through the underbrush at Titus's feet. Titus lunged for the tiny creature, but it hopped out of reach.

'A valiant effort,' Ven cried, having never met someone so very similar to himself. The man was always hunting.

Ven was always hunting, too, but his primary prey was a brown-and-green-eyed goddess and, when he finally found her, he would not kill her, but festoon her body with kisses.

Fortunately, Ven had managed to find other prey as well. On the first day of his partnership with Titus, Ven had landed two deer in the forests south of Londinium. The men had sold the hides in the city and with his proceeds Ven had been able to buy a hat and a decent pair of trousers.

Since then, however, they had not sighted a single animal. The forests of southern Britannia seemed unexpectedly empty and now even the tiny bird fluttered away.

'I blame the Romans for our ill fortune,' said Titus, returning to the edge of the fire with his pot of water. He scooped in a handful of grain.

'You blame the Romans for our poor hunting?'

'For Romans hunting is a sport, much like everything else. There is no appreciation for tribal hunting boundaries, or any control on the take. The Romans are wretched, greedy men.'

'But you are Roman yourself.'

'Aye, and so are you, in most ways at least, may Taranis forgive you.'

Ven gasped at the invocation of the barbarian god of thunder. 'In my heart I am pure Brigante,' he vowed.

It had been an ongoing debate between the two men. Who was more Roman: Ven the Barbarian Roman or Titus the Roman Barbarian?

'Explain to me a world in which a Roman man wears trousers and invokes Brigante gods,' Ven said, 'and a Trinovante woman sends her prayers to Diana and extols the virtues of the baths.'

'It is the way you live your life that makes you who you are,' said Titus.

'What I really wonder is why these southern tribes no longer even try to fight.'

'Because they know they cannot succeed. The only time they came close to success was during Queen Boudica's revolt, when they formed a great alliance, and still the Romans managed to destroy them. Meanwhile, the comforts of Rome beckon them daily, along with the stability of a world without raids. Wine, oil, weapons, gold, education—'

Ven shook his head. 'The Romans are monsters. They paved over the sacred baths. They killed the druids. They make a desert and call it peace.'

'And yet half the tribal warriors of southern Britannia are now Roman soldiers.'

'Traitors, all.'

'They fight for the promise of citizenship,' observed Titus. 'Are they traitors, or just men who want a place in the new world?'

'This is no new world. It is the land of proud tribes who have existed for thousands of years.'

'Without the Roman peace, those tribes would be warring and raiding with each other just as they have always done.'

'The Roman peace is not peace. It is slavery,' Ven hissed.

'That woman from Camulodunum would not say so.'

'Then she is a fool.'

Now it was Ven who stared into the flames. Perhaps he was the bigger fool. The town they had visited that day was no oddity, it was a vision of the future. The great warrior tribes of southern Britannia had fought and lost, and now they were being assimilated.

Surely the northern tribes of Britannia would be no different. They would resist the Romans for as long as they could; perhaps they would even mount an alliance, just as the southern tribes had done. There were many in Rome who privately believed that the Boudica rebellion might have succeeded were it not for the Roman commander Suetonius's unique skill.

Perhaps the tribes of the north would encounter a weaker Roman foe. Perhaps they would fight and die together against terrible odds and be victorious. More likely, however, they would simply fight and die, and all so that their sons and daughters could put olive oil on their bread.

The world was turned upside down. Even if Ven's tribe had not changed since he had lived among them, it would not be long until they did—though a deep part of him hoped that they would not go down without a fight.

Freedom is the prize, he thought suddenly.

A strange longing overtook him. It was not for the deep forests or windswept hills of his home territory. It was not even for his own kin. He longed for Vita. She was the only thing that seemed to make sense any more and he would not rest until he found her.

Orla's babies would not stop crying. 'Take Bodenius,' she told Vita, handing her the boy.

Orla's husband, the Brigante chieftain, had just toppled a table full of dishware, waking both babies from their naps. Now he kicked several of the fallen goblets against the wall, causing more loud clattering. The babies howled.

'Cease, Rennyt!' shouted Orla. 'Control yourself!'

Vita feared for Orla. A Roman woman would not dare to speak to her husband in such a way without paying the price of a beating.

Vita moved to Orla's side. 'Give me little Amatus as well, Domina,' she said and gently took the second babe against her chest.

'I will not have you knocking over furniture in our home!' Orla shouted at her husband. 'Be calm.'

'How am I supposed to be calm when the cursed Roman Governor has just doubled the price of tribute?' the chieftain roared.

'What?' Orla asked, though she could barely be heard above her babies' cries. 'Quiet them, Vita!' she commanded.

'I am trying, Domina,' said Vita, fearing for the chieftain's wife. Vita stepped as far away from the couple as she could, then glanced about for some distraction. She caught Grandmother's eye.

'Sing them a song, dear,' the old woman muttered.

A song? The only songs Vita knew were banquet songs in Latin, though she vaguely remembered her mother singing songs to her in her youth. She searched her mind for a Caledonian lullaby and at last was able to remember one.

'The poor little ant thought he was so small...' she began singing softly.

'Why did he double the price of tribute?' Orla asked.

'Because the cursed Romans are bringing another legion to Britannia,' he said.

'Gods, no,' said Orla.

Vita continued softly, 'He tried to move the crumb, but it would not move at all...'

'But why do they need yet another legion here? Is two not enough?'

'Because of the wall, Orla. They have already begun to dig the trenches for it.'

'The poor little ant was really such an oaf...' Vita continued at a whisper.

Orla shook her head. 'It cannot be.' She buried her face in her hands. 'What will become of us?'

The babies were nearly quiet and Vita finished softly, 'Together with his friends they could move a whole loaf...'

Now the babies were silent, but their mother was weeping.

'Did you not hear that, Wife?' said the Chieftain.

'Hear what?'

'Your slave. Did you not hear her singing?'

'What of it?'

'Her accent.'

'She is Caledonian—of course she has an accent.'

'That is not a Caledonian accent,' stated the Chief. 'It is a Roman one. That woman is Roman.'

Orla turned to Vita. 'You are Caledonian, yes, Vita? Is that not what you told me?'

Vita took a breath. 'I am part-Caledonian, Domina, but I am also part-Roman.'

Orla let out a gasp. 'Do you see?' shouted the Chieftain. 'I always knew it.'

'Apologies, Domina, I—'

'That is how they all are, Orla!' said the Chieftain. 'They lie like thieves.'

'For shame, Vita!' shouted Orla.

'I do not want her around my children,' ordered the Chief. 'Give her another job. Laundry. Cooking. Make her go grind grain for all I care. Just do not let her touch my boys. She stinks of Rome.'

Vita handed over the twins and exited the roundhouse as quickly as she could. She ran to her laundry buckets and dived into her work. It was winter already and the cold wrapped around her hands, threatening to make them useless. Still, she could not bear to face the family to whom she was bound.

Vita plunged her mistress's tunic in the soapy water and began to scrub. Several passers-by hissed and sneered at her as she worked. 'Dirty Roman,' they called. 'Oil-swilling scum.' News travelled fast at the hill fort— even faster than it did in the Aventine, or so it seemed.

She imagined her mother suffering similar treatment beneath her Roman masters. It was no wonder her mother always seemed so sad. She had once been like Orla—a strong British tribeswoman who stood up to her male kin and lived her own life. Then suddenly all of that was taken from her. By Romans.

'Roman harlot!' someone barked. Vita sucked in a breath, resolving not to let them break her spirit. She knew that over time, the Brigantes would begin to see her as part of their community, just as the Romans did with the barbarians who lived among them.

She rinsed Orla's tunic and hung it out to dry, then plunged her own tunic into the soapy water. Though she was a slave, Vita counted herself fortunate. If she had not been discovered that day on the beach, it was possible that she might have been seized by less scrupulous captors. Even if she had made it to Londinium, it was not certain that Ven would have come to find her at all. Worse, Lepidus might have found her instead.

At least she had food in her belly, a roof over her head and furs with which to cover herself. She was lucky to be alive—something she reminded herself over and over as she scrubbed her tunic furiously, long after it was clean, as if to wash away her Roman-ness.

The sun dropped below the horizon and she found herself alone beneath a cold winter moon. Finally, the tears came, as they always did on nights when she missed him. And tonight she missed him terribly.

She pictured him running through a deep forest somewhere, chasing after a deer in the moonlight. No wonder he was called Hunter: he was so fleet of foot. Surely not even a deer could escape him.

Though, somehow, Vita had managed to escape him utterly.

She had not even had a chance to say goodbye to him—or to convey her gratitude. She had not been able to kiss him one last time and tell him that she loved him with all her heart.

He was the worthiest man she had ever met. He was kind and honourable, caring and valiant. He stirred her soul and ignited her lust. She owed him a debt that could never be repaid—for reminding her who she was, for making the world new again, for bringing her back to life.

Now, however, she had to let him go. To cling to his memory would be to invite misery. Love and longing were not just dangerous emotions for a slave, but for anyone who found herself inside one of life's prisons.

She had to forget him. It would take time, but she knew that she could convince her mind that he never was and thus ease her own suffering.

Never again would Vita want what she could not have. It was that very desire that had led her to commit disastrous mistakes—first with Magnus, then with Lepidus. If she had not tried to recover her dowry, Magnus would not have tried to kill her. If she had not broken her contract with Lepidus, she would not have been enslaved. The path to her freedom had been laid out before her twice and twice her own avarice had been her undoing.

Never again. Now Vita understood that she had overreached and the gods were having their say. Vita's mother had been a slave and now Vita would be, too: a just punishment for her ambition and greed.

She would not resist her bonds. She would serve her new family as best she could. Instead of yearning for what she did not have, she would be grateful for what she did have. She would no longer seek to escape her life, but to accept it.

When Vita at last returned to the roundhouse, all of the family was asleep. She fetched her blanket and curled up on top of her bed mat, just next to the door. A few paces away, Grandmother was snoring softly. Vita could not manage to stop her weeping and she feared awaking the old woman. She buried her face in her hands.

'Are you all right, dear?' she heard the old woman whisper.

'I am all right, Grandmother. Gratitude,' Vita whispered back.

'You are trying to accept that something has been lost,' said the old woman.

'Yes, I am,' said Vita, expecting the kind old soul to offer her words of comfort.

'In that way you are like the Brigantes themselves—trying to accept what they have lost to the Romans.'

'I suppose so, yes,' said Vita.

'A dangerous game, acceptance,' Grandmother said, then she rolled over and returned to her sleep.

Chapter Thirteen

It was the *kalends* of January when Ven first glimpsed the ditches. The day was cold and clear and he and Titus had just climbed to the top of a hill that had been recently cleared of timber. The northern limits of the Roman province of Britannia spread out before them, a tapestry of brown fields and green forests.

Cutting a path from east to west across the landscape was a familiar escarpment of rock. Ven knew the feature well, for when he was a boy he had often climbed the escarpment's stone-pocked slopes and used them as lookouts for game. He never could have imagined its undulating heights might one day play host to his tribe's ruin.

And yet there was the harbinger for that coming ruin right before his eyes—in the form of ditches.

They ran across the landscape like a trio of earthen serpents. The first, closest ditch lay at the southern base of the escarpment and was obviously the shallowest of the three. Ven might not have recognised it at all had it not been for the stumps of the trees that had obviously been felled to mark its path. It could not have been more than the size of a shovel in depth, a kind of demarcation line for something greater to come.

Ven wondered what that thing might be. For all of his architectural and military knowledge, he could not explain the purpose of that southernmost ditch.

The purpose of the northernmost ditch, in contrast, was abundantly clear. It was a first line of defence. Located just beyond the steep northern side of the escarpment, the northern ditch was large and full of souls—an endless line of men in military dress.

Ven noticed the stains of tribal tattoos on some of the men's arms and guessed them to be auxiliary soldiers— probably recruited from the southern tribes. The ditch they were digging was as deep as the men were tall and flanked by even higher berms. It was less a ditch than an earthen wall, a formidable barrier in its own right.

The final ditch snaked between the two other ditches on top of the escarpment itself. It climbed over rises and plunged into canyons, tracing a path across the territory that Ven had once called his home.

Ven could see groups of men gathered at intervals along this third ditch. Some were moving large wooden cranes into place while others appeared to be stacking stones. Still others were standing inside the ditch itself, digging relentlessly.

'There will be the wall,' Ven remarked, though surely Titus had guessed as much. 'Hadrian's masterpiece.'

Titus grunted. 'Now I remember why I never come this far north.'

'And why is that?' asked Ven.

'Same reason the Princeps is building that wall. You northern Brigantes are a troublesome group.'

Titus was gazing beyond the northern ditch to a hill fort in the distance: the northernmost hill fort of the

Brigante tribe. Ven recognised its tall spiked fence and thatched roofs instantly. The Brigante Chieftain and his entourage made his home at the hill fort along with hundreds of others and, as a boy, Ven had travelled there often with his father for meetings. Seeing the hill fort now, after so many years, brought a strange pain into Ven's heart.

He turned away only to discover another familiar sight: a sprawling Roman settlement about a mile south of the southernmost ditch.

The core of the settlement consisted of an ordered collection of buildings: barracks, granaries, stables, workshops, offices, latrines and ovens surrounded by a large stone wall. 'That is the Roman fort of Vindolanda,' remarked Ven. 'It has been here since before I was born.'

'And will be here long after you are dead, I imagine,' said Titus.

Outside the fort, a town had grown up: a haphazard variety of dwellings that appeared almost comical against the fort's stern angles.

'A day's trip to the east of here is another fort called Coria,' remarked Ven. *Where a wicked man makes his home.*

'I have never been to Coria, either,' remarked Titus. 'They say the soldiers there pay twice as much for beer.'

'Perhaps they would also pay twice as much for furs,' said Ven.

Titus shook his head and gazed out at the sprawling forest. 'Doubt that.'

Ven gazed west as far as he could see. 'There are still many more forts to be constructed and many more soldiers to begin work. There will be twenty-two forts in all supporting the wall, along with a smattering of fortlets and other *castra*,' Ven remarked.

'For a barbarian, you know quite a lot about Roman military installations,' said Titus.

'Well, I drew up the plans for the wall myself,' said Ven.

'Ha!' Titus slapped Ven on the back. 'Good one! Now let us get out of here, by Hades. Did you not say your old settlement is near? I could use a warm stew and a soft bed tonight.'

The two men continued their journey, and by sunset they were standing outside a cluster of small roundhouses beside a quiet river north of the wall.

He found the finest-looking roundhouse and knocked on the door. A buxom, stern-faced woman answered. She held up a sharp *gladius* and frowned. 'Who are you and why to do come here?' she growled.

'I am Ven, son of Tovin and Enica,' Ven said in his best Brigantian Celtic. 'I come from this place. Please, lay down your weapon. I am not your enemy.'

The woman held the blade even closer to Ven's throat. 'No, you are not, but the man next to you is. Tell him to leave.'

'He is my friend and will do you no harm. I give you my word as a Brigante.'

'He is Roman. Tell him to leave or I will cut his throat,' said the woman. 'I give you my word as a Brigante.'

Ven turned to Titus. 'I am sorry, friend. It seems that our association ends here.'

'As I feared it would,' returned Titus.

'May you find wealth and happiness.'

'I already have,' said Titus. 'It is you I worry about.'

Titus turned away, then paused and turned back. 'Remember, it is the way you live your life that makes you who you are,' he said.

Ven felt as if he had just received some rare and precious wisdom. He bowed his thanks, but when he returned to standing, Titus had disappeared and Ven found himself locked in a pillowy embrace. 'Cousin Ven!' the woman cried. 'I never thought I would see you again! It is me! Cousin Ertola!'

'Cousin Ertola?'

'Girls, come and meet your cousin Ven!' A handful of young women emerged and stood behind the woman, the youngest of whom stared up at Ven with enormous unblinking eyes.

'Armea, give your cousin a proper greeting.' The girl gave a lavish bow while Cousin Ertola shouted over Ven's shoulder.

'My cousin Ven has returned!' she cried joyously. 'Come, everyone! Meet my cousin!'

Ven turned around discover several dozen souls standing all around him. A tall, heavily tattooed woman stepped forward and gazed at Ven doubtfully.

'I am Adamanta, wife of Tenus, the late leader of this settlement,' she stated. 'And you are?'

'I am Ven, son of Tovin and Enica. I hail from this very soil.'

'No other kin travel with you?' asked the woman.

'None at all,' said Ven. He thought of Vita. 'I am sorry to hear of your loss.'

The woman grunted. 'There is no time for condolences. The Romans have begun to swarm like bees in our territory. They took my husband's life only a month ago, along with many others.'

'What reason?' asked Ven, feeling his teeth begin to clench.

'Governor Nepos doubled his tribute demands without notice. Sent out a cohort from Vindolanda. They tried to steal an entire herd of our cattle. We had to fight back.'

'How many dead?' asked Ven.

'Too many,' said Adamanta. Ven looked out at the gathering of Brigantes—a collection of the very old and the very young. 'Is that why there are no warriors here?'

Adnamata narrowed her eyes. 'Obviously I am a warrior.' She glanced at her bandage-wrapped hand. 'I am merely wait for my injury to heal. I will then join the others at the hill fort where they are currently amassing.'

'Are you planning another raid?'

'Not a raid—a proper fight this time. The last stand of the Brigantes.'

'Allies?'

'Not a one,' said Adamanta, her lips a thin line. 'It seems that all the southern tribes have been purchased.'

'And the northern ones?' asked Ven.

'Enemies all. They cannot be trusted.'

'Without allies, it will simply be the last of the Brigantes.'

There were several loud gasps, but Adamanta's stare was unwavering. 'There is no other choice. When we resist their demands, they threaten to enslave us, but when we fulfil their demands we become slaves already. Will you not help us fight back?'

'Listen to me,' said Ven. 'The Brigantes can prevail, but not without allies. We need the tribes of the far north on our side—the Votadini and the Selgovae and the Damnonii and all the rest.' *The Caledonii*, he thought.

'Those tribes would never come to our aid,' said Adamanta.

Ven shook his head. 'I am not skilled in battle, but I am skilled with words, and if your chieftain will allow me, I am certain I can help forge such alliances. It is

your only hope. I can also mingle with the Romans.
Get information.'

'You wish to wield words?' Adamanta looked Ven
up and down, then frowned. 'A waste of good warrior,
I say.'

'Just listen to the man, Adamanta,' said Ertola. 'Perhaps he can help.'

Adamanta pursed her lips. 'Why did you come here,
Ven of Rome?'

'I am searching for a woman,' he admitted, for he
knew he could not lie. 'She was stranded on the coast
south of Londinium a few months ago—a short, stout
woman with brown-green eyes.'

Ven noticed the little girl standing beside Ertola tug
on her mother's skirt.

'Stop, Armea!' said Ertola.

Meanwhile, Adamanta was shaking her head. 'So you
did not come to defend your threatened tribe?'

'I confess that I did not understand the threat until
today,' said Ven. 'So, no, that is not why I have come.'
Ven remembered Titus's parting words. *It is the way you
live your life that makes you who you are.* 'But I tell you
now that it is why I will stay.'

Ertola put her hands together delightedly, and there
were soft sounds of approval from the people all around.
Ven felt his spirit swell. Now that he had said the words
aloud, he understood the truth in them. He had spent
an entire life doing penance for what he had lost. Now,
finally, he had been granted a chance at redemption.

'Then what does it matter whether or not you find
this woman you seek? Are there not bigger challenges
to pursue now? The safety of your kin?'

'I will help the Brigantes,' Ven repeated. 'I give you
my word.'

'Then you are welcome here,' said Adamanta. She stepped back and gave him a deep bow.

Ven was ushered by Ertola and her family to a small roundhouse just outside the settlement. When Ven stepped inside, he was surprised to discover several tables and chairs, a large raised bed and a finely appointed hearth currently occupied by a lidded pot.

'This home belonged to one of the men we lost,' Ertola explained. 'We have been loath to clean it.'

'I am so sorry, Cousin,' said Ven.

'I am just happy that the gods have sent you to us,' said Ertola. She kissed Ven's cheek. 'Make yourself at home now. We can speak more in the morning.'

Ertola and her girls swept out of the roundhouse without seeing young Armea hiding behind one of the chairs.

'What are you doing there, little one?' asked Ven, catching sight of the girl.

'I know where the Roman lady is,' she whispered.

Ven's stomach jumped into his throat. 'I beg you to tell me,' Ven whispered back.

'My mother says I cannot say it aloud,' said Armea.

Ven crouched down. 'Then perhaps you can whisper it in my ear.'

When Ven first sighted the woman, she was standing over a large granite stone, attempting to grind grain. She stood outside a large roundhouse at the far end of the hill fort, struggling with her task. She was lifting the grinding stone too far off the pestle stone, not letting the stones do the work. Her sandy brown hair fell forward, covering her face.

But why was a woman grinding grain at all? Was that not why they attached donkeys to grinding wheels?

And why did she labour outside the dwelling on such a cold winter's day?

Ven walked closer, hoping she would not notice his interest. It had been only days since Armea had told him about the half-Roman, half-Caledonii woman residing in the northernmost Brigante hill fort. According to Armea, the woman had been gifted to a Brigante chieftain by scouts many months ago.

Still, Ven was careful not to cling to an unlikely hope. Armea was a girl of only ten who seemed to delight in secrets. There was no telling what kind of falsehoods she might tell for her own amusement.

Ven pulled his cloak around him against the chill. The night before, there had been a light snow and the sky remained grey and threatening. Many of the hill fort's denizens were returning early from the market held in the nearby fort of Coria and there was a tumult of moving horses and people shuffling goods from carts.

A man wearing a chieftain's golden *torc* and an array of fine furs swung down from one such cart and shouted something at the woman, though Ven could not determine what he said. She nodded vigorously and returned to her task.

It seemed clear the woman was a slave. A Brigante man would never have berated his wife so publicly and a Brigante wife would have never taken such a scolding without returning a scolding of her own. Besides, only a slave would be relegated to doing work outdoors on a chilly day like today.

The man unhitched one of his donkeys and lead it behind his house. At least that explained the reason for the woman's thankless task. Grinding grain was a donkey's work, but clearly the donkey had been away that day.

As Ven stepped closer, his heart moved slightly up

into his throat. The first thing he noticed was her hair. It was longer than before, but she had pulled it back behind her ear, leaving her neck almost entirely exposed. He knew that neck. He had once rubbed it gently.

The woman remained bent over her task, but he could see the small details of the lower part of her face. Those lips—so shapely and clever. He understood those lips, for he had kissed them once.

Stepping closer still, he noticed her rather serious nose. It pointed sternly to her lips, which she discreetly moistened with her tongue. Lust shot through him.

It had to be her, though there were several differences in her appearance that worried him. Her jaw, for example, was still as soft and round, but there was a slight hollowness to her cheeks. Her arms were thinner, too, and the tunic she wore seemed rather loose, despite the warming garments she wore beneath it.

She looked very much like Vita, but there was less of her.

Tears welled in his eyes. She had been made into a slave, had been subject to privation and hardship and all manner of laborious works. Though the tribes of Britannia were easier on their slaves than the *familias* of Rome, the position was still a miserable one, and part of him prayed the woman was not Vita and that he was mistaken.

Then she looked up at him.

Gods, it was her. Her face was like a cracked egg: he could see the fissures of hardship, the lines of endurance. Still, her brown-green eyes had not lost their shine, and when they locked with his own eyes a small explosion took place inside his heart.

She cocked her head in disbelief. 'Ven?'

He put his finger to his lips and shook his head

gravely. Every part of him wanted to take her in his arms, but he could not do it. Too much enthusiasm would convey her value to him and as it was he was not sure he had enough coin to purchase her.

'You there,' he said. 'Do you belong to the owner of this house?'

'Yes, sir,' she said, squelching a smile on the verge of explosion. She bowed meekly.

'Get him for me now, woman. I wish to make a deal.'

Chapter Fourteen

He insisted on carrying her across the threshold of his small roundhouse, a journey of less than six paces, and she laughed as he settled her down on top of his bed of furs.

'Why do you laugh?' he asked, feigning confusion. 'Is it not Roman custom for a man to carry his bride across the threshold of his home?'

'But we are not in Rome, nor am I your bride.'

'Not yet,' he said, his eyes flashing. He bent to kiss her lips, then changed direction at the last moment, planting a kiss on her forehead instead. He bent to start a fire.

She stood in the middle of the room, blinking. 'I am finding it difficult to believe I am not living inside a dream.'

'Do you require some sort of proof?' he asked.

'I believe I do.'

He switched to Celtic. *'Chroesawer, duwies,'* he said. *Welcome, goddess.* Returning to Latin, he gestured to the low platform of his fur-lined bed. 'Now take off your shoes and have a rest. I think you will find the bed especially soft.'

Vita was happy to do as she was told, stretching out atop his furs and marvelling at the near-instantaneous warmth they granted. 'I feel as if I am floating on a cloud,' she said.

'I have been floating on a cloud since I met you.'

Vita smiled and shook her head. 'First rhetoric and now poetry?'

'Goose feathers,' he said.

'What?'

'That is what you feel beneath you. The bed mat is stuffed with them.'

Vita nuzzled against the down-filled pad, feeling luxurious. During her enslavement at the hill fort, one of her duties had been to stay awake beside her owner's hearth each night, feeding the flames until all six members of his family were asleep.

She had been granted the use of a fur for the cold hours and had mostly kept warm, but it did not change the character of the floor of the dwelling. It was always hard, always cold. 'I do not think I ever want to leave this bed,' she said.

'That is a relief, because I do not ever want you to.' He was bent beside a pot perched on a metal grate over the central fire. 'You are my guest for life.'

'Guest? But you paid the chieftain good coin for me. Do you not own me?'

He laughed. 'On the contrary, Vita, I fear it is you who owns me.'

He lifted the pot from the flames and poured a creamy liquid into a cup, which he placed on the table beside the bed. Exiting through the thick hide door, he returned in seconds with an armful of logs, which he dropped into a container beside the fire. 'I may have to go cut some more wood,' he remarked, studying the half-full container.

'You must have travelled over ten miles today. Are you not exhausted from the ride?'

'Not at all.' His eyes danced in the firelight, making her stomach dance, too. 'Let me go see what more I can gather,' he said and stepped outside once again.

When he returned, he dropped an armful of branches on to the logs, filling the container. 'There,' he pronounced. 'Enough wood to last us all night.'

All night, she thought. It was impossible to believe. Just yesterday she had gazed up at the grey winter sky, certain that its colour would never change. But now here he was and they had all night.

'I did not believe this day would ever come,' she said. She felt a tear slide down her cheek. 'I nearly lost hope...' She studied his face. It was as she remembered it, still as handsome and unexpected as the first day she saw it. Big eyes, broad cheeks, wide mouth. A playful grin and a nose too smart for its own good.

'I would never have ceased my search for you, you know. Our reunion was as inevitable as the sunrise.'

'You did not doubt that you would find me?'

'Never once.'

'But how did you know I had not died?'

'I just knew. I cannot explain it.'

'I tried to forget you,' Vita said. 'I tried so very hard, Ven. I longed for you. I made myself miserable.'

'You tried to turn your heart to ice. It is what a slave must do.' Ven smiled. 'Unfortunately, your heart is warmer than most.'

'I have learned that what my heart wants is often very different than what my mind wants,' Vita said.

'What I have learned is that the world can change in an instant and that all we have is this moment. We must seize it.'

'*Carpe diem?*' She shot him a sly grin.

The small room was already warm from the heat of the fire. Its smoke seeped through the high thatched roof like water through a sieve. Vita pretended fascination with the disappearing smoke while Ven removed his tunic and undershirt and placed them over a chair.

Now he stood before her wearing only his trousers, which were tied low around his narrow hips, revealing two remarkable, downward-plunging sinews that she felt certain came together somewhere beneath the cloth. Those fascinating bridles of flesh acted as a kind of frame for his stomach muscles, which were stacked like logs up the length of his torso.

They were so thick and strong, those muscles. How much she wished to climb them.

And so she did, with her eyes. They led her northwards, deep into the untamed territory of his broad chest. There a forest of curly hair spread over the contours of two thick, muscular plates. She longed to run her fingers through that soft forest, then to bury her nose in it and breathe deeply.

But for now she only lay back in admiration. He had grown stronger and more substantial since she had last seen him. His arms had certainly thickened. So had his chest. It seemed to bulge with latent force, as if he might be able to hold back an entire tribe of angry ex-husbands.

He stared down at her thoughtfully. 'Just look at us: a Roman and a barbarian, both taken from their homelands, both enslaved, both freed by the other. I think we are the only two people in Britannia who have lived such strange fates.'

'Perhaps in all the civilised world.' She glanced around her. 'Does a dirt-floor roundhouse in northern Britannia still count as the civilised world?'

He laughed. 'I hope not. I do not plan to behave in a civilised manner at all tonight.' His eyes flashed and there went her stomach again.

'What is that?' she asked, glancing at the cup on the table beside her.

'Honeyed goat's milk,' he said. 'It is even better with biscuits, but am afraid I am a terrible baker.'

'And I am a terrible cook!'

'I do not believe that.'

'My mother refused to teach me. She said that cooking was a skill for slaves, and that her daughter would never be a slave. Life is strange, is it not?'

He held the cup out to her. 'Drink now. You are far too thin.'

Vita put the cup to her lips, keeping it there long after she had finished drinking in order to discreetly watch him pull down his trousers.

She had heard that the Celtic warriors sometimes went to battle completely naked. Now, as her very own Celtic warrior stood before her in only a loincloth, the reason seemed clear: it was to inspire awe.

'How long have you lived in this house?' she asked. She lifted the cup to her lips once again, but accidentally gulped the liquid, resulting in a spasm of coughs.

'Are you all right, Vita?'

'Yes, of course. Perfectly fine,' she sputtered, stealing another glance at him. *It is fascinating how the size of your desire seems to be testing the threads of your loincloth.* 'You were saying about the house?'

'I have lived here for only a handful of days,' Ven replied. 'I was fortunate my cousin remembered me.'

'And if she had not remembered you?'

'She would not have given me this house. It belonged to a warrior who died.'

'I am sorry to hear. How did he die?'

'He was killed in a fight…with a Roman soldier.'

His words lay heavy around them and, as Vita drained her cup, she searched her mind for another subject. 'We have so much to catch up with. Tell me, how did you escape Londinium? And how did you manage to find me at the hill fort?'

Ven grinned. Saying nothing, he reached down and untied the knot of his loincloth. It slid to the ground without a sound.

And in that moment there was no question in the world that could have seized her curiosity with greater urgency than that of how. Just—*how?*

She fixed her gaze on the fire just beyond him. 'The fire is really going now,' she remarked. 'Just look at the size of those flames!'

An unfortunate choice of words. She glanced at the table, then at the bench, then at the ceiling, as if to study the thatch. When she finally gathered the courage to look into his eyes again, she found them full of mischief.

'Your eyes are green tonight,' he said.

'Impossible.'

He stepped towards her. 'Why impossible?'

'When my eyes are green does it not mean that I am unhappy?'

'Not unhappy, just neglected.'

'Neglected?'

'I believe I can remedy the situation.' He glanced down at himself, inviting her to do the same.

By all the gods in all the heavens. Here he was in his entirety—and more gifted than any fantasy she could possibly conjure. She resolved to count her blessings, or, rather, to count his. He was real and he was all hers. She pulled off her tunic, then slipped beneath the furs.

Ven slipped into bed beside her and gathered her into his arms.

'We have so much to talk about,' she said. 'Tell me, how did you lose the Scythian? Did you travel on foot here? What about your tattoo? How did you find food?'

'Ah, Vita,' he whispered. 'Just kiss me.'

Kiss him? Well, she supposed she could do that. She pressed her lips against his and was instantly surprised. All of the stoic calm he had displayed at their reunion, all of the quiet tenderness of their ride home, all of the gentle playfulness with which he had unclothed himself had disappeared. In its place was a man whose lips were trembling.

They continued to kiss jealously, hungrily, for what must have been a thousand years and, when they finished, Vita realised that her lips were trembling, too.

She had finally accepted that she would never see him again. Months ago, she had tucked his memory away in the deepest corner of her mind and resolved never to retrieve it. She had been certain that the gods were punishing her then and convinced herself it was deserved.

Now, it seemed, the gods had changed their minds, for now she had everything.

'I no longer trust the gods,' she said. He was tracing her lips with his fingers. 'The moment I accepted my fate, they changed it.'

'In that case, perhaps this your reward. You satisfied them.'

'I yearned for you, Ven.'

'You yearned for this,' he said. He enveloped her in

his arms and seemed to breathe her it. 'You yearned for life.'

'If I yearned for life, then life is you,' she replied. 'It is when I am with you that I truly live.'

She could feel his emotion welling up, threatening to overwhelm them both. 'I did not know how long it would take to find you,' he whispered. 'It was as if the best part of me had disappeared. And then today when I saw you...'

His words were clearly failing him and unfortunately so were hers. On their ride from the hill fort, she had squeezed him from behind as if to reassure herself of the truth of him. As the miles passed, shock had been slowly replaced by emotion, until she could not squeeze him tightly enough. Memories flooded back and tears spilled down her cheeks.

Still, it had been so many months since she had seen him and she had long ago learned her lesson about false hope. He had ridden hard, trying to get home before dark. They had not stopped once, not exchanged a single word. There had been no way for her to know if his feelings had changed.

Clearly they had not and a dam seemed to break within her. She had been strong for so long, not letting herself feel anything. Now, as he kissed hungrily down her neck, she realised that she could become human again. She could bury herself in his furs and let her heart melt.

'I will keep you safe,' he cooed. 'From now on.' He caressed her arms. 'Never again will I let you get away.' He closed his eyes and bowed his head as if making a solemn vow, then proceeded to move his hands down her waist. His concentration seemed to deepen as he traced the shape of her hips, then reached around her to grip her bottom.

He pressed his forehead against her stomach. 'It seems that I have dreamed of touching you for so long that I must convince myself you are real,' he said.

'I am real,' she said in Celtic. She ran her fingers through his hair and gently massaged his head.

'Ah, that feels good,' he said. 'But tonight is not about making me feel good.' He moved his head slowly downwards until she could feel his warm breath tickling the soft hairs between her thighs. What was he doing down there?

'Do you remember the massage I gave you at the baths?' he asked.

'I think about it every day.'

'I am going to give you another massage now—one that is going to make you feel even better than the first, but the rules are the same.'

'What rules?'

'You must trust me and you must try to relax. Do you think you can do that?'

Vita laughed nervously. 'I can certainly try.' She did not wish to leave the silence unfilled. 'I remember how relieved the muscles of my back felt after that day. The way you were able to press in beneath my shoulders. Was that a special technique you used? I remember the way you…'

She could not finish her thought, for it seemed that while she was speaking he had slid his tongue between her legs. Had he really just done such a thing? Perhaps she had misapprehended his action. Perhaps that was not his tongue.

No, it was certainly his tongue. But a man's tongue did not belong between a woman's legs. Did it?

In truth, it felt unspeakably good—so good that she could barely sit up on her elbows to voice her concerns. What did he think he was doing? Was he sure about this? And why was it suddenly impossible for her to actually say her questions aloud?

He squeezed her thighs reassuringly and she read his mind. *You must try to relax.*

Right. Yes. Relax. She sucked in a breath, exhaled.

But really, how could she not respond to a thick hot tongue sliding in and out of her? And if she could not speak her words aloud, then why did it seem so easy to moan? It was hard to determine where his tongue ended and her pleasure began. He was caressing her from within, but was evoking something beyond relaxation. It was as if he were undoing something inside of her. She feared she might simply melt into the sheets.

'Oh…' At least she could say that much.

She lay back and concentrated on the thatch, trying not to think. The smoke from the fire wove through the layers of thin branches and it was as if she were one of them. She was utterly helpless as his tongue wove its way languidly around the most intimate parts of her. How did he know how to make her feel this way? What treatise had he read? What scrolls had he studied? Or did it just come naturally, like so many of Ven's gifts? Massage, hunting, fighting and…this.

Though surely what he was doing was forbidden, for nothing legal could possibly feel this good. If only the Roman Governor knew about this, surely he would find a way to tax it. At the very least he would demand tribute from practitioners such as Ven, for what was tribute if not a means to balance the power?

And the power was clearly in Ven's hands, or, more specifically, his tongue. Now its movements were growing faster, more purposeful. They seemed to be stirring something inside her—coaxing her lust. Whatever he had unravelled inside her was being suddenly respooled. It coiled up from her depths like a snake from a basket. It seemed ready to strike.

And then he did something unexpected. He ceased.

He braced himself over her and gazed into her eyes. She had been robbed! She was still throbbing for him. Her lust had become a dull ache. In only a few more moments, he would have pushed her over the edge.

'You wicked man,' she said.

He grinned down at her shamelessly, as if his handsome face and sparkling charisma could somehow make up for his tease. Well, perhaps it could, but she would not make it easy for him.

'You wicked, wicked ma—'

All at once, he thrust his hips forward, continuing to hold her gaze as he pushed himself inside her and... *Oh, sweet Minerva.*

All the gods in all the heavens. What more was there than this? Bliss catapulted through him and his moan was echoed by her own. Could it be that she was already there? He certainly was. He had made love to her many times in his dreams, yet nothing could have prepared him for how he felt just then, as he slid inside her and felt her tight wet heat.

He had lost control of the situation. He had meant to surprise her, to watch her eyes grow wide with sensation. But now a million spears had been hurled into the air and he was trying to outrun them.

He did not have a chance.

He pushed into her again, his control disappearing. He wanted her primally, like the first man who had ever made love to the first woman at the beginning of time. There was only this desire and its resolution—this need that was more powerful than a hundred legions and the mighty queen who could fulfil it.

He held himself outside of her for as long as he could, feeling nothing but want, knowing nothing but the vague regret that he had not brought her to her pleasure. He braved a glance at her. Her back was arched off the mattress.

'Please, Ven, I beg you.'

He had somehow brought her to the precipice. He looked into her eyes. They were flooded with light. She was not just waiting for him, but begging him to go on. He thrust himself into her, not holding back. She cried out, trembled, gripped his shoulders. He thrust into her again and again.

This woman—she was everywhere. Her flesh, her breath, her sweat. He continued to thrust as her howl became a cry that merged with his own and then all at once they were one.

Bliss exploded between them. Primal, divine, eternal. They were ranging through the heavens laughing at the gods, travelling on swift legs that morphed into soft, downy wings.

He collapsed on top of her and buried his head in her hair. There was nothing but this moment. There were no other people in the world but them.

He kissed her again—a long, slow, wondrous kiss for which Ven quietly thanked the gods. He had expected to live out his days in a frozen forest, had never even dreamed that he might wander on to such a warm, windy beach.

'Vita,' he uttered. He switched to the tongue of his truth. 'I love you.'

Chapter Fifteen

The next morning, before Vita had opened her eyes, before she even knew her own name, she knew happiness. She could feel it settled over her like a soft fur. She cuddled against it, wondering how long it might stay. She silently invited it to stay for ever.

She felt his tender lips on her forehead. 'Vita, I must go. Our herd of cattle have broken into one of the Roman hay corrals outside the fort at Condercum. I have been asked to translate and help to resolve the matter.'

Vita's heart sank. 'When will you be back?'

'Certainly before dark. I have told many of the residents about you. I am certain they will welcome you as one of their own.'

'Is there anything you would like me to do while you are gone? For your home, I mean. I would like to make myself useful.'

Ven tucked a piece of her hair behind her ear and looked into her eyes. 'Please do exactly what you like. This is no longer just my home, it is your home also, and I wish for you to be comfortable in it.' Then he was gone.

Vita looked around the empty roundhouse. Her home? A feeling she did not recognise bubbled inside her, a kind of festival inside her heart. It seemed impossible that just a day before she had been labouring in misery in someone else's home. And now she was living in *her* home?

She glanced about the circular space and found everything necessary to make a life: a table and bench for eating, shelves containing cooking supplies, a collection of tools in a small wooden bucket. A hearth, a pot, an axe, a basket. A feathery, warm, impossibly comfortable bed.

Her home.

She dressed herself and put another log on the fire, then arranged the bed furs in a way that pleased her eye. She plucked several items of clothing from various surfaces, folding the clean items and placing the rest in a laundry basket.

She put the pot of goat's milk on the fire to cook and then spied a bag of grain on one of the shelves. She was shaking the grain into the milk when an idea struck. Biscuits! Ven had said that he did not know how to bake. As a slave, she had managed to learn a few recipes, including biscuits. She decided she would surprise Ven with a batch of them.

She ate her breakfast standing up, so enthusiastic she was to begin her day. She decided to do the laundry first and get it hanging, then enquire after the communal oven for her biscuits. Making the dough would be easy, as she had spied a tub of animal fat on Ven's shelves— *their* shelves—as well as a bag of finely ground grain. Perhaps she could even find some early mushrooms to accompany the pastries.

She set off down to the river with her laundry, bouncing as she walked. To do laundry in Rome she would have had to fetch several buckets water from the fountain, then hang it on the roof, a laborious process involving much lifting.

Here in Britannia there was water wherever she turned. Britannia's rivers and streams were like Rome's fountains and aqueducts—only much more beautiful and requiring no maintenance at all. More beautiful still were Britannia's grand, glorious trees—elders, sycamores, yews and gracious old oaks, one of which shaded the sandy beach beside the river where she began her laundry.

As she scrubbed, she turned to admire its ancient, gnarled roots and wise grey bark. It did not surprise her that the Britons held such trees sacred. Crouching now beneath its mighty limbs, she felt as if she were standing beneath the arches of the holiest of temples.

She was halfway through her task when she sensed someone step behind her on the small sand bank.

'You are Ven's woman,' a woman said, startling Vita. 'The slave from the hill fort.'

Vita jumped to her feet. 'I am Vita, yes.' She bowed her greeting. 'Apologies, I did not hear you.'

Vita stood upright, taking in the blonde woman's formidable height. She was wearing a warrior's arm band and several arm tattoos in strange geometrical designs. 'What are you looking at?' barked the woman.

'Apologies,' said Vita. 'I admire your tattoos.'

'They are not for you to admire,' she said. 'And you are not allowed to do laundry in this part of the river.'

Vita gazed down at the small sand bank. A collection of footprints suggested it was often used for such things.

'Apologies,' said Vita. She gathered up her things.

'You speak with an accent,' said the woman. 'A Roman one.' The woman spat on the ground beside Vita's sandal.

Vita stared at the disgusting expulsion for several moments, unsure of what to do. 'I have kin in the north,' Vita said at last.

'Which tribe?'

'The Caledonii.'

The woman spat again—this time beside Vita's other sandal. Vita's heart was beating. She felt as if she had just come upon a bear in the forest. She kept her eyes averted to the ground, waiting for the creature to pass.

Eventually the woman left her alone, thank the gods, and Vita gathered her clothes and returned to the house.

The encounter had disturbed her enough to make her fear going into the settlement, so she busied herself cleaning and organising the small space until Ven returned that evening.

'I have missed you,' she said, embracing him.

'Not half as much as I have missed you,' he said. He searched her eyes. 'There is something wrong. Are you all right?'

'A woman found me beside the river today. She told me I could not do my laundry there. I think she wished to fight.'

'A tall blonde woman?'

'Who is she?'

'The wife of the former leader of this settlement. She lost her husband very recently in a skirmish with the Romans. I am sorry, I should have warned you. There are some members of this settlement who may be hostile to you at first. They know you are under my protection, however, and they will not harm you. They will come to care for you in time. Once earned, a Brigante's affection is for ever.'

He pulled her to him and lifted her skirt. 'Ven!' she gasped.

'I have been thinking about you all day.'

'And I you,' she said. She felt his hands beneath her loincloth, then the gentle heat of his fingers caressing her softly and all her worries seemed to melt away.

'You *have* been thinking about me,' he remarked. A deep, growling sound hummed inside his throat and he pressed her against the wall.

She offered no resistance as he kissed down the front of her neck, then lifted her tunic above her breasts. 'There are so many parts of you I have not yet kissed.'

'You must get to work in that case,' she said. Her laugh became a moan as his mouth moved on to her breast.

She had nothing to which to compare the sensation. Pleasure radiated throughout her body as he softly kissed her flesh.

'This is divine,' she said.

'This is just the beginning.'

He began to caress her nipple with his tongue— slowly, at first, so she could become accustomed to the sensation, then with increasing speed.

'What are you doing to me now?' she asked, as if to suggest it was the first time she had experienced such a thing. 'Oh, gods,' she murmured as he increased the pressure of his tongue. He wondered if, in fact, it was the first time.

He began to knead her other breast with his free hand. She moaned, then sighed, watching him with a half-lidded curiosity. 'Has no man ever done as I am doing?' Ven murmured. She shook her head, as if the question itself puzzled her.

Magnus Furius, he concluded, was not just cruel, he was a fool.

'Relax, my goddess,' he said, as he moved his lips to

her other nipple and watched her head collapse backwards. He had imagined this moment many times, yet he did not envision the pure joy he would take in it.

He wondered how long he could keep himself from her. His desire was already so full that it pained him, but he had vowed not to take his pleasure until he coaxed hers.

He gently removed her loincloth, then lay her down atop his furs and drank in the sight of her: her abundant breasts, her wide hips, her small, round navel.

He marvelled at the shape of her—so very different from his own. Where he had bones and angles, she had curves and flesh. He knew he should not be staring, but the soft forest of curls between her thighs would not release him, nor would a desire so keen he could not order his thoughts.

He straddled her hips. He made a heroic pose and she laughed and her momentary distraction gave him the perfect opportunity to return his attention to her breasts. He gathered them in his hands like flowers.

'I love these,' he admitted.

She sat up on her elbows. 'Then they are yours,' she said.

He buried his head in her cleavage and she shrieked. 'You really do love them, don't you?' she asked.

'They are not of this world.'

'It is strange to think that in another life, we would be enemies.'

'Our tribes would be enemies...but we...' He released her breasts and leaned down to kiss her lips. He wanted all of her right then and he pressed herself against her.

'No, no, no,' she said playfully. She swung her leg around his body and manoeuvred herself on top of him. 'There will be no further lip kisses until my debt is paid.'

She leaned down as if to kiss him, but instead whispered in his ear, 'Please remove your tunic.'

He did as he was told, removing his bothersome tunic and casting it aside. Ah, that was much better. He might have removed his loincloth as well, but he did not wish to alarm her.

'Now turn over and lie on your stomach.'

'My stomach? Are you certain?'

She nodded gravely and he could do nothing but obey. She would certainly change her mind as soon as she saw the scars criss-crossing his back. They terrified any soul who had the misfortune of catching a glimpse of them.

He lay flat on his stomach and waited to hear her gasps of horror, but all he heard was the soft pattering of rain atop the roof.

Then he felt her lips. They moved down the length of his spine in a soft, tender rhythm. 'What are you doing?'

'Kissing your scars.'

'It is a rather large area to cover,' he remarked, though he did not want her to cease.

'I have many kisses stored up inside me,' she said. She moved to the edge of his shoulder and kissed a diagonal line downwards, placing the last kiss at the top of his hip. Moving to the middle of his back, she placed another line of kisses along the edge of his shoulder blade. She seemed to be following the scars themselves, as if tracing the story of his misery.

And somehow, changing the ending.

By the time she was done, he was yearning to hold her. He twisted to the side and reached behind him, but she remained seated firmly astride his buttocks. 'That was divine,' he said, trying to coax her back to the bed, but she refused him.

'That was just the beginning.' She reached for something on the bedstand and soon he felt drops of thick liquid being scattered over his skin. 'Try to relax,' she said.

He could feel the delight in her fingertips as she began to knead his weary shoulders. Each of her gentle squeezes seemed to release some hidden demon, while each of her soft caresses seemed to banish it for ever. 'You have never received a massage, have you?' she asked.

'Not ever,' he admitted.

'And yet you give them to others all the time.' She moved her hands down the long muscles of his back.

She worked with a methodical tenacity, kneading the bands of muscle in alternating columns. He could feel her concentration, could sense the generosity in each sweep of her hand. She wanted to make him feel as good as he had made her feel at the baths. To pay her debt.

He feared she was paying it back with interest. Her touch was gentle, but so very precise. She found the tiny knots beneath his shoulder blades with the instincts of a hunter. She pressed those knots and held them, willing them away. He nearly shouted with ecstasy.

'You are rather good at this,' he said.

'I had a rather good teacher.'

She worked her way down the length of his back until reaching the crest of his buttocks where she paused. He held his breath and waited, wondering and also fearing what she might do next. 'I am the baker and you are the bread,' she chided, then began kneading him in lavish round strokes.

He chuckled softly, unsure what was funnier, the fact that a Roman woman was currently kneading his buttocks or the fact that he was enjoying it so much.

Then he felt the soft dribble of oil on his upper thighs. She slid her soft fingers down between his legs and touched his desire. His breath caught as she stroked him gently and whatever relaxation she had coaxed in him quickly came to an end.

Angst swelled inside him. Something else swelled, too—nearly to the point of pain. He wanted to have her right then, but he could not, for her hands were now completely wrapped around him.

Lust raced through him. 'Be careful, Vita,' he warned. 'You are driving me mad.' He reached for her and this time she did not resist. She tumbled on to the mattress beside him, laughing wickedly.

'May I do this, Vita?' he asked. He was already untying his loincloth. 'It will be very fast.'

'Yes,' she breathed. 'I want you, Ven. Please.'

He moved astride her and in a single motion he was with her. He plunged into her depths, wanting to bring her along with him, but feeling as if he were already losing himself.

This woman—she was everything. He felt it with each thrust, with each gasp. He could not stop for her. He could not even slow down. This was the end of the world and its beginning. Every second was a sensation. Every sensation was not enough.

'Vita,' he gasped, but he had already taken off into the air, catapulted towards his own undoing. Then he was there, reaching the crest, an explosion of ecstasy, followed by a cascading fallout of bliss.

He slumped over her—equally helpless in his descent. Icarus himself falling out of the heavens. 'That was selfish,' he mumbled. 'I am sorry.'

She was staring up at him with eyes of adoration and it occurred to him that he did not deserve this woman, this moment. He did not merit feeling this cursedly happy, and yet…he would take it.

He was a starving man given manna from heaven. He would not question it. He would not push it away, not any more. He would accept it humbly, gratefully. He had been starving for so long; now, finally, he would eat.

Her hair was hanging across her face in the manner of a siren. He reached out and moved it behind her ear. 'Gods, your eyes,' he said, 'they remind me of—'

But she would not let him finish, for she was pressing her lips against his.

They made love once more that evening before dinner, then again afterwards—a long, slow congress followed by the most wondrous sleep Vita had ever known.

When she awoke the next morning, she felt changed, as if a part of him remained with her.

It was at once glorious and unnerving. Each time they made love she felt closer to him. When he told her he would be gone again that day she felt strangely bereft. She needed to do something to occupy her mind—some project to help her return to herself. Then she remembered—the biscuits!

She would make a dough and then venture out into the settlement in search of the communal oven. She would introduce herself to as many people as she could find and do her best to make a good impression.

It would be a way she could erase yesterday's strange encounter with the tall woman and begin again. She would not be afraid. She was under Ven's protection after all. She would show this group of Brigantes that not all Romans were wicked, and, when Ven returned, she would not only have delicious biscuits to share, but a story of her triumphant day.

She made up her dough and placed it in a cloth, which she set inside a small handled pot. Thinking again, she pinched off a small piece of dough and hurried down to the stream, where she placed it beneath the oak tree and asked for protection. Finally, she set out towards the central cluster of roundhouses.

Built around an open area in which several chickens ran free, the centre of the settlement reminded her very much of the Brigante hill fort, but smaller. Hearth smoke emanated through the thatch roofs of the low round-houses and several loose sheep meandered about, but there was nobody to be seen anywhere.

'Hello?' Vita called, but no one emerged to greet her.

She heard the sound of bleating emanating from a barn and stepped inside to discover a rather desperate-looking goat with an udder swollen to the size of her own head. Setting her dough on a small table, Vita put her pot down beneath the crying animal and began to milk.

'What are you doing there?' shouted a voice from behind her.

She turned to discover an old man leaning heavily on a cane. 'That is my goat and you do not have per-mission to milk her,' he said. He pointed his cane men-acingly at Vita.

'Apologies, sir. It is just that she was in pain. I could not bear to hear her cries. Here is the milk.' Vita stood and held out the bucket to the old man. 'I am Vita. I have recently come to live with Ven. It is nice to meet you.'

The man glared and Vita. 'They say you are a slave of the hill fort chieftain.'

'I was a slave,' said Vita, 'but now I am free.'

'Not free,' said the old man. 'If Ven bought you, then you are his slave now.'

'I beg your pardon, sir. I am not his slave. I am his...' What was she, then? His lover? His good friend? His Roman curiosity?

'You are certainly not a Brigante,' observed the man.

'I am certainly not a slave.'

'Get out of my barn.'

Vita hurried past him, fearful of the cane, which he seemed to wield rather like a sword. When she emerged from the barn she was near to tears. She poured out the goat's milk on to the ground, scattering a group of chickens and drawing the attention of a girl stepping out of one of the homes.

'Why did you do that?' she asked Vita.

'Do what?'

'Pour out that goat's milk?' Vita read innocence in the girl's expression.

'It was…tainted,' explained Vita. She walked towards the girl, determined not to lose faith. 'I am Vita,' she said, bowing politely. 'It is lovely to meet you.'

'Are you the slave from Rome?'

'I am no longer a slave,' Vita clarified, 'but, yes, I am from Rome.'

'What is it like?' asked the girl.

'Well, it is very crowded.'

'How crowded?'

'About a million souls,' said Vita. The girl cocked her head. 'It is so crowded that they do not allow carts in the city during the day. Do you know why that is?'

'Why?'

'Because so many people fill the streets that there is not enough room for them!'

The girl's mouth hung agape.

'How many people live here, in your settlement?' Vita asked.

The girl looked at her fingers, then held them up. 'This many people, three times.'

'You mean thirty.'

The girl nodded shyly.

'And how long have you and your kin lived here?'

'Since I was a baby. There are excellent grazing grounds just down the river.' The girl pointed towards the river and Vita turned to peer through the trees.

'Ah, yes, I think I see them,' she said, but when she turned back to address the girl, she was no longer alone. A short, large-chested woman stood behind her, her arms braced on her formidable waist.

'Can I help you?'

'No—ah, yes. I am Vita.' Vita gave a deep bow.

'I know,' the woman said. 'What do you want?'

'Ah, I was just looking for an oven. I wish to bake some biscuits.'

'No oven here, I am afraid,' said the woman. 'You would have to go back to the hill fort.' The girl turned to the woman as if to protest, but the woman shot her a look.

'Thirty souls and no communal oven?' Vita asked.

'Not a one.'

'But the hill fort is more than ten miles from here.'

The girl tugged at her mother's sleeve. 'Mother, what is a mile?'

'It is the way the Romans measure how much territory they have conquered, Armea,' the woman replied, then spat on the ground. She narrowed her eyes at Vita.

Vita bowed her head. 'Well, thank you anyway,' she said. 'It was nice to…' she continued, but the girl and her mother had already disappeared behind the door.

Turning back towards Ven's house, Vita glanced down at her pot. Curses, she had left her dough in the barn.

Turning back towards the barn, she spotted the old man standing at its entrance. She could not give up now.

She just needed to be friendly, to show the old man her good intentions.

She started towards him. 'May I retrieve what I left inside? It is a round of dough. For biscuits. Do you like biscuits?'

'This is not your barn,' he said, though he seemed to be speaking of something more than the barn. 'Go home, Roman.'

Vita felt a little piece of her heart break as she bowed and conceded defeat. She returned to Ven's roundhouse on feet made of lead and lay in bed for a long while. As a slave at the hill fort, no one had questioned her right to go about her day. She had been merely invisible: not a threat, but a tool. Now that her status had changed, she seemed to have become an enemy.

She should have anticipated it. She represented everything that the Brigantes hated—a free Roman woman with roots in a rival tribe. She was as suspicious as the legions currently amassing at the forts of Coria and Vindolanda. As long as the Romans had its army in the north, she feared she would not be accepted.

The old sibyl's words echoed through her mind. *'There are many kinds of prison.'*

Arriving home, she put a pot of water on the fire and tossed in a handful of grain. She added some dried vegetables and a bit of fat, along with some salted venison and herbs.

By the time Ven stepped through the door flap that evening, the roundhouse had filled with a rich aroma.

He flashed her a lusty grin. 'I am starving and that smells divine.' Her mood instantly lifted. He crossed to where she stood over the fire and peered into the pot. 'Who says you cannot cook?'

'Perhaps my cooking improves the further I travel north.'

'Perhaps your cooking improves in proportion to how well you are loved.' He stood behind her and wrapped his arms around her waist. 'I missed you today,' he said. He kissed down her neck, causing her whole body to radiate with heat. Inside she was beginning to feel a bit like the soup.

'How was your day?' she asked.

'Not good, I am afraid.' Ven crossed to the bench and began to remove his boots. 'The Roman soldiers refused to release the Brigante cattle. The chiefs are furious. There is talk of an attack on the legion stationed at Eboracum, a five-day ride to the south of here.'

Vita stared into her soup. She knew nothing about war and battle, but she did know that few tribes in history had ever defeated the Roman army. 'It would be a waste of Brigante lives,' she said.

'That is what I tried to tell them, but they did not heed my words.'

'Are you not uniquely situated to give good advice about Romans?'

'There are a few who do not trust me. Some of the Brigante warriors think that I am secretly working on the side of the Romans.'

'They think you are a spy? But why?'

'Because I speak like a Roman and act like a Roman and I...'

'You live with a Roman,' said Vita. Her heart sank.

'You must know that it is not your fault, Vita. Every day their lands grow more threatened. Governor Nepos has been demanding more tribute from the tribes. Often he sends whole centuries to collect it. They humiliate the chiefs and inflict needless violence.'

Vita nodded. It was as if he were not describing Rome's behaviour, but Magnus's. 'You are indispensable to your tribe right now,' she said. 'You know that, do you not?'

'I know,' said Ven, exhaling. He shook his head. 'A friend once told me that a man is how he makes his life. I have come to like who I am in recent days. This life, my tribe, you—it feels right.'

Vita's heart filled with joy. It seemed that her love had found his purpose and was finally beginning to forgive himself.

'Come now, darling,' Ven said, brightening. 'Tell me about your day. Give me some good news.'

'Well, I nearly fetched us some goat's milk,' she said cheerfully, 'and I almost made us some biscuits.'

'Almost?' Vita smiled, though she knew Ven could see through her façade. 'The house has certainly never looked better,' he observed.

Vita looked around, feeling bored. There was only so much cleaning and folding and tidying she could do.

She fetched a bowl and spooned some soup into it. 'I was thinking I would explore the forest tomorrow,' she said, 'consult with the oaks, you know, perhaps gather a few mushrooms.' She crossed to Ven and placed the bowl on the table beside him, but he showed no interest in it. He frowned at the doorway.

'Please just keep to the settlement for now, Vita—at least until this business with the cattle is over. There are angry tribesmen roaming about. I would not want…'

Vita sat down beside him and placed her hand on his. 'I understand that it will take time,' she said. 'I am patient.'

He stared into her eyes, then took her face in his hands and kissed her more tenderly than he had ever done. Feeling bold, she let her tongue slide sensually into his mouth.

'Gods, Vita,' he breathed, deepening the kiss. Soon their tongues were sparring and Ven's hand was reaching slowly up her skirt.

Days ago, she might have stiffened with nerves, or played coy, but now she opened her legs invitingly. 'What are you doing to me?' he growled into her ear. He lifted her up and carried her to the bed.

'What about dinner?' she protested.

'It is not soup I hunger for any more.'

It is me, she thought in wonder. *Me.*

The next morning when she awoke, he was already putting on his boots. 'I agreed to help a kinsman clear a field and there is still the matter of the cows. I will be back before dusk.'

Vita glowed with pride for her strong, honourable Brigante, yet she was already bereft. 'Be safe,' she said feebly. She followed him out to his horse.

'Ah, I nearly forgot!' he said. He reached in his saddle bag and held up an object so small she could barely see it. 'It is a gift for you.'

'What is it?'

'It is a needle and thread—for your sewing.'

Vita gazed at the wondrous instrument, her heart filling with gratitude. 'Really?'

'My cousin procured it for me. A small but mighty spear.' He winked at her and her stomach did a flip. 'And there is something else—just a moment.' He dug inside the saddle bag to produce a thick mound of green wool.

He heaved it into her arms and she instantly felt its fine quality. 'How did you come by this beautiful cloth?'

'I traded a fur for it.'

Vita was near to tears. 'How can I ever thank you for this, Ven? It is wonderful! You are wonderful!'

'Not wonderful, darling, just in love.' He kissed her hard, then swung up into the saddle and in seconds he was gone.

Vita had filled that day with sewing. And the next. And also the next and she was content. Soon they settled into a comfortable rhythm. Ven would leave in the morning to attend to tribal business and Vita would remain at the house, keeping herself busy.

The needle and thread were her solace; the woollen fabric her muse. She contrived to sew a cape so beautiful that the people of the settlement could not help but give her a chance. It would be for the girl she had met that first day—little Armea. A green wrap to warm her small shoulders. A peace offering.

Meanwhile, Vita discreetly kept to their house, choosing the hour just before dark for trips to the river. She managed not to encounter a single soul.

If her days were sober and solitary, her evenings were filled with untold delights. She sensed that Ven was unique among men, not just for his admirable gifts, but for his insatiable desire to use them.

It was as if he had sealed up all of his lust for her in a wine amphora and had finally broken the wax. Vita could drink as much as she liked.

Fortunately, she had a healthy thirst. She had begun to learn his body and how she could please it, delighting in every small discovery she made. He was always overjoyed by her efforts, often rather vocally so, and seemed not to begrudge her lack of experience.

Besides, she was gaining experience quite rapidly now. By summer she would surely be an expert, for they could not seem to get enough of each other. She never felt more alive than in his presence. When he was gone, her body missed his. It did not matter what she was doing, she always found her thoughts drifting to her tall, strong barbarian warrior with that dangerous look in his eye.

It seemed that he thought of her, too. He always brought her things from his travels. A feather here or a pretty stone there. He would present his gifts as an after-thought, however, usually the following morning, be-cause when he saw her at the end of a day all he wished to do was kiss and touch.

It was almost shameful the way they carried on. On the bed. On the table. On a nearby patch of grass. There were many nights when dinner went uneaten, news un-shared and words unspoken because their bodies had far more urgent business.

And yet it was not only their bodies that seemed to be converging. Each time they made love, Vita felt as if she gave him another piece of her heart. She sensed that he was giving her pieces of his in return and she grate-fully accepted them, not believing it could be true—that a man as good and noble as he could find her worthy of his love.

But there it was, all around her, even when he was not near. It seemed to fortify her, to root her in the ground, and somehow also to send her flying. Part of her did not care if she ever saw another living soul again as long as she had this wondrous man by her side.

And by the gods, she was going to make him biscuits.

One morning after he had left, she dug a hole in the ground and lined it with stones. She poured a dozen smouldering coals into the hole, covering them with a long plank lined with sticky rounds of dough. She topped her invented oven with another long plank and in less than an hour she had the most delicious biscuits she had ever tasted.

Setting aside Ven's portion of biscuits, she took the rest and divided them into two bundles. She placed the bundles in the doorways of the old man she had encountered and also the mother and the daughter. Surely they would appreciate a little sustenance and would know that Vita meant well. She settled into her sewing for the rest of the afternoon, congratulating herself for her neighbourliness.

That night when Ven returned, he wore a look of puzzlement.

'What is it?' Vita asked.

'Did you see the outside of the house? It appears as if we have been pelted with a rain of biscuits.'

Stepping outside, Vita saw her biscuits in pieces all over the dirt. A few still clung to the clay siding, like ugly smears of plaster on a wall that would always be cracked. She broke down in tears. 'They loathe me, Ven.'

'They do not loathe you, they just loathe Romans. I am not even a Roman and still they do not trust me.'

'But I *am* a Roman!' She glanced at him in his long woollen trousers and dyed blue shirt. His hair had grown so long that it hung about his head in ropes. He was a Brigante through and through. It was she who did not belong. 'What am I going to do? I am not wanted here. My life is so endangered that I cannot even roam the forest. I cannot do as I like. I cannot be free.'

Ven shook his head. 'Tell me, what is the one thing that is more valuable than silver or gold?'

'I do not know. Nothing.'

'Silver and gold together, remember? Electrum. That is what you are. Roman and barbarian. You see both sides just like me—a diplomat. You must not forget your own value. You can help these people just as much as I can.'

Vita gazed at the destroyed biscuits. 'It appears that my diplomacy is now fodder for the birds.'

'Come inside now,' Ven urged, ushering her away from the mess. 'I wish for you to show me what you have sewn today. And what is that smell? The gods themselves could not cook so well.'

The next morning, Vita awoke to discover Ven gone. Outside, his horse remained hitched, indicating that he had not gone far. Vita took a moment to pet the old mare's long face, then caught sight of Ven striding back from the middle of the settlement. His eyes flickered with rage.

'What is wrong?'

'Roman soldiers from the fort at Coria have slaughtered our herd.'

'What?'

'Last night. There was a large feast at the fort. They killed all twenty cows. Fed the entire fort. The chieftains are on the edge of war. I must fly to the hill fort now and try to stop something terrible from happening. I may be gone for several days. Will you be all right?'

'Of course,' said Vita, biting her tongue. *Please do not leave me here alone.*

What a selfish thought. Ven was trying to prevent a war and all she could think about was a few grumpy neighbours. Still, there was a knot forming in her stomach and a deep foreboding overtook her. She feared she would not see him again.

'Please be careful,' she said. 'If there is violence, do not involve yourself.'

He placed his four-horned saddle on top of his mare. 'I hope to prevent it before it can take place.'

He was such a good man, the noblest in all of Britannia, and she needed him to know what was in her heart.

'Ven?'

'Yes, dear?'

'You are the best of men. I mean, you are my best man.'

She shook her head in frustration. He laughed gently and kissed her lips. 'And you are my best woman. You are also my only woman. Always will be.'

He mounted his mare and gave her a kick.

'Wait! Ven!' she shouted. He was riding away from her. Soon he would be gone. 'I love you!' she shouted. She saw him turn and grin.

And she never saw her barbarian warrior again.

Chapter Sixteen

When Vita awoke that night, the roof was ablaze. She jumped out of bed and found herself coughing amid heavy smoke. She could hear the menacing roar of the flames above her and saw the red of flames beginning to penetrate the roof.

She dashed around the house, gathering as many of Ven's belongings as she could until she heard a loud pop. She rushed away from falling embers as the roof collapsed above her, trying to keep her panic at bay. Ven had very few things to call his own and could not afford to lose any of them. She had to save as much as she could.

She lunged about, keeping her eye on the roof, the flames her only light. She scooped up clothes, tools, food, furs—anything that could fit into her arms—and threw them into a pile outside the door.

Her sewing! She ran back inside and grabbed her basket of fabric just as a blazing timber came crashing to the floor.

Vita threw herself from the collapsing building and rolled on to the ground. The fire was growing in strength and she stood alone, watching the flames consume everything. Nobody from the settlement came to her aid, though surely they could smell the smoke. She was all alone.

How could this have happened? What wicked god had decided to destroy her small, fragile world, just as they were beginning to make it her own? His world. Theirs.

Vita searched her memory, trying to determine how she had failed. She had completely squelched the hearth fire that evening and had not even lit a lamp. There was simply no source within the small roundhouse that could have produced such a dangerous blaze. Besides, if she had started the fire herself, the house would have been burning from within, not without.

It did not make sense. Vita stalked about the yard, searching for clues. Finding nothing, she started towards the settlement and gasped. It appeared that the fire was spreading. Three small blazes raged right in the middle of the very road.

Vita ran to put them out, then realised that they had nothing to do with a spreading blaze. They were not fires, but dropped torches.

She felt ill. She could imagine the wicked souls who had utilised them, their guilty shadows escaping back to the settlement whence they came. She picked up a torch and peered into the shadows.

Ven's house had not caught on fire, it had been set on fire, likely by three of Ven's own kin. They had waited until Ven was away. They had probably been planning it for days.

They did not want her there. It did not matter how hard she tried. She would always be Roman and they would always be Brigante. Their hatred for her went back nearly a hundred years, when the late Emperor Claudius first called this land his own. It was not going to change with kind words and biscuits.

She felt a hand tap her shoulder and turned to discover the old man from the barn. His wrinkly eyes danced beneath the torchlight. 'If you are not gone by tomorrow, you are a dead woman,' he whispered softly. He glanced behind him. Several figures stood just beyond the flames, quiet as ghosts. 'Leave this settlement now or lose your life,' one said.

The old man yanked the torch from her hand and she watched him and the other figures march back to the settlement by its eerie light.

She was not going to cry. She would not pity herself or wallow in her powerlessness. Nor would she blindly brush the incident aside, hoping things would get better. She had done that for years back in Rome. It was a dangerous thing, acceptance.

She found a piece of hide and spread it out upon the ground. She would not ask Ven to fight for her. He had bigger things on his mind, like saving Brigante lives and preventing a war. She would not ask him to take her side in this or in anything else.

But she would be a fool to continue to live a life in which she could not leave her home, or speak with her neighbours, or go and explore the forest in safety and peace. She could not let her soul wither as she had allowed it to do back in Rome. In another year, there would be none of her left.

She began to place small necessities at the centre of the hide: biscuits, a knife, a loincloth. Vita loved Ven more than she had ever loved anyone, but how could she live with him in this dangerous, threatening place? She added more supplies: a flintstone, a drying cloth, a hairbrush, more biscuits.

She was not safe and could not even be in charge of her own life. Ven had liberated her—that was true—but as long as she lived in fear, she never would be truly free.

She laughed bitterly. It seemed that she had chosen happiness over freedom once again, without even knowing it. *'Seek your freedom first,'* the old sibyl had told her. *'Everything else will come.'* Perhaps it was her destiny to live the lesson over and over again until she finally learned it.

Vita spotted her basket of sewing. She pulled the needle from the fabric and admired it. *'A small but mighty spear,'* Ven had called it. How dear he had been to obtain it for her. How hard he had tried to help her get free from her invisible prison.

Holding the needle between her teeth, she placed the fabric on top of her other belongings, then gathered the hide around them into a neat, portable ball. She sensed her life repeating itself as she secured the makeshift travel bag with a knot.

Locating the shovel, she dug a shallow hole beneath a nearby tree and placed all of Ven's belongings inside. She covered the pile with his collection of furs, which she secured in place with rocks. She knew he would not be home for many days and she wished to protect his things from damage.

The moonlight poured over the makeshift cache and she stared at it for a long while, her body trembling. Impulsively, she pulled the last fur off the pile.

She knew he would not mind. He would want her to be warm on her journey, though warmth was not the reason she wrapped it around her shoulders. She wanted it so she could be reminded of him always.

Because she was leaving him.

There are many kinds of prisons, the old sibyl had

warned her, and then Grandmother had warned her again. Freedom was the prize and so Vita sheathed her small, mighty spear and lifted her leather bag, then strode off into the darkness.

It was raining the day Ven journeyed home from the hill fort and he was smiling like a fool. He was returning home to his love after all—his own beautiful Vesta, the keeper of his flame—and could not get his mare to run quickly enough.

He shook out his wet hair and grinned up at the sky. He thought of Vita whenever it rained like this. 'This reminds me of the day we met,' he would always tell her. It had become a kind of jest between them, for it rained most days in this part of the world. Whenever it would begin to pour, he would peer outside and say, 'This reminds me of…'

'…the day we met,' she would always finish. It was their private joke. He never got tired of it.

The rain had stopped by the time he reached the settlement, though Ven was soaked to the bone. He could not wait to step inside their little house and see her scolding grin. 'You are a wet rat!' she would say and he would lift her off the ground and kiss her well.

At first he thought that the blackened ground was an illusion of the light. He encouraged his mare closer, confused. Had he taken a wrong turn? He glanced back to the settlement and observed the road in its usual position. He was in the right place, but his house was not. It was gone. It was…burned. *Vita.*

He wheeled his horse around and charged back into the settlement. 'Where is she? he shouted. 'What happened?'

He did not know who answered him. There seemed

to be a chorus of voices speaking to him from far away. 'We do not know what happened,' they told him. 'We do not know where she is.'

'My house is burned, my woman is gone and nobody knows what happened?'

'We are sorry,' they said. 'Truly sorry.'

'Vita!' he bellowed. He galloped back to the burn, fell from his horse and lost his stomach. Had she been killed? *Gods, no. Please.* Ven gazed up at the heavens. 'Mighty gods, I will do anything you ask, just tell me she lives.'

He rushed around the burn, nearly sightless with despair. There was no sign of her demise, thank the gods. Glancing towards the forest, he noticed a pile of furs beneath a tree. He rushed towards them, fearing the worst, but when he lifted them he discovered nearly all his belongings.

He searched through the pile for her sewing. He knew that if she had left on her own volition, she would have taken her sewing with her. His heart clenched as he sifted through his things, praying he would not catch sight of the thick green fabric attached to a silvery needle. After searching for a long while, he collapsed into the mud and wept.

She was alive.

For some reason, she had left him. He thought back to the last thing she had said to him before he had ridden away: *I love you.*

He did not understand. Why did she leave? What terrible circumstances had compelled her to abandon the man she loved? He could not waste his time thinking about it now. He would soon find out because he would soon find her.

He searched the site for her footprints, but they had

been washed away by the rain. Surely she had headed towards the road. Once there, there were only two directions in which she could have turned: north or south. If north, she would have headed for Caledonia, her mother's homeland. If south, she would have either headed for the Roman fort at Coria, where Lepidus was stationed, or the closer Roman fort of Vindolanda. Both places were less than a day's travel south on horseback.

Ven returned to his mare, his heart beating. He had to find Vita before she reached one of the two forts. Brigantes were not welcome inside such places—especially ones concealing former Roman slave tattoos.

Ven did not wish to consider the other possibility: that she had headed even further south. It was a five-day carriage ride south to the Roman fort at Eboracum, the largest Roman fort in the province, and five days more to Londinium, its greatest city. If she sought sanctuary in either of those cities, she would be much more difficult to discover.

Ven gathered his breath and tried to stay calm. He would find her—that was all that mattered. He was a hunter, after all. Sooner or later he would catch the woman he loved.

He gathered his furs, mounted his mare and made his way south towards Coria, searching behind every tree and stone.

He had reached Coria's sprawling fort at nightfall and slept fitfully beneath a waning moon. The next morning, he asked discreetly after Lepidus's residence and waited outside its walls. Eventually a tall young man emerged wearing fresh bruises on his cheeks. Ven described Vita and asked the young man if he had seen her.

'I have not seen her,' he vowed. 'I am sorry, sir.' He would not meet Ven's gaze.

'If you tell me the truth, I will give you a fur,' Ven promised, but the young man only shook his head. 'I am begging you,' said Ven. He lifted his leather cap and revealed his slave's tattoo. 'You may trust me. I was a slave for your master for many years.'

Finally, the young man looked Ven in the eye and Ven spotted the wetness of recent tears. 'I know who you are,' he whispered back.

'You know me?' asked Ven.

'You are all my *dominus* speaks of: a tall man with green eyes and a forehead tattoo. He beats me because I am not you. He has set a large reward for your return.'

Ven stepped backwards, stunned. 'Will you betray me, then?' Ven asked. 'Collect the reward for yourself?' He gave the young man a glance. His legs were nearly as long as Ven's.

'I am a Parisi,' the young man stated.

'Our tribes are enemies, then,' said Ven.

The young man shook his head. 'Do not fear, I will not betray you.'

Ven nearly embraced him. He placed his finest fur in the young man's arms and gave him a grateful bow. 'Sell this fur and when the time is right, leave him,' he said. 'Promise me.'

Then Ven disappeared from the *vicus* of Coria like a shadow in the midday sun.

He arrived in Vindolanda before midday. He sneaked into the settlement without detection and discreetly asked after Vita, but none had seen her. He considered waiting for the local tavern to open, then thought better of it. He had a terrible suspicion that she had headed south to the much larger fort of Eboracum. If he left now, he might still be able to apprehend her on the road.

On his way south, Ven peered into the windows of every carriage he passed, and when he arrived at the sprawling settlement of Eboracum, he did not even stop to eat.

For days he canvased the streets outside the fort, searching the eyes of pedestrians. He spoke to every shop owner and carriage driver he could find. He lingered outside the bath house, watching the legionaries come and go. Sometimes, he would stop them. 'Excuse me, but I am looking for a woman,' he would say.

'Aren't we all?' they would reply with a laugh.

Soon it was on to Londinium. There he lingered outside the public latrines and lurked around the marketplaces. 'Have you seen a short, round woman with brown-green eyes speaking the accent of Rome? She sells capes.' He repeated the query perhaps a hundred times a day and always the answer was the same.

He bribed every tavern owner he could find, growing desperate. 'There is another *denarius* for you if you can lead me to her,' he promised. He waited and waited for news to surface until all his furs and his *denarii* were gone.

He made his way back north into the forest outside Eboracum. He did not wish to linger in Londinium, but nor did he wish to return to his people in the north. He could not face his kinsmen, whom he now felt certain had driven Vita away. He knew that if he returned to the hill fort, he would be quickly consumed by his duty to his tribe.

He was standing in the middle of the island of Britannia, caught between duty and despair. He was neither here nor there. He could not decide where to search for Vita next.

'Where did you say you came from?' the young woman asked Vita. She could not have been older than fifteen, though the scar on her face suggested those years had been long.

'Rome,' Vita said.

'You do not look like you are from Rome.' The young woman glanced at the fur around Vita's shoulders. 'What is that?'

Vita blinked, feeling the stir of emotion. 'It is all I have left of him.'

The young woman frowned. 'Avidia!' she shouted. 'There is a woman here looking for work. Seems a bit mad. Says she is from Rome.'

'Can she cook?' a familiar voice called back.

'Hardly at all,' Vita shouted in return.

There was a gasp, then the sound of a crashing pot. A woman rushed out from behind the wall wearing a grin as wide as she was tall. 'Vita!'

'Avidia!'

The two embraced, paused to behold one another, then embraced again. 'The gods are great,' Vita said.

'They are indeed, for they have delivered you to my doorstep,' replied Avidia. 'I have hoped for this day for a long while, never believing it would actually come to pass.'

'Nor can I believe it!' Vita gazed into her friend's eyes, which were clearer than she had ever seen them. Her cheeks seemed rosier, as well, and there was an uncharacteristic lightness to her voice.

'But how do you find yourself here, dear Avidia, at this grassy edge of the world?'

Avidia turned to the young woman. 'Gislinde, put out the closed sign and lock the door, then see yourself out. You have the day off today and the tavern will be closed. I need to catch up with an old friend.'

'Yes, madam,' said Gislinde, shooting Vita an apologetic nod. Avidia produced two cups from behind the bar and set them out.

'It is like not time has passed,' Vita remarked—except that Avidia did not produce an amphora of wine. Instead she filled each cup with milk from a goatskin bag. She held her own cup high. 'A toast to two poor women from the Aventine who got themselves free! Hear, hear!'

'Hear, hear!' Vita echoed, and drank down her cup. It tasted almost as good as the goat's milk that Ven had warmed for her just days ago. Almost.

'Sit down now, Vita,' Avidia said, beckoning to the bar stool. Vita gazed at the high-legged obstacle as if it were an un-mountable horse. 'Go ahead,' urged Avidia, laughing. Giving herself a running start, Vita jumped up on to the high stool.

Avidia laughed riotously. 'You have not changed, dear Vita.' She pulled up a stool. 'Now tell me how you landed in my tavern on this lovely day of spring.'

'A priest!' said Vita.

'Is it not always a priest?'

'On the road to Eboracum. He stopped his cart for me and told me that Eboracum was in danger of a raid. He offered to bring me north to Vindolanda instead.'

'I know the man,' Avidia proclaimed. 'Drinks here regularly. He was coming to make a sacrifice to Ceres, yes? To protect the new granaries for the fort?'

'Exactly!' said Vita. 'He mentioned a woman from the Aventine had recently opened a tavern here. I hardly dared to hope.'

'So the benevolent gods did indeed guide your path.'

'I had not thought of it that way,' said Vita. 'Since when did you believe in the benevolence of the gods?'

'Since I opened my own tavern and paid off all my debts,' Avidia said with a twinkle.

'But why open a tavern here, outside a military fort?' asked Vita. 'Why not one of those busy tourist towns in southern Gaul?'

'A wise woman once reminded me that not everyone can cook—and especially not soldiers.' She shot Vita a significant look, then gazed into her cup. 'I do not even remember your visit on the day of the Vulcanalia. When I finally awoke, the owner of the tavern told me that you had come in need of aid. I could not forgive myself for failing you, so I vowed to pay my debts and try to find you.'

'But how?'

'It was the Massilian wine you gave me. I did not drink another drop of it. Instead I sold it slowly to deep-pocketed clients. It took me a month, but I was able to pay what I owed the tavern owner and pocket enough for my travel.'

'But how did you know where to look for me?' asked Vita.

'I went to your home. A rather pregnant young woman answered the door.'

'Lollia,' Vita said. 'My husband's lover.'

'I thought so,' said Vita. 'I asked her where you had gone and she said she did not know—only that your husband Magnus had requested your departure.'

'That is one way of putting it,' said Vita.

'I tried to depart myself, but she would not let me go. She said that she had not been to the baths for days and that she dearly wished to gossip, so I stayed and listened while she unburdened herself to me.'

Vita grinned. 'About what exactly?'

'Men!' laughed Avidia. 'She said that they were wretched creatures and not worth the leather of their sandals. She described her husband, Lepidus, who had recently left her for the Roman fort of Coria.'

'But what did you do when you did not find me in Coria?'

'I decided to look for work. Someone told me that there was another fort a day's journey away from Coria that dearly needed a tavern. I suppose the rest is history.'

Vita looked around at the small timber building. 'How did you find coin to rent such a place?'

'My cooking, of course! The prefect who oversees the fort was in need of a proper Roman cook. I sold my services to his family and was able to save enough to pay my first month. I still cook for them sometimes and he keeps quiet about the tavern, drinking being forbidden to soldiers,' she said with a wink.

'You kept yourself free,' said Vita wistfully.

'You speak as if you did not.'

'It has been a bit of a challenge for me,' Vita said, then told her tale of hardship and woe. By the end of it Avidia was near to tears.

'You were enslaved.'

'It was not for long. The Brigantes treat their slaves better than the Romans do. I was not beaten or humiliated. I always had enough to eat and a blanket to keep warm.'

'Did you escape?'

'I was rescued by a man.'

Avidia grinned. 'A certain tall, strong barbarian-warrior type who goes by the name of Ven?'

Vita nodded.

'You are welcome to tell me that I am a genius,' said Avidia.

'You are a genius,' said Vita, raising her glass.

'But where is the man? Let us pour him a drink, by the gods!'

Vita felt her stomach twist into a knot. She forced a resolute grin. 'I had to leave him. His tribe would not accept me, you see. My life was in danger.' Vita stared at the wooden beams of the roof, imagining them ablaze. 'I fear I have nowhere to go,' she whispered.

Avidia tossed her curls. 'Well it just so happens that we are in need of a new waitress. You would not happen to speak any Tungrian, would you?'

Gratitude flooded into Vita's heart. 'I am afraid I was ill the day my *grammaticus* taught Tungrian,' she said. 'But what I lack in Tungrian I make up for in dumplings.'

Avidia leaned against the bar, as if to prevent herself from fainting.

'I have triumphed over them, Avidia! I have also conquered stew and mastered bread. And biscuits! Just a few days ago, I made Ven an excellent batch of biscuits...'

An unwanted memory pulsed into her mind and she could not blink back her tears. Moments slipped past, then Vita felt the assurance of Avidia's hand squeezing her own.

'I do not know why I am crying,' said Vita. 'I have secured employment at the edge of the Roman empire. I should be dancing across the floor.'

'A rather difficult proposition when one's feet do not even reach it.'

Vita laughed and wiped her cheeks.

'This pain will pass,' Avidia said. 'It will just take time.'

'I fear as if I have broken my own heart,' said Vita.

'I may be something of an expert in that particular phenomenon,' said Avidia with a sign.

'Well, at least I am in the hands of a true professional.'

Avidia held out her hand. 'You once saved me from despair. Now I shall save you.'

Vita jumped down from the stool and the two women embraced. 'Come, let me show you the tavern,' said Avidia. 'We will make you some porridge and I can tell you all the *vicus* gossip.'

'Porridge flavoured with gossip—a delicious combination.'

'Ack!' shouted Avidia. 'The story I told you about Lollia—it is not complete. I forgot to tell you the most scandalous part. When she was telling me about her troubles with men, she confessed that she was planning to divorce Lepidus.'

'That is rather scandalous, though I must say it does not surprise me.'

'Would it surprise you to know that she was planning on leaving Magnus, as well?'

'Really? So soon? I heard that she was in love with him.'

'I do not think so. Her baby is certainly not his.'

'What?' Vita gasped.

'She let the truth slip without meaning to,' said Avidia, lowering her voice. 'Then she swore me to secrecy. The father of the child she carries was not sired by Magnus or by Lepidus. It belongs to some mercenary bodyguard—a man she called the Scythian.'

Chapter Seventeen

Vita found she enjoyed working at the tavern for it kept her busy day and night. She did her best to contribute what she could, which included making new aprons for Gislinde and Avidia, and new cushions for the stools and chairs.

'Cushions!' Avidia had shrieked when Vita surprised her with the gift. 'Surely our sales will go up, for now our customers will want to stay and drink all night.'

The words had been prophetic. The cushions really did seem to increase the tavern's business, though that was not the only reason for its success. Every day more soldiers were coming to live and work at the fort. The construction on the wall across Britannia—Hadrian's Wall, as the soldiers called it—had begun and Vindolanda was going to be one of the major supply forts along its route.

Thus Roman infantry soldiers travelled north from Eboracum and Londinium, and other parts of Britannia, joining the Tungrian and Batavian auxiliary troops already stationed at Vindolanda and filling the tavern every night with their revelry.

Nor was it only men who frequented the tavern.

Women visited, too, and were especially appreciative of Avidia's ability to manage the unruly soldiers. They came from all parts of the empire, often in tandem with a father or brother, and made their lives in industries that supported the military men.

Some of the women were soldiers' wives, for although Roman soldiers were not allowed to marry, they often did so in secret. Despite the army's insistence on abstinence, it seemed that the soldiers were particularly good at finding mates. This far away from Rome, most *pater familias* could not exert their right to choose wives for their sons. Men and women chose freely whom they wished to marry, with little concern for status or culture.

There was one exception to this custom of tolerance: Brigante men. The Brigantes were considered a dangerous threat and even small parties of Brigante men were intercepted when trying to enter the *vicus*. Tensions were high throughout Brigante territory and there were constant rumours of skirmishes and raids on Roman settlements. Vita knew that if Ven tried to look for her here, he would not be allowed to find her.

And that was well. It was best that she remain far away from him. By staying with him she was undermining his authority within his own tribe—an authority he needed in order to prevent them from suffering more deaths.

She knew how badly Ven wished to do good for his tribe—not just for the ones who lived, but for the ones who had died as well. She knew that it was this important work that would allow him to finally forgive himself for his failures so long ago. To stand in the way of his path would not only be selfish, it would be loveless, and Vita loved Ven with all her heart.

He could not be Roman and she could not be Brigante and it seemed clearer to her every day how danger-ous their love had been. The only thing that could have come of it was woe.

Freedom was the prize and now that Ven was free to do what he must for his tribe, Vita was free to live her life, too. No more invisible prisons—only a very real wall and Ven and Vita on either side.

It did not matter, or so Vita told herself. What mat-tered was cleaning up this mess, or fetching that soldier's beer, or finishing these lines of stitching before the lamp-light ran out. She kept herself as busy as she could and thus managed to keep her longing at bay.

Her capes had begun to sell faster than she could fin-ish them and, by the time that spring arrived, she found that her pockets were full. Very full.

She should have been delighted. With the money she had earned from the tavern and her sewing, she could buy whatever she wished. The problem was that she did not wish for anything at all.

That was not true. She wished to know that he was all right. Was he eating well? Had he found a new place to live? Did he miss her the way she missed him—so badly that it felt like a stone inside her stomach?

She decided to rent a room. The tavern floor was rather hard and there was a small room attached to the wheelwright's shop that was being offered at a fair price. On her first night inside the small dwelling, she could hardly believe her good fortune. After nearly a year of searching, she had finally found a room of her own and without even looking.

The space had a large hearth and a fine raised bed for which she was able to make a cushion in no time. She purchased a simple table and chairs from the local wood smith and was able to acquire an old cooking pot from Avidia's stores.

She was surprised by the privacy the room afforded. She could leave out her sewing and not worry about it getting stained and the place warmed up quickly even during a freeze. It was a true sanctuary amid the bustle of the *vicus*, yet she did not feel the kind of joy she might have expected at such an acquisition.

On the contrary, most nights she felt rather lonely in the room. She tried to keep herself busy with her sewing, but often found herself thinking of Ven. She especially dreaded the moment she arrived home each night, for it was when she missed him the most.

Some nights she would lie in bed and construct elaborate fantasies about him. She would envision Ven as a soldier and she his secret wife. There were many women in town who enjoyed such arrangements. They were easily recognisable by small apartments they kept—often accompanied by children.

Soldiers' wives led hardworking lives, but they struck Vita as a rather merry group. Most days they would go about their work in the *vicus*, selling and trading and gathering gossip. Then, every fifteen days, they would reunite with their husbands for three days of secret reunion.

A married soldier would always arrive outside his wife's room at night, in order to avoid detection. He would tap his fist against the door, then disappear into the private dwelling without a sound. Normally, he did not emerge until three days later, when he would sneak back to the fort under cover of darkness.

Tap, tap.

Vita imagined what it would be like to hear that gentle sound upon her door—the harbinger of the man she loved. She envied secret wives, though she knew she could never be one herself—not unless the Roman army suddenly began accepting Brigante recruits!

Still, she indulged the fantasy nearly every night, picturing Ven arriving on her doorstep after fifteen days had passed and quietly giving the sign. In the vision, she ushered him inside soundlessly and sat him down before a bowl of soup. The soup was always presented, but it was never consumed, for they always had more interesting things to do.

Vita had passed most of the rainy spring months basking inside those rosy visions. Then one morning in May, the rain finally ceased. The sun came out from behind the clouds and shone over the lush green hills outside the fort, making them sparkle.

The three women emerged from the dark tavern and lifted their faces to it and for the first time in months, Vita felt the sun on her face. 'It feels better than the sun of Rome, does it not, Avidia?'

Her friend nodded. 'Like the sun god finally had a bath.'

'I had nearly forgotten there was a sun,' remarked Gislinde.

'The tavern is closed for the month!' Avidia pronounced suddenly. 'We all need a change of scenery. Let us go down to Londinium and do a few errands.'

Gislinde jumped and clapped her hands. 'I have always wanted to see that fabled city!'

'Londinium?' Vita asked the girl. 'But what about Rome?' Gislinde frowned, as if it was the first she had heard of the place. Vita turned to Avidia. 'But why go all the way to Londinium? It is such a long way and not without risk.'

'Work is not everything and risk is the very spice of life!' replied Avidia. 'We must keep ourselves moving, Vita—lest we grow stale and blue with mould.' She flicked a bit of dust from Vita's shoulder and shook her head. 'Besides, we are due for some procurement around here—pitchers, cups, and the like. And Gislinde here could use a new tunic.'

Gislinde shrieked. 'A new tunic!'

'Procurement?' repeated Vita, still confused.

Avidia expelled a long sigh. 'Vita, we are going to go shopping.'

Avidia and Gislinde took less than a day to prepare for their trip to Londinium—a ten-day journey by carriage. 'Are you sure we cannot convince you to come?' Avidia asked Vita.

'I am rather tired of road trips,' Vita replied. 'Besides, I had enough of crowded streets back in Rome.'

'How quickly your definition of crowded has changed!' Avidia remarked.

'I would much rather navigate around the wise old rocks and trees than the grumpy old matrons and merchants,' said Vita.

'Promise me you will at least get outside,' said Avidia. 'Take yourself for a stroll, Vita. Get out of this muddy *vicus* and enjoy yourself for a change. It will be good for you.'

The next morning after seeing the two women off, Vita decided to take Avidia's advice. She headed north, in the direction of the wall-to-be, and caught sight of a group of soldiers hard at work halfway up a ridge.

They were gathered around a wall nearly as tall as she, each performing a different task. She saw some of the soldiers mixing concrete while others were chiselling and placing stones, while still others hauled rubble from a set of nearby carts.

Vita watched and wondered at the men at work. The wall they completed would be a true feat of engineering.

And the end of the Brigantes.

Vita walked over to the masons, who greeted her with a collective grin.

'Tell me, what is the true reason for the wall?' she asked the men.

'To keep out the barbarians,' said one.

'To keep us busy until the next war,' said another.

'To keep Gaius here from wandering too far from the fort at night,' said another. The men laughed.

'I think it is a tourist attraction,' said a man operating a large chisel. 'Egypt has its pyramids, Olympia its statue of Zeus and Britannia shall have a lovely wall. People will come from all over the world to stroll its scenic ramparts. They will stay in our inns and drink in our taverns.'

The man tipped an imaginary beer to Vita and she laughed. 'Well, in that case, build away,' she jested, aware that their levity came at the expense of an entire tribe. She wished there was a way for the Brigante way of life to survive this invasion, but she did not see how. If she and Ven could not even survive such a clash, how could they?

'Will there be a walkway on top of the wall?' Vita asked. 'A place for soldiers to patrol?'

'They have recently decided to add a walkway, yes,' said the man mixing the concrete. 'The new Chief Architect has added it into the plans.'

'You speak of Lepidus Severus?' Vita asked, her curiosity stirring.

'No, I speak of his replacement, ma'am,' said the soldier. 'Lepidus Severus was recently relieved of his duty.'

Vita trained her expression. 'For what reason?'

'Incompetence, ma'am,' said the soldier. 'Apparently, his slave did all Lepidus's work. After the slave escaped, Lepidus was unable to complete his drawings.'

Vita did her best to conceal her shock. She stepped back and bowed to the group. 'Gratitude, soldiers, for your heartening discussion.' She waved at the men and then made her way further up the slope, her head spinning.

Lepidus had not only been a wicked man, he had apparently also been a fraud. Nor was she any closer to answering the question than she had asked Lepidus so many months ago. What was the real reason for the wall?

She continued up the slope and soon found herself at the crest of an angled escarpment of rock—the highest point around. She paused and breathed the fresh air. There was a lovely view and the exercise seemed to have settled her mind.

She gazed north, admiring the fields and forests. The land seemed to stretch out before her like a great patchwork cape—one that she wished to follow to its fringe one day. She knew that somewhere at land's end were the lands of her mother's kin.

She yearned to meet the Caledonii, for she knew that they were a part of her in some sense. Not that she wished to adopt their ways—though they were probably not all that different from Brigante ways, which were not all that different from Roman ways. Really, she just wanted to be closer to her mother. She had been missing her more than ever lately.

Still, she knew she would never be accepted by the Caledonii. She was Roman—an invader—and not welcome in this land. It did not matter that Roman was just one part of her. By choosing one side she had tacitly rejected the other and she hated herself for it.

She had hoped her self-loathing would get better as the months passed, but the feeling had got worse. She heard stories at the tavern, terrible accounts of how the Romans treated the people of Britannia's tribes. Threats, taxation, starvation, humiliation—the cycle was unrelenting.

She knew that the tribes were violent before the Romans arrived. Their culture of raiding was famous throughout the world. Still, they did not deserve the Roman 'peace' that was being imposed upon them. They had not asked for it.

When she had been with Ven she had felt part of the solution somehow, as if together they might find a way for the Brigantes to be saved. She had envisioned a great alliance of the northern tribes, brought together through blood ties and diplomacy, somehow keeping the north of Britannia free of Romans.

Ha! What a ridiculous dream! It was the recent in a string of fantasies in which she had been indulging to lift her spirit. In truth, after she had left Ven, all the joy had drained out of her and she knew what a fool she was to hope to get it back. Freedom was more important than happiness and she had made her choice.

But, gods, she missed him.

Chapter Eighteen

Ven was sitting in a tavern outside the fort at Eboracum when he finally found out where she was. It was the middle of May and most of the *vicus* was out enjoying the sunny weather. It was the reason he had been alone inside the dark tavern for most of that afternoon and that had been just fine with him.

He had not even acknowledged the man who sat down next to him.

He hardly acknowledged anyone any more, unless it was to ask after Vita. Since he had lost her back in January, he guessed that he had spoken to half the population of Britannia. He had gone up and down the island, from Vindolanda and Coria in the north to Londinium in the south, and everywhere in between. Not a single soul had heard of a woman such as she.

Coinless and bereft, Ven had returned to the forests outside Eboracum, where game remained plentiful and his Brigante tribesmen were still far away. He landed many deer, gathered much coin and returned to the *vicus* outside the fort often.

In truth, he was miserable. He frequently forgot to eat and sleep did not come easy. Whenever he closed his eyes, he saw her. Sometimes she was rising up from a tranquil pool. Other times she was floating above it. And other times she was simply pulling back a door flap and beckoning him inside.

Always there were her eyes—luminous and full of facets. They haunted him, those eyes. They would always haunt him, though he still could not think of what they reminded him of.

He ordered another cup of un-watered wine and decided to consider the issue. He had just taken his first sip when the man sitting beside him decided to speak.

'Hello, there,' he said and Ven nodded grudgingly. 'I am Priscus. Gaius Lucius Priscus, to be precise. I am—'

'I know who you are,' said Ven. A busy wine merchant, Ven had seen Priscus in the tavern many times before. The man ordered a cup of beer.

'Here is to the Roman peace and all the business that it brings!' he said. He raised his cup in the air and then waited for Ven to do the same. 'Here, here!' shouted the merchant.

'Here, here,' Ven repeated joylessly. He watched Priscus drink down the contents of his cup in a single gulp.

Ven shook his head.

'Does something vex you?' asked the merchant.

'In fact, it does,' said Ven. *Of the dozen other chairs in this tavern, why have you chosen the one next to me to sit in?*

'You are a vendor of wine, yet you drink beer,' Ven observed. 'Why?' He tried to sound curious. It was too early in the day to fall into a fight.

'Does a fish drink the water in which it swims?' boomed Priscus, apparently delighted by his own cleverness. Ven produced a tight grin of acknowledgement, yet the man continued. 'I would be a fool to consume the wine I trade, for it is ridiculously overpriced.'

Ven gazed into his cup. He had never even considered the price of the wine.

'You would cry at the prices they charge in the north,' Priscus continued. 'Do you not wish to know why?' he asked, but he did not wait for Ven's response. 'Because they are moving thousands of soldiers to the forts along the River Vedra and the demand for wine has spiked. They are building a great wall there, you see.'

'So I have heard,' said Ven. He took a long drink from his cup. It pained him to hear about the construction of the wall. With the arrival of each new soldier, the tribute demands on the Brigantes increased. With each stone, the northern and southern Brigantes were being driven further apart. He yearned to help his brethren, but he could not do it until he found Vita.

Ven took another long drink. He should have been with his tribesmen right then, not sitting in some dark, sour-smelling tavern outside Britannia's largest Roman fort.

Still, he could not reconcile his life. If he was protecting his tribe, then he could not be there to defend Vita. If he was protecting Vita, he could not work to defend his tribe. He was only glad he did not own a mirror, so he did not have to look at himself in the eye.

'A working soldier tends to be a thirsty soldier,' Priscus was saying. He tapped his cup on the bar, but it seemed that the barkeep had gone outside to enjoy a bit of sun. 'Some taverns are better than others,' he growled.

'And which is the best tavern you have encountered in Britannia?' Ven asked, beginning to feel his wine.

'Oh, that is easy. Of all the taverns I service, the one

in Vindolanda is the loveliest,' the man said. 'Pretty bartenders, good food, prompt service. They even have cushions on the chairs. Can you imagine that? Cushions!'

'Cushions?' Ven echoed. He finished his wine, trying to find his enthusiasm.

'The place is full of Tungrians, of course. Their cohort is stationed at the fort. Coarse, ill-mannered men I find them. But if you can get over their grunting and burping you will encounter generous servings and very reasonable prices. And if a man over-drinks he is promptly offered biscuits.'

'Bishcuitsh?' Gods, was Ven already slurring his words? It was only just past midday.

'The place is always full of customers and one would never guess who is the owner.'

Priscus waited patiently for Ven to ask the identity of the owner. Perhaps if Ven waited long enough the man would just go away.

'Women!' the man blurted. 'It is run by women. Two Romans and a Batavian.'

Ven instantly sobered. He had long given up on finding Vita, but it had become a habit to listen closely to any information about Roman women.

'Describe the Roman women, if you would be so good.' Ven whistled outside to the barkeep. 'Pour this man another cup of beer, would you?' He stared at Priscus. 'Go ahead. Describe the women.'

'Well, they could not be more different,' said Priscus. 'The one woman is tall and thin with curly hair and a quick temper. The other is short and round and rather handsome. She is the one who brings the biscuits.'

Ven squeezed his cup. 'About the round woman,'

he said carefully, 'can you remember the colour of her eyes?'

The wine trader paused, searching the rafters above him. 'I believe they are green. Or perhaps brown? Why do you ask?'

Suddenly, Ven laughed—a long, riotous laugh apparently disturbing enough to give the merchant reason to depart. 'What is the matter with you, friend?' he asked Ven as he headed for the door. 'Was it something I said?'

It took Ven four days to reach the hill fort on horseback—a trip that normally would have taken six. When he arrived outside the entry gate he was met by three Brigante guards who immediately pulled out their swords. Ven raised his arms. 'I come in peace. I wish to speak to the Chief. I am Ven of—'

'We know who you are,' one of the men interrupted.

'Then why do you draw your swords?'

A large, red-bearded man stepped out from behind them. 'It has been a long time, Ven,' said the Chief. 'Many months.'

'Well met, Chief Rennyt. I hope I am still welcome here.'

'You tell me,' said the Chief. He tugged at his red beard and frowned. 'We had just begun to formulate a plan for our defence and then you disappeared.'

'I was detained in my efforts to locate a woman. I made a vow to protect her, you see. I could not forsake her.'

'The Roman woman? Vita?'

'She was run out by the people of my settlement,' said Ven. He realised his hands were still in the air. 'I swore to secure her safety. I could not let her—'

'You love her,' said the Chief.

Ven bowed his head. 'I do.'

'Stand down, men,' the Chief commanded and the guards sheathed their swords. He motioned to Ven. 'Come.'

When Ven stepped inside the wooden gates of the hill fort, he was welcomed by smiles and looks of surprise. 'It has been a long time since we have seen you, dear,' said an old woman. 'You did right in returning.'

'We shall not be conquered!' someone cried, saluting him. Several others gave him welcoming pats on the back.

Ven felt his spirits returning. 'Why do they greet me so warmly?' he asked.

'Because of what you represent,' said the Chief.

'And what is that?'

'Our last hope.'

Soon Ven was standing inside the Chief's roundhouse greeting the man's wife, Orla, and his twin boys. 'I will not rest until I know my boys will not have to kiss the foot of Rome.'

The Chief's wife and sons retired to the far end of the space, leaving the two men beside the hearth fire. 'I have sent a party of warriors north to investigate alliances. It is likely that we will postpone our battle with the Romans until next spring.'

'A wise decision,' said Ven.

'You should be with that party, you know,' said the Chief. 'Our allies will be more likely to join us if they learn about the threat of Rome from someone who has lived with Romans.'

'I believe I have an even better idea,' Ven said. 'It will require us to fetch the Druid priest. And he must bring his body ink.'

* * *

Two days later, Ven was back in Eboracum, standing outside the gate to the fort. 'What business do you have here?' asked one of the guards.

'I wish to enrol in the army,' said Ven, relinquishing his sword. 'I wish to fight the northern Britons.'

Soon Ven found himself in the well-appointed *tablinium* of the *legatus* in command of the Sixth Victrix legion. Ven looked around at the elegant statues that decorated the corners of the room. For a moment he felt as if he were back in Rome.

'So you wish to join the ranks?' asked the *legatus*. He was standing at his desk dressed in a red tunic covered by a fine leather cuirass. The lavish piece of armour traced the muscles of his chest with alarming precision, though Ven wondered if the man was truly as strong as the garment suggested. Perhaps Ven was not the only one putting on a ruse.

'What is your name?'

'Venator of Gaul, sir. Ven.'

'Hunter? I have never heard of such a name.'

'A Latin translation of my given name, sir. I come from a family of hunters.'

'You say that you are from Gaul. Which tribe?' the *legatus* glanced absently at a scroll.

'The Garumni, sir,' Ven lied.

'A wife? Children?'

'None, sir.'

'Other languages?'

'A bit of Tungrian, sir.'

'Can you ride a horse?'

'Unfortunately, no,' Ven lied. The Tungrian cohort

stationed at Vindolanda was not a cavalry unit and Vindolanda was where he wished to be.

The grave patrician looked up from his scroll. 'Why do you wish to enrol in the Roman army?'

'Because I know that the Romans cannot be beaten.'

'And how do you know that?'

'I have seen what they have done in Gaul, sir, and I know that it is the same as what they have done everywhere else. I have read the histories.'

'A historian, are you?' the *legatus* said. 'Then you will appreciate that we are trying to learn from history here in the north. I am sure you have heard of this little wall we are building?'

'Yes, sir. To separate the Romans from the barbarians.'

'That is what the world thinks.'

'That is not the reason, sir?'

'Of course not, for there are plenty of barbarians on either side of the wall. We are trying to separate the barbarians *from each other.*'

Ven nearly laughed. Of course that was the reason. Why had he never guessed it? The wall was being built across the territory of the Brigantes and their potential allies. The Romans were trying to prevent such an alliance from ever forming. An alliance of the tribes was the only thing that could threaten their hold on the north.

'We cannot afford another Boudica rebellion,' the commander said.

'Certainly not, sir. It is a brilliant idea,' Ven said. 'The wall, I mean, not the rebellion.'

The commander nodded thoughtfully. 'I wish I could take credit for it, but it was Emperor Hadrian's idea. He has read more histories than you or I combined. Divide and conquer, he always says.'

'Roman strategy at its finest.'

The commander sighed, as if bored. 'Due to our construction schedule and current needs in the north, I am afraid I would require you to be stationed in this region for your entire career. You were not hoping to travel, were you?'

'No, sir.'

'You will be required to swear allegiance to Rome, of course, every New Year, and to worship at the shrine of our Divine Emperor. Do you have any problem with that? I know those Gaulish gods of yours can be rather jealous.'

'No problem, sir,' Ven said. Besides, there was only one goddess that he truly worshipped.

'You are rather old to be enlisting. You are aware that this is a twenty-five-year commitment, correct? Citizenship is granted only at the end of that period of time. You must be sure that you find such a commitment to be worth the prize.'

Ven thought of the true prize, which had nothing to do with citizenship. 'I find that it is worth it, sir.'

The commander sat back in his chair. 'Why do I feel that you are speaking of something else entirely?'

The man was smarter than he seemed. Ven searched his mind for a way to put him off. 'It is not citizenship I am seeking, sir,' Ven said. 'I would like to be a part of something larger than myself.'

Such as the last stand of the northern tribes and my role as their informer.

'I see that you have a tribal tattoo.' The commander gazed at Ven's forehead. 'What are those strange figures across your forehead there?'

'They are deer,' Ven said, his heart beating. Time slowed.

'A rather fresh tattoo.'

'A recent hunt.' The commander raised a brow. 'I have others,' Ven added, though it was not true. He moved to lift his tunic. 'I can show you them if you like.'

The commander frowned. 'No, no, that will not be necessary.' He glanced back down at his scroll. 'Army rules stipulate that you cannot marry, nor can you drink, nor carouse with whores. Is that clear to you?'

Ven nodded gravely, wondering how Britannia's hundreds of taverns managed to get by. He supposed he could ask one of the many of the women he had seen in the streets and doorways, children clinging to their skirts, looking very much like wives.

'You will be stationed in the north with an auxiliary unit of Tungrians who are helping the the Sixth Victrix build the wall. It is something greater than yourself for certain, though you will never be a barbarian warrior again.'

'If I can help build Hadrian's Wall, then my life will have been worth living,' lied Ven.

The commander smiled and held out his hand. 'In that case, welcome to the Roman army.'

It took Ven two days to ride to Vindolanda, though the *legatus* had given him five. Before heading down to the fort, Ven paused at the top of a familiar rise. It was here that he and Titus had stood months ago and witnessed the wall's beginnings. There had been much progress since then: the sides were nearly half the height of a man in places and actively being filled with rubble and cement.

Ven noticed that work had also begun on the southern ditch, the existence of which finally made sense. The wall was being built to keep the Brigantes on either side of it from joining forces. Thus the defensive ditches were necessary on both sides of the wall. They were the first line of defence against the one thing that could defeat Rome: unity.

Soon Ven was standing at the entrance to the *vicus* before a group of guards. He presented his enrolment papers and they stepped aside, heralding his passage with a Roman salute. 'Welcome to the First Tungrians,' their leader said.

Ven nodded his thanks. 'Can you tell me the residence of a tavern keeper called Vita Sabina?'

'Just by the wheelwright's shop,' the man said, pointing the way down the main street.

'Gratitude,' Ven said and raised a salute of his own.

His legs grew weaker as his made his way down the street. His hands appeared to be trembling. What in Hades was wrong with him? It was not as if he were headed for the whipping pole.

Still, he could not help but feel nervous. Finally, the time had come to see her, his one true love, and he did not even know if she would open the door.

Perhaps she would not even recognise him. He had shorn his hair since they had last met and got a new tattoo. He was wearing the standard red tunic of the military now, along with a chainmail shirt and scabbard belt for his newly issued dagger. He was no longer her barbarian warrior, nor even her rebellious slave. He was a soldier in the Roman army.

It was for that reason alone that they could be together and that reason alone that he would never regret what he had done. He had vowed to her that he would never let her go again and he would honour that promise to the last. If she could not come to him, he would come to her.

He spied the sign for the wheelwright and turned towards it, his heart beginning to pound in his throat. It had been the right decision to come here, no matter what happened between them. Even if she did not wish to see him again, he would still be living near. He could watch out for her from a distance. He could keep her safe.

Meanwhile, he could help his kin by providing them with information about the Roman threat. He would keep his ears open in the barracks and on the march, looking out for Brigante interests. He could warn them when the tribute collectors were coming and where the next cattle thieves would strike.

Still, it was not for his kin that he had committed the next twenty-five years of his life. He had done it for her. It was all for her.

She made him laugh, made him lust, made him think. She forgave him for the worst of his sins and had taught him to forgive himself. She was the only person in the world who understood the load he carried, for she carried it, too. Part-Roman, part-barbarian.

When he had finally escaped Rome, he thought he had gained his freedom. He had been wrong. The truth was that she was his freedom. He loved her, more than anyone he had ever known, and nothing—not even Hadrian's towering wall—could ever keep them apart.

Those eyes—sometimes brown, sometimes green. He would see them soon and, hopefully, they would see him. He knew what they reminded him of now. He had known it all along, deep in his heart. They reminded him of home.

He lifted his fist and knocked on the door.

Tap, tap.

* * * * *